Penelope Farmer is the author of *Standing in The Shadow* ('Intelligent and deeply felt' *British Book News*); *Eve: Her Story* ('Moving and provocative' *The Times Educational Supplement*); and *Away From Home* ('Often funny and always beautifully written' *Daily Telegraph*). She is married to a neurologist and lives in London.

Also by Penelope Farmer in Abacus:

AWAY FROM HOME
EVE: HER STORY

Penelope Farmer
GLASSHOUSES

A SPHERE BOOK

First published in Great Britain by Victor Gollancz Ltd 1988
Published by Sphere Books Ltd 1989

Copyright © Penelope Farmer 1988

All rights reserved.
No part of this publication may be reproduced,
stored in a retrieval system, or transmitted, in any
form or by any means without the prior
permission in writing of the publisher, nor be
otherwise circulated in any form of binding or
cover other than that in which it is published and
without a similar condition including this
condition being imposed on the subsequent
purchaser.

Printed and bound in Great Britain by
Richard Clay Ltd, Bungay, Suffolk

ISBN 0 1234 1234 0

Sphere Books Ltd
A Division of
Macdonald & Co. (Publishers) Ltd
66/73 Shoe Lane, London EC4P 4AB
A member of Maxwell Pergamon Publishing Corporation plc

ACKNOWLEDGEMENTS

I would like to thank the following glass artists in particular, for their endless time, patience, technical help (and friendship): Anthony Stern of Anthony Stern Glass; Deborah Fladgate. I also thank Brian Blanthorne for his information on working cold glass.

I acknowledge, gratefully, the five weeks I spent in retreat at Hawthornden Castle, Midlothian, writing the first draft of this book at a speed only made possible by the care of its staff (and by the tolerance of my abandoned husband).

Finally, I want to thank Tom and Dodie Howarth, of Ashover, Derbyshire, in whose garden at Alderwasley the second pot of coin clippings was found.

*For my father, Hugh Farmer,
for his eightieth birthday,
with love*

Chapter One

" 'Tis a concrete of salt and sand and stones . . ."

Grace's alchemies were not her mother's. She was a glass-blower; even during her brief marriage to Jas she had not pretended to be a cook. This made it all the more surprising, practically insulting, when the first thing that met this strapping farmer's daughter (and proud of it) on turning the key in the lock of the cottage she had bought with some of Reg's money — the lock set too close to the doorframe, she had scraped her knuckles painfully in the process — was the smell of food. Not old food, either. Food in the process of being cooked. Roast meat, for instance. Still worse, there arrived, so instantaneously it might even have preceded the smell, the thought of the only real cook she had known; not Jas' mother, of course, who was a mere dilettante as far as Grace was concerned, so not worth rating; rather her own equally — and still more unfairly — unrated, almost always disregarded mother. Of whom, so far as she knew, she'd had scarcely a willing thought in years.

She was imagining things, of course. Nothing was cooking. The chill air in the kitchen still chillier — it was certainly damper — than the air outside, the stove was not only dead, the stained aluminium lids over the hotplates, like the sills of the windows set deep into thick stone walls, were filmed with dust. Even so, despite herself — everything she did these days seemed despite herself, not least the fact that she was here, in this house, its owner — she walked across to the Aga stove and laid her hand upon its chipped enamel surface. It was stone cold. As were the two hot plates, as were the ovens when she opened them, the smell persisting; of bread was it? — and some kind of meat — pork? rabbit? The ovens were also empty, it went without saying; she put her hand in, right to the back in each case, to make sure. From the bottom one the fingers of her right hand came back tinged, slightly, with rust.

"Makes you hungry, the smell in here, don' it?" said the boy who had humped two suitcases into the room after Grace. "Smells like me mum's kitchen. I don't think." He was smiling. His smile more uncertain than cheerful, he went on smiling when Grace rounded on him, stamping her feet on the stone floor, shouting at him in the Somerset burr that her years in London had blurred but never eradicated entirely, what the hell was he doing? What could he be thinking of? The place had been empty three whole months.

God only knows what had made her so angry. Terry was used to Grace. He cringed, perfunctorily, but that was all. A gaunt, at the same time potentially tall boy of barely eighteen, taller than Grace, by the look of it still growing, his too short trousers, his shock of thin pale hair, like an unevenly cut lawn, gave him a shrunken, half-starved look. A Dickensian, crossing-sweeper of a boy Jas was to call him; not Grace. An avid reader in her youth — books were one of the few ways she had of getting at her father — she had nothing against books, not even against Reg's Everyman Ruskin that he was always quoting at her. It was just that on leaving Somerset she had decided, with a certainty reinforced when Jas departed, that nothing in the world was of use to her, or at least worth wasting her energy upon, except her strong muscles, her skilled hands, her calculating, critical, imaginative eye; and, above all, the mysterious, uncharted places in her head which drew hand and eye together sometimes when she needed them to do so; if not always often enough.

For similar reasons she rejected, here and now, the hangdog, yet triumphant resentment in the look the boy gave her. Just as she rejected the intolerable memory of that sad woman, her mother, standing at the kitchen table, her cheeks stained ruddy by the wind off the Bristol Channel, her hands still ruddier from gutting a chicken. Such a bright strong image was at variance with the image of her that Grace usually carried, or rather, more usually, pushed aside; even though a lack of colour, almost a transparency were, precisely, the qualities she loved in the material she worked in. What could that alchemy, for goodness' sake, the mysterious way such disparate, earthy elements fused to make the glittering purity of flint glass have to do with her spineless mother?

Not that she reflected on it. Any more than she reflected on the fact — the way things turned out maybe she ought to have done — that it was partly because of her mother that she was here, now, in Derbyshire. Her mind having been finally made up when she had noted, on some eighteenth century gritstone tombstones five miles or so from here, her mother's name. Earsby, almost but not quite obliterated by the weather.

How cold Grace felt suddenly in this empty kitchen. An out-of-date calendar hung crookedly on the wall above the stove. As she stared, blankly, at the stained and spotted picture of Kinder Downfall in full spate, courtesy of Matlock Hardware, her anger subsided, she put out an apologetic hand and ruffled the hair on the boy, Terry's, head. Noting as she did so, her irritation almost tender, the scrawny, unwashed look of his neck. With much the same rough tenderness she used to stroke the greasy layer of wool on the butting heads of the cade lambs it had been her job to feed each spring. The next moment, removing her hand, she was bawling at him to take their suitcases upstairs before the removal van arrived, as it was bound to any minute.

Hairy Terry they used to call me, Terry is thinking. That's a joke, I'm not hairy at all, more like a half-plucked chicken according to my mum, some of my mates've been shaving since we was fifteen or younger. A beardless boy is Grace's description. I don't like that any better. Grace is OK, though; better than most. Amazing Grace I call her. Or rather my mum did, straight off, the first day I came home from working in the glasshouse, and told her the bosses' names. By then, at six in the evening, she'd already had one too many. "Grace — my God, Grace," she screeched, laughing fit to bust, why I couldn't see, but then most of mum's jokes aren't funny to no one but her, next thing was she was waltzing round the table humming the tune, Amazing Grace, waving her arms so she knocked over the cup of tea I'd just made her (fat lot of chance *her* making *me* a cup of tea). With her bleached hair, that she's taken to tying up in two wispy scarves, with her necklaces and bracelets, with her high heeled pink slippers that kept tripping her over, she looked barmy, if you ask me. (Which she doesn't. All she ever asks *me* is to make her a cup of Nescaff or else go round the corner for twenty fags.) She thinks it's Grace is barmy. She thinks I'm even barmier.

The other fellers work in factories or the co-op or some garage or other, what am I doing then frigging around with that stuff, she wants to know. My mates call me barmy too, so did I before I started. Bit of a laugh, I thought. Get me off the streets for a week or two, be good for a giggle down the boozer. By then I'd been hanging around for nearly a year, who was going to give me a proper job, what did I know how to do, fucking nothing, I weren't even good for a punch up, and don't they make sure you know it? I was bored enough by then to piss in the river for a living. Her Malignancy up in Number Ten don't care a fuck about the likes of me so far as I can tell. I hates her.

But I was lucky wasn't I? More luckier than my mates. Who'd've thought before I went to the glass I'd find it so fucking amazing. Hard work, mind. And uncomfortable at times; you cook don't you, the heat of the furnace pretty near kills you, the glass itself can burn you nasty if you're not careful. And when it's cold it cuts you; broken glass in a glasshouse turns up where you least expect it.

It's also tricky. It takes a bit to get the hang. At first I didn't seem to be getting it at all, for two pins I'd've chucked the whole thing in. But I didn't. There'd've been no chance of going back. The day I started Grace tells me she'd had it up to here with youth training, the way the yobs she'd had gone and mucked her about. Never mind a social conscience, I was the last of them she'd take, she says, and that was flat. They'd all been yobs, she says, all useless. If I was a yob, I'd better forget it. And I were a yob too, but I weren't going to tell her. Not after what I'd felt the very first moment I walked in there, on a cold winter's morning, and caught the heat of the furnace and set my eye gaping on its magic golden eye; and that was even before I'd noticed amazing Grace herself.

But then I always did like being warm. There's no chance of being cold in a glasshouse, not when the furnace is on. The kind of flats the council gives losers like Mum are always fucking freezing, I'm used to cold, whether I like it or not. But I wasn't going to be cold here, what I was going to get sometimes was more heat than even I thought I needed. Try and keep me away though. Especially once I seen Grace; a bit topheavy as they go, broad shoulders and long thin legs, like the figurehead on the Victory at Portsmouth, or Superwoman minus the cloak — there she stands thrusting an iron rod into that great hot hole. You can snigger if you want, my mates would, that's for sure. But why should I care any longer? If it's sexy, it's sexy. Which it is and isn't exactly, but so what? Out of this hot orange-white hole she was fetching this incredible *stuff*.

I can't quite believe it is glass yet, can I? Glass is hard, it's clear, I always thought; so how could you blow it, I wondered, when they'd told me that's what Grace did, what she'd be learning me. And now what she's brought out of the furnace looks more like syrup than anything. It glows yellow and orange, it drips off the iron just like syrup. And all the time it's changing colour. There's blue and green and orange glows together, it's fucking marvellous I tell you. I never saw nothing like it in my life, nor what she was doing to it neither. I don't take my eyes off for a minute. But then, nor does she take her eyes off it, nor the bloke that's working with her, a funny, wizened little bloke, what I don't know yet's her gaffer. Did I say working? It's more like dancing, the way they're hopping around one another, both with a look in their eye like a cat watching a mousehole, dead still, but lively, at one and the same minute.

First she takes the stuff out of the furnace, twists it round a bit on her rod, like she was trying to keep syrup on a spoon, then she dunks it on a table and rolls it round some more and flattens it a bit, then she holds it back in the furnace. There's a funny kind of chair with arms, quite near to the furnace; she sits down there and lays the rod on the arms to steady it, keeps rolling it with the one hand, works on the glass with the other, using all kinds of weird things — a pinkish pad, made of I don't know what kind of paper, kinds of huge scissors, kinds of huge wooden spoons. And all the time she keeps getting up and putting it back in the furnace to heat it. Not forgetting the time she starts swinging the iron round like she was a drum majorette with a baton. In particular not forgetting the time she puts her mouth to the end of the iron and blows and it all swells up, like the soap bubbles Mum blew when I were a tiddler, before my old man hopped it and she took to the bottle; just like the bubble gum I used to nick from the Paki shop after school.

At which point I get the message. I see this stuff is the glass really and when they said blowing, yes, they meant it. I want to jump up and down with the marvel, I want to yell like Chelsea were thrashing Fulham. And then she puts the bubble back in the furnace and twists it about a whole lot longer; and the old man gets more glass and sticks bits on; and so on. The long and the short of it is in less than twenty minutes from the time I walk in the door, there's a great big glass goblet on the end of her iron, what she knocks off very careful; the old geezer's put some gloves on, he picks it up and shoves it in a kind of oven and shuts the door.

Then they start over again. But this time it's the old bloke does the work, and Grace is his helper. And it's still just as amazing, though less of the great mystery, I know who they are now, that the old man's Grace's gaffer, Reg, dead Reg these days, an' we miss him. And I know, because they just told me, that the table where they roll the glass is called the marver, and the oven where they put the glass to cool down slowly is the lehr, and the iron they put on the bottom of the glass, that leaves the mark there, so's you know someone blew it, is the punty. I don't keep names in my head usually, no, not never, what's the point, but I keep these ones, I keep repeating them over an' over all the time I'm watching. And not just because they say they ain't going to tell me nothing no more than the one time.

Of course there's no Reg no longer. Nor's there going to be anyone else come to that, the other assistant decided to stay in London. It's me gets — will get, once we're started — to do the things Grace did for Reg and Reg did for Grace. And all for peanuts. (She's not mean, Grace, not really; it's just that it takes loot to set these things up and Reg's loot won't last for ever. And, besides, being Grace, she's careful.)

It don't matter. She's got me hooked and she knows it. In one way it's just a job like any other, you do the same things all day long sometimes, stands to reason you get pissed off in that heat. In others, most others, it ain't the same at all. There's not a moment day and night I can forget the smell and sound of her glasshouse. The hiss of the wet paper as the hot glass sears it, the clatter of the irons, the roaring of the furnace, the little tinkle, tinkle of the glass cracking on the blowing irons we set back in the water trough to cool 'em. The hot, strong animal stink of it; hot metal, scorched paper, the smell of heat.

Grace remembered quite clearly the gusty summer afternoon when, laying her head against the flank of her father's favourite horse, she decided to run away. She was twelve years old. And weeping.

Not to run away at once, of course. Even with the images still unbearably fresh in her mind, of her father's square hands feeding the irreplaceable papers into the Rayburn stove, of the three of them watching the flames flare blue then white. Even while planning what to take with her, working out bus timetables and so forth, Grace remained a practical girl at heart. Little by little she began to consider, more calmly, a less immediate future. She was not, she thought, whatever happened, going to spend the rest of her life the way her mother spent her life, acting as her father's skivvy, or anyone else's.

Why did she stay, she wondered? Perhaps that was the moment, also, that she began to despise her mother because she had not managed to run away. Unable to admit for one moment that she, Grace, might still need mothering sometimes, she could have accepted being abandoned for such reasons. No matter how badly their father bullied her and Winifred, his daughters, it was nothing to the way he bullied Peggy, his wife, their mother. They were quite safe in bed at night, for instance. Whereas they could hear him sometimes — they had heard him last night — shouting at her into the small hours; sometimes, like last night, they heard some less definable sounds from the bedroom also, which since they included moaning ones almost certainly made by her mother, Grace assumed meant no more good to her than the others.

The food would be less good if she left. But so what? (Grace stopped weeping now. Took a dandy brush, began, almost mechanically, grooming the flank her tears had stained.) If anything she resented the way her mother tried to make good cooking compensate for everything else. In fact she resented all her mother's attempts to protect her from their father; largely because they were in vain, for the most part. Worse, because they brought down still more bullying, set her mother cringing before him just the way she had been cringing an hour or so earlier, when, hearing the shouts, Grace had opened the kitchen door to find her trying to protect the precious drawings. Uselessly it went without saying. At least half were already in shreds upon the kitchen floor. It was when he saw Grace standing there looking at him, in silence, that her father had snatched up the rest, strode across the kitchen, and opened the Rayburn door to show its burning heart. And all the time he had gone on shouting and shouting. Silent for a moment while they watched the papers burn, he started up again the moment the door clanged to, yelling the same things he'd been yelling before: "No daughter of mine," "arty stuff," "practical farming folk" — and so on.

The joke was — not that Grace was yet old enough to see it — that by "practical farming folk" he meant them, the family he — and she — had been born into. Whereas this dark-haired, dark-eyed, almost piratical looking lot, descended from Spaniards, most likely, washed up after the Armada, or else more recently from Spanish smugglers, weren't practical at all. Unlike their long-headed blue-eyed commonsensical Saxon neighbours, they didn't have the knack somehow, their farms survived barely, no matter how hard they made themselves — and their children — work.

And how they worked; never-endingly, it seemed to Grace, who did her reading and drawing at school or late at night long after she was supposed to be asleep. Hating her father meanwhile with such passion that she also hated, openly, anything or anyone associated with the name father. God for instance. From the intensity with which Grace loathed God, you'd think she'd spent all her life among her mother's stern Methodist family, up on the Brendons, rather than been cradled down here, below, by the pink, Anglican, closely cultivated folds that rolled down to the Bristol Channel.

It did not help, it made things worse, that apart from the fair hair bequeathed her by her mother's side of the family, Grace looked just like him. She had, moreover, along with his physical strength, inherited his love of and understanding of horses. A love she'd tried to resist at one time, as she resisted everything else that emanated from him, but without success. Never mind it was her job to tend her father's beasts almost unaided — heaven help her if one flank was less glossy than it should be, if one mouth was fed an oat more or less than it was due. Never mind it was the horses took such money as the family had, made their lives still more of a struggle. Never mind that her father insisted on her riding from almost the time she could walk, and that as riding master was harder on her than ever. No matter how long he schooled her, on the youngest horses very often, rather than the pony officially allotted to her and Winifred, no matter how often they threw her, he showed her none of the pity or consideration he gave the horses. Up she would have to get, and on she would have to go; her determination to do so — from an early age she never let him see her cry — so total, that she once rode with a broken collarbone the whole of a summer afternoon.

She was a match for him, all right. In this as in most things. The trouble was that he knew it. And that because Grace loved his horses, they were the first things she started drawing.

It was drawings of horses, of course, that he'd torn up. It was for the horses that, standing by the kitchen door, outwardly impassive, she'd inwardly raged and hated as the flames leapt in the depths of the Rayburn stove on which her mother performed her culinary miracles. It was on a horse's flank that, throwing down the dandy brush suddenly, in the first outward manifestation of rage she had shown all afternoon, Grace once again found herself weeping, not only comforted but saddened this time by its sweaty, prelapsarian pungency against her hands, her hair, her face. Because she knew already it was horses she was going to have to lose. Knew that art, not equestrianism, was her most likely means of escape. Not because art so particularly aggravated her father. But because, even then, she knew she was very good at it. And because equestrianism, on the other hand, would not take her away from her father but nearer him.

As the years went on, Grace saw to it that her art got even better. Unlike her sister Winifred she was a clever girl in all things, fortunately for her. She sailed through her schoolwork; though her father stuck out for the practical subjects at O level, he couldn't control things entirely. Alongside science and metal and woodwork — Grace, with the approval, for once, of her father, who had no son to learn these useful skills, was one of the first girls not diverted into needlework and cookery — she took not only history but English literature. She also, unofficially, haunted the art room; the art master himself paid her O level fee; she passed spectacularly.

Grace should have left school then, in theory. But her headmaster was from a farming family himself, he not only knew the language, he was clever at using it. He persuaded Mr Tucker — Grace never knew how he did it — that if she stayed on for A levels, she'd make any agricultural college she wanted. So Grace, aged sixteen, went on into the sixth form.

Not, of course, that she had any intention of proceeding to agricultural college. Alongside her science subjects, she took art, unbeknown to her father.

Aged sixteen-and-a-half she turned to ceramics. Its tactile and earthy nature suited her perfectly. Not only was the earth, metaphorically speaking, in her blood, the need to handle the clay so firmly, wedging and kneading it, let out all the fury she kept locked inside her under different names and guises. Though she mastered the use of a wheel — with difficulty — something about the co-ordination needed she found dispiriting, even oppressive — she did not continue to use it; she moulded her pots rather, or coiled them. Her masterpiece, or so she thought, and her art master agreed with her, was a huge oval dish, glazed dark green and black except for the pale blue ram's head in the middle, a furious, even mythic-looking thing with its curled horn, its one eye relentlessly glaring. It took her weeks to make altogether. At weekends she skived off farm work and took the bus into Minehead to work on it. Her father thought she had a boyfriend; he'd have hit her even harder if he had known that what she actually had — with the art master's blessing and the caretaker's connivance — were the keys to the school and the art room.

Aged seventeen, she had all her hair cut off by a barber in Minehead. This time her father took a belt to her, did not just use his hand. Though the prettiness of his younger daughter had clearly given him some simple pleasure, he'd been baffled by the elder girl's likeness to him, even before her visit to the barber revealed an emperor off a Roman coin, made it still more apparent. (He might want Grace to work like a man, he seemed to be saying, as he beat her; but she damn well had to look like a woman.)

Aged eighteen, she got straight As in her A level subjects. Armed with the certificate, fifty pounds — twenty she had scraped together herself, the rest she had taken, without compunction, from her father's desk (had he ever paid her a single penny for all her work?) — her portfolio of photographs and drawings, a carrier bag containing two sweaters, three t-shirts and her spare pair of jeans — and of course, wrapped carefully, in newspaper, the ram's head dish — she took one bus to Taunton and another to London; at no point looked back.

For the first month, dossed down in a youth hostel in Holland Park, she worked at a variety of evening jobs. By day she went round hammering on the doors of every art school her art master had told her the name of. It wasn't the conventional way of setting about it, she knew, and if she had not known, would soon have discovered. But she also knew — or rather suspected — that sheer persistence can sometimes work wonders; more so if allied with a talent of which she had no doubts whatever.

This conviction, the persistence with which she applied it, paid off. The big Somerset girl, with her burring accent, but surprisingly light, female voice, her ram's head dish safe in a supermarket plastic bag, her ever more battered portfolio of work, and her seeming capacity to wait, all day if necessary, in a hundred outer and unwelcoming offices, intrigued more than a few of those she pestered. In due course several offers came her way. After much thought, she undertook the foundation year at Camberwell; where she continued to support herself at first, working nights and weekends. In time, one mentor managed to prove her unsupported and got her a grant from the local authority. He also found her lodgings in Kennington, with a professor of philosophy at London University, whose wife, a successful sculptor, kept animal specimens in her freezer till she was ready to draw them. (Being sent on harmless errands in that household, to fetch kippers or frozen peas, also meant, very likely, confronting the open yet glazed not to say accusatory eyes belonging to dead foxes or badgers.) The sculptor took one look at Grace, gave fluting cries of delight, as from some bird she was drawing, and recruited her, too, as a model.

Nor was she the only one of her family to notice the rather primitive yet striking beauty the gaunt, ungainly Grace had developed. Jas, the oldest son, then learning to blow glass at the art school where Reg taught twice weekly, observed it the first time he saw her. Every so often he would drop in to eat with his parents. Imperceptibly — too imperceptibly for Grace to notice — he started coming more frequently. And that was how it began. Not quickly at first. Bit by bit. Little by little.

Chapter Two

" 'Tis the most plyable and fashionable thing in the world, and best retains the form given . . ."

There's a load of fancy rubbish talked about glass these days, to Reg's mind. Grace, who went to New York once, to see what's going on, tells him functional's a dirty word among the gaffers there. So much for them, then, he thinks. As if the best of glass, to my mind, isn't a fine goblet made to an eighteenth century pattern; clear stuff, too, to show the colour of what you're drinking. You can keep your fancy sculptures, twisted bits, this and that, what the dog had for breakfast and the feline for dinner, no good but to sit on a shelf and be looked at, and only then in a dim light and you're not sober. I don't hold with that at all, nor does Grace when she's honest. If the stuff looks good, I don't hold with it. Even she admits most doesn't.

Glass is a craft, that's what I think, and always have, no more nor less than inlay, say, or wood turning; the more skill of course, the finer, I give you that. Wherever you got to, no matter how good, how long you been at it, you get it right, you get it perfect. With glass, what's more, you get it perfect quick, and no messing about. *And* you get it exact. You work it too soon or too late, don't get it in the lehr fast enough, you cool your lehr down too quick, so the pieces don't anneal proper, crack, crack, that's it, you're going to lose the whole caboodle.

Always a new apprentice come, just to show him, I'd do my party trick, I'd make a few Rupert's drops; that's glass allowed to drip and to cool on the spot. You can smite those drops at the broad end with a hammer till you're purple, won't make a happorth's difference. But tap 'em at the other, they blow up in your face. That's an extreme, I say, just the same you be careful, one bit of harry-be-quick, my lad, you're done.

Where I started of course, in the factory, all of us in a line, gaffer, gatherer, servitor, marverer, finisher, you get each task right then and there, fast, and pass it on, same job each time, time after time. You don't try fancy stuff, standing in a line, you'd hold the lot up. It's man by man, gather to lehr, morning, noon and night, the heat of the furnaces frazzling each man out, till he can't take no more, no longer, can't take the clumsiness of no one, knocking out his rhythm, spoiling the work, losing him money soon as he knows it. No, you do your job; you get it right; that's the beginning, that's the concluding of it. I tell you.

Which don't mean to say you haven't to get the feel of the stuff; haven't to get to like it; more than like it, often enough. I were fourteen when I started, back at the factory in Middlesex; the one that got its closure when the gaffer retired, more years ago than I care to remember. They did moulding there as well as blowing. But it was the blowing got me, right from the commencement, not that I were set to blowing for a while. Not that it does your lungs a power of good, haven't I my wheezes to show for it; the ones are going to do for me, sooner rather than later? I sound like her pa's old combine, Grace is kind enough to tell me. I don't care to inform her it'll get her too in the end, if something else doesn't. I have my conviction she knows it.

It was just a job for me in the early days, like I said. But it got me bit by bit; got me more than it did my workmates, I always were the odd one out. My mates, so far as I have the knowledge, did not take the train to the metropolis their days off, they didn't enter them museums holding their caps like they couldn't be certain what they were doing, damaging their eyes all day peering into rows of glass cases. But I did. I don't know how frequent. Frequent, certainly. And I went in libraries too. Set myself down among all those whey-faced gents with fading hair and imbibed all the literature I could lay hands on; about Venice and Ashdown Forest; Jacob Verzelini, George Ravenscroft, the one first put lead in crystal. An' if I didn't dare go into antique shops, what's a working-class lad like me got to do with antique shops, I perused all the windows, there were some as thought sometimes I was planning a felony, called the police. Till it got so I could look at a piece and tell you straight where it came from, what epoch it was blown in, more or less. And it got so I knew what kind of glass I liked the best.

And I tell you what I liked, which is a curiosity, it's not as if I'd ever drunk the substance, let alone liked it. I liked wine glasses; in particular eighteenth century wine glasses; goblets and rummers, any sort you think of. They had an eye those days of yore, they knew what glass liked and what it didn't. They knew it took to air and to turning; liked to be blown; liked to be decorated in spirals; and though it comes to be solid in the end, must look like it were blown in the fire and turned there. Jas would say I'm talking just the way he used to, but that's not truth, my talk's plain, it states the fact, it's not fancy; I don't philosophise, the way he were always doing.

But then that were the trouble with Jas; he talked too much. Aside him going off leaving his wife, and in the family way to top it. And leaving glass, his other wife, he always said; that's not the sort of thing I'd ever catch myself pronouncing. Didn't I always tell him trouble would come of putting things that way? How could he tell if he were the faithful type? And he weren't as it turned out, though he swore he could be. Him an' his little mouth, though the rest of him were all so wide and open; his round face and curly locks; the wide shoulders of him perched on little legs; like a bull were Jas. And like a bull could be turning nasty.

Like I said, I like my glass plain, and preferably in goblets; any kind of stem almost — baluster, inverted baluster, ball knop or acorn knop, drop knop or flattened; foursquare stems I like, the kind sets the glass to the table; also airier, more delicate stems, that look to lift a piece right off it. Colour I don't like in glass, except it's a colour twist, a spiral set inside in the stem, showing how it were twisted in the making. Even then I like an air twist better, showing the same, but in the glass only. A fine tall goblet with a good broad foot and an air-twist stem, not even a knop to it, that's the king of all glass, as far as I'm concerned, can't be nothing in the universe more beautiful than that; never mind what you call it. What's words compared to that, I ask — I can't love words the way Jas used to; what is the use of words, I ask you, but to distinguish one thing from another; ball knop from acorn; air-twist from colour.

The long and short of it was, I got a fancy to try my hand at those artefacts I'd grown so fond of. I was a skilled lad now. I could blow up a piece with the best. After work, in friggering times, when we could make what we wished to, when my workmates went in for all kinds of fancy making, animals, birds and such like, all decoration and squiggle, I tried some eighteenth century goblets, nights I could find another to assist me. Though I hardly knew often quite where to commence it. It were a question of attempt and fail, fail more usual. But in the end I had it. The gaffer himself got to hear, he used to come down and watch me. He showed me more books than I'd found — even gave me some from his own library. And it were him first quoted me John Ruskin, the gent made more sense of glass than any, if you want my humble opinion. In fact he made more sense of most things. The only books in my house, save my big Bible, come from my family, are the collected works of Ruskin that my gaffer gave me. Never mind he was a wordy bloke, till Jas I never met anyone like him, for what he said I can even forgive his being wordy.

The quality of glass, Johnny Ruskin says, is one, ductility, and two, translucence. That is you can pull it out to different shapes, that is it lets light through, assuming you don't stop it. You make glass, don't acknowledge these, you lose it; that's what he says and I believe him. Cut glass is barbarous, he says, there too I am in concord. Gilded, enamelled glass is barbarous, too, I say; so's sticking glass in a mould and bringing it out all odd-shaped and wrinkled, the sort of thing Grace is beginning to complicate. I tell her. She won't listen. She never does, unless it suit her. And I sigh and let her go, the way you do a daughter, I suppose, not that I'd know much concerning daughters.

Jas was like a son to me, though, I acknowledge. I came across him after the old factory folded, after the old gaffer retired. The gaffer believed in what I did, he saw me right, set me up on my ownsome, with a line even for my living, making the little blue bowls to put in salt cellars, the silver kind they sell at places like Asprey's. Betweenwhiles I pursued my eighteenth century stuff, call it repro if you like, why should I care, it looked good then, it looks good now, and I adapted it to my own ways and uses, the way the old gaffers used to. And I had a market for every single piece. The gaffer saw to that. He'd let me train up likely lads all along, the best of 'em I took to the new place with me.

Weren't long after, they thought to teach my kind of work at one of the colleges; and weren't no one knew how to do it, excepting yours truly. So they asked me to teach it; there I was then, learning all kinds of fancy lads with letters to their names, and fancier ideas about Art and that. Put 'em in the sort of line I was apprenticed to, they'd not live a week, I tell you. Still I learned them all I knew, and some of 'em come good enough, I'm granting.

Jas was one; but the only one I invited to my place, let work there along of me and my likely lads. And he liked it; oh how he liked it, he was all talk of ductility and translucence, Johnny Ruskin had nothing on him, I tell you. But he did love glass; loved it as much as I did. In foolish moments I saw myself passing on through him. In the most foolish of all I stopped the whole production line one morning – the lads weren't pleased, but why should I have been caring — they watched jealously, every man jack of 'em, while I led Jas through to the cupboard at the back of the glasshouse, that not one of them had ever seen open. And brought out, all ceremonial, a great leather tool bag. They weren't the tools I used, I'd had my own too long to want to change when the gaffer gave me these in parting. But for his sake I've always kept them careful — he's been dead these twenty years. 1820 was the date stamped on the handle of the shears in that leather bag, alongside the name of their first maker and owner. In this business you honour your tools; they are important.

Jas took them saying nothing, they might have been his due. At the same time he always showed he knew what they were worth. He continued to use them as long as he stayed with me. Finding those tools set back in the same cupboard I took them from was how I knew he wasn't returning, not to me nor the glass nor Grace. Not in my lifetime anyway, so I felt it. After might be a different matter, I always knew, but that's nothing to me any longer, my only concern is what happens to my glass, after, and maybe not even that much.

I gave the tools to Grace in due time though not with such ceremony. I think she were pleased. At least she smiled at me and used them. What would the gent who made them have said, I wonder, to see his tools in a woman's hands? About what I said, I should imagine, when Jas first offered her the blowing iron and taught her how to gather. And what a sad job she made of that. It didn't come easy to Grace, no, it did not come easy, not like it did to Jas. If you could have told me I'd have her working with me all these anni domini, if you'd said I'd have given her the old gent's tools, you could have blown me down with a feather; because she was so slowsome, so cackhanded in the start; still more, of course, because she was a woman.

It was February and pouring with rain when, twelve years or so after Jas had fled with his actress, after she'd lost her baby and taken to the glass and Reg, Grace got off the bus on the A39 at the turning up to Luxcombe. Fortunately she carried an umbrella. If there was anything that showed her how things had changed that did, even more than the still incomprehensible fact of her mother's death. Umbrellas were for city folk. In all the years she had walked up this same lane on her way from school, with her mother in the beginning, later by herself or with Winifred, not one of them, she thought, had ever had such protection. On wet days they huddled in the hoods of macs and jackets, bowed their heads against the spears of rain and hurried home that much faster.

The lane seemed gloomier than she remembered, if a little

shorter; its almost crimson sides were no less steep and no less overgrown in places. When she reached the village she did not continue past the cottages down to the farm, but turned straight in at the gate of the little fourteenth century chapel just up the road, which her mother, despite her Methodist upbringing, had so assiduously attended, and waited alone at the back for people to start appearing. One glance at the coffin when it was set down on the trestles in the middle of the aisle was enough. None of the wreaths of flowers on it were from her, which seemed appropriate somehow, if to be regretted, especially by herself. She looked at no one throughout the service; noted only the miserable drip of the rain off the yew tree beyond the window; the red of the plough on the adjoining hill blanketed by drizzle.

Even afterwards, at the graveside, she and her umbrella remained apart. Which isn't to say that there weren't, in such circumstances, one or two other umbrellas — someone had even been bold enough to try to shelter Mr Tucker. Or that Grace did not at last steal a glance or two at her father and then wish that she had not. Not because he still failed to acknowledge her presence by so much as a flicker, but because he had shrunk over the years, it seemed to her; or maybe he just seemed to have shrunk, his shoulders being so bent. His cheeks and nose were netted with red veins, so were his eyelids she noted when he closed them, the coffin being lowered in. Could it be tears that were leaking from underneath? Was he actually weeping for her mother? Assuming she could believe it, she could scarcely endure it. Maybe, she hoped, it's not tears, maybe it's rain only.

She did not know the parson either. A young and awkward man, he attempted, vainly, to fill the gaping spaces in the family with words clearly not meant to be perfunctory but sounding perfunctory. Grace felt sorry for him in a way, at the same time as despising him. He, more than anyone or anything, perhaps because of rather than in spite of the fact she had never clapped eyes on him before, represented a world from which she was now, definitely, excluded. "Our dear sister," he called her mother, staring down into her grave.

Earlier he had invited them to remember her good works, and to be grateful for the fact she would now be resting in peace. But of course she wasn't his sister, he was young enough to be her grandson. Just as the images of comfort he came up with, of crops growing and being cut down in their natural courses — "You folks here, in such a place, are much more fitted to understand and accept the seasonal processes of God" (pronounced Gawd) "than those of us brought up in a city" — only showed that he still belonged to the city, thought Grace, recalling, reluctantly, for the first time in years, local tragedies that had little to do with any comfortable kind of sowing and reaping; like the man from the next door farm, driven mad by a nagging wife, who had shot himself under a walnut tree. Or like her mother, for that matter, who sowed seeds that brought up nothing to nourish her except the bitterest of weeds.

She was not prepared to ask herself if she cared that she was now excluded. She had spent too many years pretending none of it existed. Yet afterwards, walking back down to the main road, unable to shake off the as yet unendurable memory of the pale wood of the brass-handled coffin descending into a bleak rectangle of red mud, she tried in vain to replace it with the memory of the wet white cloth of the parson's vestment pulled out from under his cloak by the same wind that had dragged at her own black scarf, lifted the thin hairs from her father's head.

Did her mother's kitchen, she wondered, smell of food when the mourners entered, like the kitchen of the good wife in a local legend? (A reputed witch, commemorated in a tablet in the church, trusting no one else to bake her funeral meats, she had returned in person to oversee them even while her corpse was being buried.) She could never know, of course. Back in London, the only trace of the day was the red mud on her shoes, on the hem of her mac, which she scraped away as fervently as if it was not earth but blood.

The second time Grace came back to Somerset was for the funeral of her father. It took place in midsummer, during haymaking, long after the farm had gone so far downhill the Crown had threatened to take the lease away from Mr Tucker unless he handed it over to his son-in-law, Bill, Winifred's husband. Who now, so far as Grace could see, at a swift if shrewd glance round, ran it both diligently and successfully. This did not stop her resenting, more than she might have expected, how plain Bill made it, throughout the day's somehow desultory proceedings, that all he could think of, all he wanted to get back to, was his hay.

They were not burying her father. They were cremating him, which was fair enough, she thought. (She loved and respected fire and remembering her incinerated drawings could not wish her father worse or better.) They were not even bringing his ashes back to the chapel graveyard to be buried alongside her mother in the place where he'd lived his whole life.

"He said he'd no choice where he spent his life, but was damned if he were going to lie there for eternity," Winifred whispered to Grace while they were waiting. This was also fair enough, Grace thought, though, looking around her at the municipal lines of the crematorium garden, she could not see how he or anyone could think it was any better. All the same that one last act of defiance, no matter how pointless, made her understand fully, perhaps for the first time, the miracle of her own escape.

Jas's family was quite a different matter. As Grace knew long before she knew much of Jas, despite seeing him come and go often enough in this, to her, almost intolerably over-coloured, over-stuffed household. There were objects on shelves and pictures on walls she actually cared to look at, yet at the same time distrusted. (Back in Somerset, her father allowed hunting prints and calendars only, anything else he called clutter. Eyes and notions could not change their habits that quick, she discovered to her dismay; maybe ever.) There were lights that did not eye you coldly, yet were bright enough to read by, and Indian covers on most of the beds. Clutter or not — and she could not help being disconcerted sometimes as well as disapproving at this family's seemingly extravagant and almost always noisy goings-on — she loved her own room, at the top of the house. The colours on her quilt were earthy ones that reminded her of home. She had a chair and a desk; in time she dared tack up a poster from a Lucie Rie exhibition alongside the Matisse print that she never felt sure enough of her status in this household to take down, though she disliked it. She set her ram's head dish on the mantelpiece, sellotaped round it, as time went on, drawings and photographs of other pots she'd made or thought of making.

When Jas came to eat a meal with his family, he usually sat by his mother at the far end of the table. Grace assumed he did not notice her — it had not yet dawned on her that she always would be noticed. She also assumed — the fact did not interest her much — that whatever notice did come her way was likely to be unfavourable. She noticed Jas, though. She had never met anyone like him; the way he talked, for instance. Words in her family were kept for practical matters, whereas he used words as if he was making pictures; they came in rivers; they evolved into landscapes she would have said, if she'd known how to. If she mocked his family sometimes, mostly in protection of herself and her daily shaken perspectives, she could not, would not, mock Jas, let alone enjoy their mockery of him. "Oh Jas," they said. "Shut up, Jas." "Let someone else get a word in edgeways, Jas." Sometimes, usually, he laughed back. Occasionally, though, he took umbrage, his small mouth curled and sulked in a way she did not care for, but could not avoid seeing.

One night, late, there was a knock on Grace's attic door. When she opened it she found to her surprise — she had not even known he was in the house that evening — Jas standing there, staring at her.

"Can I come in?" he asked, almost humbly; or at least without his usual assurance — she was too taken aback to make anything of it.

"If you like," she said brusquely. Though her tone made it sound more like "if you must," she realised at once, between alarm, astonishment and pleasure at his having sought her out, it wasn't what she meant. She was still more disconcerted when she saw how her confusion seemed to have reassured Jas; how he flung himself down on the rug in front of her gas fire with much more of his usual ease. "Sit down," he said. "I've come to talk, that's all. Not rape you. I'll take the bed out of the room if you like. If you'd find that less disturbing."

"Who said I imagined any such thing?" said Grace, plonking herself down on the bed in question. "Talk if you're going to, I'm good at listening. Much better than at talking."

"I had noticed," Jas said. And to the tune of the gas fire's pop pop pop, proceeded to talk till past two in the morning. In due course he developed a ruddy cheek where the fire scorched him. Grace could not take her eyes off that unsightly blotch of colour — it did not stop her joining him on the hearthrug at last, when it grew too cold to stay sitting on the bed.

"Did you ever see glass blown?" he was asking.

"I never thought of it," she said. "Why should I?"

"Wouldn't you like to?"

"Yes, maybe I would." But at this moment, still, even though she had begun to open to the mysterious words in which he talked of his obsession; even though she had never before in her life wanted to do anything except for itself, she wanted it because of Jas, mainly.

"I'll take you to Reg's glasshouse one day," Jas said. "He doesn't like women much. But you, I think, he could put up with."

He looked at her then, in a way he had not looked at her before. She did not know if she liked it. What she did like, apprehensively, was the growing understanding that this visit wasn't to be the end of things. That Jas was likely to be seeking her out again. It did not matter that after a minute Jas himself seemed to have forgotten it. Once more the alchemies involved in glassmaking, the fusing of different substances to make glass of all colours, had carried him off.

His enthusiasm reminded her, in passing, of her mother for ever exclaiming to her two daughters about the mysterious and wonderful things that occurred to eggs, for instance, when you applied heat to them; reminded her also, more comfortably, of the mix of chemicals in her own ceramic glazes. The way you could combine one colourless substance with another, to produce, say, a brilliant yellow, had always struck her as not as odd as it looked, but, rather, almost organic; like shoving in a pale seed and getting back a poppy. It was so inevitable, in fact, you only had to learn what to do and how to do it. If you failed sometimes to get the effect you wanted, it was, invariably, for some good scientific reason. There was not the slightest mystery about it, the way Jas made it sound, for all that the terms he used — ductility, viscosity, translucency — were scientific enough, for all that he talked of such things as observable chemical reactions.

Grace said — she would have said some of the other things if she could, but did not know how to — "You put things in very fancy ways sometimes. Her's quite simple and scientific really. Her's not magic."

Jas grinned at her. She had never noticed before just how white and even his teeth were. His mouth looked as if it was not big enough to hold as many teeth as it had to. His tongue, as pink and moist as a puppy's between his lips and teeth, but fatter, bred in her suddenly an overwhelming urge to reach up and touch the curly hair that might have been the pelt on some animal she was supposed to be tending; apart from being, probably, not only longer but softer.

"But it is magic, in a way," Jas was saying, smiling to himself slightly, as if he knew precisely what she was feeling. "People always used to think it was magic."

Softly, never taking his eyes off her — though the words he used were almost as academic as those used by his father, his tone grew more intimate by the minute — he added, "The glassmen were thought to be magicians, didn't you know? But then of course they'd seem like magicians. So did all the other masters of chthonic arts, like the alchemists and smiths." He rolled the word chthonic round his tongue in a way that made it clear he liked it; yet he must, Grace thought, have suspected she'd never have heard it before let alone knew its meaning; just as he must have seen that for her, at this moment, he was the only magician that counted. ("Contrary to appearances, there's always been a romantic, almost Mills and Boon element in you, Gracie, in regard to me," he was to accuse her later.)

"There they were," he went on, "secreting metals in the fires, transforming them into something else, who knows but if in the end if they could hit on the right formula, they mightn't have been able to convert all metals into gold. Just like some furnace Midas." Touching her bare arm for the first time, not looking at her, he added, "Turn even your flesh to gold." She shivered at his touch. It never occurred to her to take her arm away.

"More like Goldfinger," she said. "And I'd be dead. If you left me no space of skin for breath."

"You sound as if you still don't trust me," he protested.

"Trust you? I never thought about it." And it was true that she had not, not in the way he meant. The way she was feeling at the moment — the way she had never felt before in her life — she distrusted herself much more. Touching the livid patch that had arrived on her own cheek by now, its warmth both terrified and exhilarated her. (What would her father have said at the sight of Jas, for instance? The thought made her feel triumphant, briefly.)

"Glassblowers used to wear animal skins to protect them from the heat," he was saying. "Imagine a man at such a fire, wrapped in a deerskin complete with antlers, wouldn't anyone have thought he was a magician?"

"He'd have got rid of the antlers, of course," objected Grace, firmly. Yet she did not object in the slightest when, not long after, at around five past two — the candles Jas had lit uninvited some while back jerked and jumped, guttering right down; clothes, hung on hooks against the walls, made headless shadows on them that moved as Jas did, as the candle flames did in the breeze they created between them — he led her from the fire, laid her body down on the earth colours of her eiderdown, and started to undress her.

"Blow out the candles," was all she said, snatching vaguely at some notion of modesty she never knew she had, let alone reflected on, until it came welling up from heaven knows where. He took no notice. By the time the last candle flared and went out, he had already, more or less skilfully, relieved her of such virginity as her horses had left. It wasn't much; she hardly bled a drop. Indeed, although a few hours earlier she'd barely conceived of such a process happening to her, let alone with him, she now took it as much for granted as she had used to take the old ram's tupping of her father's ewes. As she took for granted the easy pleasure it gave her. Not only the first time; also the second and the third. Problems with orgasm, it turned out, were not for her.

"Why did you bleed so little, Gracie?" was Jas' only demur. It was the first time he called her Gracie — the first time she objected to it. He was teasing but not entirely; she could feel his slight but genuine chagrin. Maybe till now, he'd never managed to seduce a virgin. "Are you *sure* I'm your first lover?"

But she did not really believe he doubted her; any more than she cared if he did, providing that he kept on fucking her. Not only was he too triumphant at such a conquest, a moment later, God help her, she could hardly believe it, was telling her she was beautiful, not like anyone else. Worse still he was saying, "I think I'm in love with you, Gracie." Which seemed much more like rape than the other, even though, so far as she'd considered the matter, she'd always assumed seduction to be the same as rape.

Touching his face, running an amazed finger along his red lips, letting him entrap it between his fine white teeth, she forgot the promises he had made not to molest her; saw belief in what he said as no less reasonable a strategy for the moment than any other. Even though in her book it was the most unreasonable of strategies. Even though, thank God, this man was as arrogant as her father. But much more confident, she assumed. But then she had no one, except her father, against whom to measure him. (She did not, perhaps unfairly, never having noticed how the man used to look at her, count her art teacher at Minehead.) Still worse, she had nothing, apart from the savours of their two spent bodies, apart from the gleam of the almost gutted candle on the ram's horns, on its stony eye, to guide her. And even that savour, those horns, that eye she herself had, in one way or other, created.

Terry was a week or two in the glasshouse, getting the smell of it, before he so much as touched a punty except to put it away or fetch it, let alone a blowing iron.

Apart from Reg, who was too old and sick to come in every day, there was the other assistant, poovy Jeremy. Him I couldn't stand, with his ginger hair and fancy pants, nor could Reg I'm glad to say. Jeremy didn't seem to like glass that much; he never thought of nothing except getting what he called his oats, even the glass he made friggering round for himself was sexy: bowls like arses, little lids like tits; he were worse than all my mates, I tell you, and that's saying quite a lot. Still he weren't a bad worker, I give him that. If Reg weren't around with Grace, working with her on that eighteenth century stuff, Jeremy'd help her on the great bowls she went in for, that he called her skyscapes and firescapes, though she never did, she just called them her bowls. Really heavy they were, I didn't know how Jeremy held them straight on the punty when she knocked 'em off the blowing iron; she'd trapped swirls of colour in the glass, they were like stormy days, like the middle of volcanoes.

My job meanwhile was tidying up, sorting this an' that, making coffee, putting the irons back in the rack. Else, the days Helen the secretary came, I polished stuff in the showroom, swept the floor, took letters to the post. Bit by bit, though, I got to helping with the glass, got to be part of the dance proper. I found I knew the steps without knowing I'd learned 'em; when to hand her things, for instance, when the pink pads were dry and needed spraying with water.

One evening after Jeremy went off to meet his floozy, she even started teaching me to gather. I'd thought to do it easy, it looked money for old rope when she were at it. Of course it weren't; all I got on the iron every time was a thin little coating. It were her fixed me a proper lump in the end; before I knew it she had me sitting in the chair, twisting the iron with one hand — of course I couldn't keep it steady — while with the other I tried to shape the glass with the pad; then she made me roll it in colour on the marver, then coat it with more glass in the furnace; till I had a paperweight of sorts, magic if you ask me, even though it were me what did it; even though it were shaped bleeding funny.

Another evening she began teaching me to blow; of course at first I couldn't get so much as a blister. She showed me over and over, in the end when my breath were running out it did swell up a bit, I got a bowl of sorts, a little one; but it weren't flat at the bottom, it wouldn't stand up ever.

What I do now stands up all right. I can make a fine goblet from gather to foot to finish, I'm even making scent bottles Grace thinks she should be able to sell. Just the same it's those things I made first I'm proudest of, never mind my mum laughed fit to bust; the paperweight looked like a bent cock, she said, she would, wouldn't she, why couldn't she marvel at the colour trapped inside it, not even ask me how I did it?

Weren't long after, Grace made me set the punty on the foot of the goblet she were working. I hadn't expected that. I were so scared I dropped it; it goes without saying poncy Jeremy thought that a giggle, if not the best joke ever. Grace said nothing, just pretended to clip me over the earhole. Next day she gave me the punty iron again. I didn't want it this time, seeing bleeding Jeremy waiting for me to drop it. But I didn't drop it. I held it just about OK. And to give the bugger his due, he bought me a pint that night on the strength of it, and in front of his floozy, who were a bit of all right, weren't she, even if she did like that git Jeremy. Next day Reg were in; Grace sent me for the punty this time as if it were normal, so it seemed to Reg too, quite normal, it were only me told myself I were a clever bugger, feeling the sure way I caught it, not too strong this time, not too weak; the glass didn't dip a fraction when she knocked her end off and left me holding it as to the manner born, twisting it a little to keep the thing steady and even. Glassblower Terry I were, pretty nearly. It seemed the first thing I learned to do proper the whole of my frigging life.

Which were a marvel. And it were Grace taught me. And it's why I'm here in bleeding Derbyshire leaving my mother behind at last, the only thing I ever really wanted. Grace had better not take to the booze, I tell you, I'm not putting her to bed of nights, at least not for that reason. Who'd have thought Reg'd've have left her his business, better still his house, which he'd had for ever, and turned out worth a mint of money? They didn't speak soft, never. He grouched at her more like. She usually said nothing. Granted when they worked together they might have been Reg Astaire and Grace Rogers on the telly, they were that neat on their feet; for all Reg was so slow and old, else, coughing, wheezing, spitting up lumps of yellowish gob.

And then who'd've thought she'd move out of London? It were a lot of ready, I know that, but she could afford it, her flat, his house to sell, all the prices up here much lower. We brought quite a lot of the business with us: the tools, the lehr, the glory hole, the sandblaster. Not the furnace of course, we've got to make ourselves a furnace, that's why we're hanging about, waiting; it takes six weeks to deliver the stuff. It's dead quiet up here, also; too quiet I sometimes think. And the whole time the house smells of cooking. Not her cooking, she don't do none, nor mine, I'm a dab hand at fry-ups, but this smell ain't fry-ups, it's like pies and cakes and bread, it makes me hungry. Maybe it makes Grace hungry, if that is she even smells it. Perhaps she doesn't, perhaps it's just me an' I'm going off my rocker; maybe it even *means* me to go right off my rocker.

Jas was not the first man since Grace came to London who had wanted to get her into bed. A fact that never ceased to amaze her; in Somerset no one had fancied her in the least, whereas her sister, Winifred, was never without a steady boyfriend from the age of fifteen or so. She was different, that was the problem. To make it worse she did not care who knew it, never bothering to learn the preliminary sexual arts, flirtation, for instance. Though some men therefore feared and resented her, just like her father, with others it added to the attraction of this fine figure of a woman, still firm and hard from the physical work that had been heaped on her in her childhood.

Jas was definitely one of the others. He was not even awed, he took what he wanted; which she gave him freely — having resisted everyone else, she'd have given him anything. She had not known how much she needed such things, until Jas took her virginity from her.

As for the glass; she was intrigued, all right, by what he told her. But she did not, at first, see it as having anything to do with her. Glass belonged to Jas' brilliance; her own fires she saw as much more muted. All the same, from the first moment she walked into Reg's glasshouse, she felt comfortable in there. With its heat, dark corners, dust, jumbled tools, it was much more congenial to her than the places where she usually worked. She found real workmen, for instance, like the old man who had sometimes worked for her father, whose kindness long ago convinced her she need not hate all men because she hated him. She felt at home with Reg's workers the way she did not feel at home among the youths in her art school, who argued about art forms, and raved about painters like Rothko and Robert Rauschenberg of whom she, from her no nonsense background, had felt from the beginning, had remained, extremely suspicious. She also felt more at home with Reg's workers than with Jas' racketty, not to say permissive, not to say noisy family — not only did Jas' mother not blink so much as an eyelash when he came down to breakfast along with Grace, she had even started trying to persuade her to model naked. Music ranging from reggae to Bartók came from every room in that house except Grace's. No one actually appeared to be listening to it, either.

She excepted Jas, of course, from her dismissal of his family. Seeing how he fitted in with Reg's workers, she liked him more than ever. It was also she, more than anyone, who supported his decision to give up art school and work for Reg full time, failing to see the danger in the restlessness indicated by Jas' eager pursuit of such a change of plan. More and more frequently she came to watch him work; did not care in the least, if she was aware of it — possibly she was not — that Reg tolerated her presence because of Jas and Jas only.

It was not that Reg was so old-fashioned as to think women belonged in the home. Women belonged anywhere they liked, as far as Reg was concerned, provided it was where he wasn't. Appalled to find women in his art school class, he taught them because he had to, against all his principles. No good would come of it, he told anyone who would listen. Had he been a Catholic, Jas teased him, he'd've crossed himself, as in the face of the very devil.

Jas, though, as far as Reg was concerned, was not to be denied. This big girl seemed sensible enough, fortunately, didn't speak much, kept out of the way when wanted; she even took her beer well when they went down to the pub. And if Jas was teaching her a bit about the work, getting her to help him after hours, that was his affair, Reg thought, so long as he didn't have to see it. Besides, Grace was married to Jas by this time, the thing was not only more or less legal, it did, presumably, keep Jas happy. If he banned Grace, might she perhaps start trying to keep Jas away from the glasshouse? Reg was not going to risk it.

Jas was not only his best worker by now, not only got glass right, he also made Reg laugh. Seeing the old man's head thrown back, his dentures slipping a little, his fingers misshapen with age, yet still powerful, gripping his tankard so tightly he might have thought his mirth likely to throw it over, Grace was not to know that no one else, ever, till Jas, had succeeded in making Reg laugh. On the other hand she could see the way Jas wrapped Reg round his little finger. She did not like that altogether. And liked still less the realisation that Jas could be, as a business man, quite tricky. (A sharp salesman, much sharper than Reg, he'd already persuaded him into one cut-price deal selling rummers to a large store.)

She saw much less clearly, of course, how Jas wrapped her, Grace, round his little finger; how else had he got her, usually so cautious, to marry him overnight? He had his mother in his pocket likewise, but she, fortunately, knew herself and Jas much better; it was she who not only bought them their flat, but, claiming it was Grace's due, given the times she had used her as a model, had insisted they put it in both Jas' and Grace's names. (Grace herself would not have insisted. The idea of someone's mother having the will, let alone the money, to buy her son a flat, let alone that such a son could be her husband, was in itself too much to take in; almost beyond her comprehension.)

It was Jas' capacity to charm her that got Grace helping him in the glasshouse some evenings, against all her inclinations, not to say better judgment. By the time Jas walked out, Grace was not only three months pregnant, she was also a tolerably competent assistant; even though she had never, for one moment, found glass easy; any more than she had found it easy throwing pots on a wheel. Her hands, by choice, worked much more slowly.

Yet, perversely enough, it was precisely the speed of glassmaking that had begun, little by little, to win her. Ceramics took so much longer; weeks sometimes, what with the different glazings and firings, never mind the interminable coiling of the clay. Nor, till the weeks were up, could you be sure what you were getting. Sometimes, if things went wrong, you ended with precisely nothing. You did not know with glass either. Sometimes glass, too, got broken; it got knocked off the iron, or it had an air bubble, or it cracked, unexpectedly, in the lehr. Yet the surprise or disappointment was revealed in less than an hour, overnight at the very most. Grace found herself liking that. She'd never felt patience burdening her before. But now, watching Jas, she began to.

When Jas left, though, that seemed the end of it. Would have been the end of it; the last person on earth Grace wanted to see was Reg, whom Jas had also abandoned. She only went to the glasshouse, a month or so after her baby had been born dead, prematurely, because she had a note from Jas, saying he was off to California. With this he enclosed a note to Reg, to be taken to him personally. Anyone but Grace would have put it in the post anyway. Not Grace though. Grace, not obedient exactly, but dogged, took the note over herself.

★

You could have knocked Reg down with a feather when that young woman turned up out of nowhere; when he turned round and saw her standing behind him.

Just after Christmas it was, the ice had already got us. I'd never expected to clap eyes on her again for certain. That had been the last of a female in my glasshouse, I thought, not unkindly, not exactly good riddance, either. Even I could see Jas had done wrong by her, if he were so ungainly as to hang a woman on him, he shouldn't have left her, not like that, not after going so far as to set a young Jas in her belly.

Nor were she a bad girl as they go, if you happen to like the sex that's female. I thought it still when I turned and saw her. Not that the sight of her gave me pleasure exactly. She was taking some paper out of her pocket, which she motioned to, but it were not the right moment, she understood it, so she should have done the times she'd watched us work, on Jas' invitation. When I'd got the piece in the lehr at last — it was a goblet with an airtwist stem as I remember — there she still was, like a statue; she'd not seemed to have shifted an inch, though looking a happorth less frozen, as far as my eyes were capable of judging. She were thinner, I thought, than I'd known her; of course she hadn't never been a Gibson Girl exactly. Maybe, I thought, her Merry Christmas were no more mince pies and tinsel than mine were.

She still didn't say nothing. Just handed me the paper; I saw at once it were Jas' writing.

"He said I had to give it you," she tells me then, deadpan, in that little voice of hers which has always surprised me, coming out of that tall girl.

"He'd no right to give you orders, not now he hasn't," I says, trying to be kindly.

"He never had any rights to give me orders," she replies; she is stony as ever.

Naturally I don't try to detain her. But of course it wouldn't have been decent to show her out as I would have been minded with all other members of the so-called fair sex. We was in the same boat, in a manner of speaking. That is to say, in our losing a son and a husband, I'd more in common with that one than with any woman save my mother. At the sight of her I was even ready to acknowledge it, though I can't say I'd thought of it sooner. If Jas weren't my son, he felt it. Was no doubt neither, he was Grace's lawfully wedded. (Not one, by the feel of her, she'd wipe easy from her mind, whether then or later, howsomever she believes it.)

Why she stayed round that morning, I cannot, of course, be certain. Unless it was because at that time of year, post Yuletide, the warmth would have been welcome to anyone save other glassmen. Unless it was because she felt lonely in that flat of hers, and found it easier being reminded of Jas here, in my glasshouse; as I did. She looked all around the place as though she had never seen it. At my witch's piece, for instance, on top of the main furnace, for what it's worth in keeping away such females. (It having been Jas' trouble, from the beginning, that he'd sooner invite the witches in than ban them.)

Though I don't name names, or hold it against her in the circumstance, there was maybe one of those witches, in a manner of speaking, not too far from where I was standing. She was eyeing the shelves now, the one with the books Jas bought what I never looked at; also the shelf with the seconds, on which were still some of his pieces. I don't doubt she noticed. It gave me the thought to offer her a cup of rosie. She looked so weakly, I considered she could do with a few lumps of sugar and some milk inside her belly, along of a good strong dose of Indian tannin. The problem was I'd a feeling she'd refuse the offer. In the end I just gave her the mug already milked and sugared. She never said thank you, more important, she drank it. Was still drinking, slowly, when I began to start working, she looked like a person thawing, her skin less like the colour of metal. Maybe, I was reflecting, it's not just females are witches; maybe some men are witches, maybe Jas spelled the both of us, the Lord only knows how he did it, I never knew no one talk such a load of nonsense.

Nor do I know what got into me after. Being between

Xmas and New Year, all I had was the one man to help me, him I paid overtime. Maybe if I hadn't been shorthanded, her life — and mine — had turned out different. When my worker got called out sudden, I didn't make him wait till the piece was finished. I didn't jack that piece in, either, win one, lose one. No, what I did was much more crazier, I looked at Grace, and jerked my head towards the punty. Without us having exchanged but the three or four words since she walked back into the glasshouse, our fate was sealed; she finished the piece with me. The man's face when he came back and caught us were a picture. Which I saw, and perhaps that did it. Before I knew, and with not exactly my approval, except I was used to her by then and getting more used by the minute, she gave up ceramics first, then her art school; she apprenticed herself to me. The clumsiest apprentice I took, ever.

For by God did she remain lubberly, not to say ham-handed; devil knows why I kept her, at times I said so. Devil knows why she kept coming, come to that; she didn't look like she enjoyed it. She was a diligent worker, I grant you, but could I get her two hands to work in co-operation, no I could not in the beginning. The sight of her cackhanded efforts sometimes made me want to weep — me weep, an old man, yes weep, like Niobe, her what you see in museums, in all them marbles, weeping for her young 'uns, what someone had taken. And as for my apprenticing a girl, Old Nick himself must have been working to make me concord it, from that beginning, that December morning. Not that anyone had a better eye, not anyone I'd found lately. Her eye was good as Jas' in a way and better, no matter how unhanded. Was no lack, neither, that she wasn't one for fancy talk; a tongue-tied woman is more than I could have hoped for.

It got so before I knew, I couldn't be doing without her; I kept no one on but her, when old age crept on, when I couldn't keep up with things no more, not except I closed down the business in its most part; the salt cellar part, that is, the factory line up. We moved into a smaller place, worked with the eighteenth century stuff only, she were good for that, by then she could get an air-twist neat as anyone, though who'd have believed it the way she was when I commenced her; all lubberly, like I said, like she had oil on her fingers not butter, the fly of glass out of her hands short and sweet as a donkey's gallop. It was staying power that did it; got her where she got to be; and if I had more patience with her than I'd ever have believed of yours truly, it was, I daresay, because, all those years, she reminded me of Jas, his lordship.

Not that I made things easy for her ever; she did not escape my tongue's lashings; the more of them perhaps because of my rememberment of Jas. Maybe I didn't feel too good about the lashings always. Maybe because of that when I made my last will and testament, I willed her all of it. Who else was there to take it, that I trusted, that I believed in? And what else did I have to give, sir, apart from my glass, apart from a roof that leak though it might was in a neighbourhood grown over the years altogether too fancy?

It was March by the time Grace and Terry arrived in Derbyshire. Not only was it snowing that morning of their arrival, though not cold enough for the snow to lie, it snowed on and off for the rest of the month. But then, in April, the weather turned unseasonably warm and dry. They'd had planning permission for the glasshouse since the end of February; by mid-April they'd set up the gas tanks, strengthened and painted the walls, laid on the electricity. The materials for the furnace still not having arrived, though, nor due for another two weeks, there was, for the moment, nothing much more that they could do.

Up at the house, of course, there was still plenty of work needed doing. Grace would have applied herself, normally. What stopped her was the smell in the kitchen which, ebb and flow as it might, had never gone away entirely. At times it seemed stronger than ever, it moved in her head as tangibly as sound; it *was* sound in the end, as well as all the rest; a sound that among the glory of baking bread, of roast meat and ragouts, of plum duff and gingerbread, separated, little by little, into words that might seem glorious depending on the way you saw them — Grace inclined to that way maybe but not entirely; or, on the other hand, might not. They were quite unmistakable, certainly. Wedlock is padlock, she heard some voice as if proclaiming. *Wedlock is padlock.*

Chapter Three

*"It only receives sculpture or cutting from a diamond or
emery stone . . ."*

Wedlock is padlock . . . The mysterious voice so unnerved Grace that for a while, during the day at least, she could hardly bear to stay in the house at all. At first she told herself not to be so stupid. Since the smell of fresh paint would, surely, drive away the smell of food, she bought paint and paintbrushes, and started, with Terry's help, to give the cottage a new coat of paint. To no avail. The smell persisted. After two days she left Terry to it and went down to her glasshouse at the bottom of the woods. Where she found she could not bear to stay for long either.

It was not the most salubrious of sites. A former nailworks, overhung by scrubby oak trees, it was flanked on one side by derelict workshops, labelled DANGER. UNSAFE STRUCTURE. KEEP OUT. On the other, a chain link fence stood between the glasshouse and a cinder wasteland; the local dump, where something was always burning, giving off an unwholesome, smoky reek. The austere Grace would have scorned, usually, to let herself be affected by such things. She had chosen this building carefully; it was, among other things, cheap. Nor would she have been affected now, she told herself, if her glasshouse had been in working order, her furnace alight. But without a furnace even, let alone fire, the place was lifeless; as derelict as the dump. She forced herself to stay a whole day doing this and that. In the evening she locked up thankfully and went home determined not to go near the place for the moment.

Next morning she thought Terry looked upset when she

said she was abandoning him; that for the second day running he was going to have to work by himself. She shouted at him. "I pay you to do what you're told. And that means work. Whatever work I choose to give you. I expect the kitchen finished by the time I come back tonight." Then she slammed out, got into her car and drove off, if she did not know where it hardly mattered. It was all landscape here and landscape was what she wanted; it was landscape she had wanted for nearly two years now to get into her work somehow, so far without success; from the moment, in that unpromising-seeming gallery, miles up Madison Avenue, she had clapped eyes on the rather too slick, rather too shiny cubes of glass, with, trapped inside them, what looked like sections of stratified rock.

Her New York trip had turned out pointless till then, commercially or otherwise. It had still appeared so when Grace walked into this particular gallery and held out the slides of her and Reg's work — without much hope — to the bald gay who seemed to be its owner.

It was not that she was a bad saleswoman usually, surprisingly enough. You could not say that she charmed her customers exactly, the way Jas used to. What she did do was convince them of her integrity, and thus of the integrity of her glass. Not in New York, however. In this gallery as in all the others, the owner glanced fleetingly at Reg's goblets, at the bowls Jeremy dubbed Grace's firescapes, or skyscapes, then said, looking the other way, as if he too knew she must have heard it all before, "Didn't they tell you, lady, functional glass is for the gift shops? Glass sculptures is what the galleries are into these days."

He wore a check shirt, sneakers, and jeans supported by a belt with a snake buckle like little boys used to wear in England to hold up their shorts. Whatever would Reg think, Grace was wondering, eyeing the somehow menacing and to her quite meaningless chic of the artefacts about her; none of which had been made with Ruskin's criteria in mind. Deformed — she considered — and twisted shapes, moulded, cut or blasted; neon rods put together to make patterns like subway maps. They only went to prove, she thought, what Jas had always insisted, that glass was of all mineral substances the one most easily vulgarised. Yet again she asked herself — almost since the moment she touched down at Kennedy she had been asking herself the same thing — what could have possessed her to use her Craft Council grant looking at developments in American glassmaking, rather than Czechoslovakian, say, or German? It was not even as if she *liked* American glass much.

(Jas, of course, was in the USA. But since he lived as far as she knew on the West Coast, not the East, and since, had she thought about it, she would have assumed this was as good a reason as any to flee in the opposite direction, it never occurred to her to imagine that Jas had anything to do with it. Jas'd had nothing to do with her life for over eighteen years.)

The gift shops to which she kept being directed had been, of course, as useless to her as the galleries. Their stock still more vulgar if anything, her own stuff was much too expensive and purist. She hated New York, she decided, putting her slides back in their envelope. The only things she'd seen so far that she liked in any way whatever — and this despite herself — were the great glass boxes rearing up from Fifth Avenue, reflecting the sky, reflecting a cathedral in one place, as well as reflecting each other.

It may have been these same glass boxes, however, that predisposed her towards the caseful of shiny cubes on which her eyes fell as she was heading for the door; the man with the snake belt already had his finger on his buzzer to let her out.

She could not say she liked even these cubes much. She did not spend long surveying them; never thought of asking for details of their maker. Yet, on the instant, those rocklike sections trapped inside them, like the undersides of landscape, told her what she'd wanted to know, without knowing it; what had been missing up till this moment, both from her glass and from her life. She nodded at the bald man, walked out of his glass door the instant his buzzer released her; flew home next day, determined, consciously or not, to do something about it.

While Reg was still alive, of course, there was not much she could do; less because of him, his possible reaction, than because she herself was not yet ready to do so. Her work went opposite ways if anything. She started turning out opaque bowls and vases, black in many cases, split by jagged lines of white like foam, or, more often, like lightning, almost all roughened in the sandblaster. Reg hated them of course; John Ruskin would have turned in his grave, he said. Grace laughed. It felt more as if she was turning in hers. This glass caught her own blankness so exactly, it pleased not only her but her buyers. She had no difficulty in selling every piece.

A couple of months later, she bought herself an ancient Morris Minor, not unlike the one her father used to drive, and started to travel the country whenever she could spare the time, looking for landscapes that might be of use to her; practically the first intention she'd been able to see clearly in herself since her determination to leave Somerset over twenty years before. But it wasn't until she reached the Peak district of Derbyshire that she found at last something of what she looked for. The very flintiness of the landscape which had so appalled earlier travellers — Daniel Defoe, for instance — drew her; the more, probably, because she came in winter, between snows, when it was at its barest and bleakest. Even given her small knowledge of geology, its structure was easy for her to read at such a time.

Jas, who knew about such things, could have informed her of precedents for moving up here; in earlier centuries other glassblowers had trekked northwards, to settle a bit further west. It was coal *they'd* been after, to fuel their furnaces; coal there was in plenty, then as now. Grace had noted the bitter coal smell from almost every chimney; she liked it, what's more.

Not that she was going to need coal for her furnace. Even to her, her decision to choose this place seemed in most respects perverse. Not least because it had hung finally on something as tenuous as finding her mother's almost obliterated name on a tombstone. She had been led, to be precise, to the south-east corner of a horseshoe formed by the gritstone, of which the northern edge was Bleaklow and Kinderscout. The dark rock of the High Peaks, almost always forbidding to look at despite its reddish tinge and perceptible glitter, enclosed more open, flowing, limestone country that had once been marine reefs and lagoons. These limestone dales were not graceful exactly, either, but much less sombre. The surprisingly deep, narrow valleys between their undulating slopes reminded Grace of those which fissured the Brendon Hills above where she came from. It was barely possible, once inside, to imagine the more open landscape above them.

This was white country, of course, pale country, by comparison with the Brendons, let alone the gritstone; so deathly that only ash trees grew on it willingly. Even so its pallor, which the very arrival of spring could not disguise entirely, appealed to her more than the pallor of the chalk downs further south. She also loved ash trees; their sprays of leaves, their graceful branches, the way the wood bent and gave when you worked it, was so different from the material she'd wrestled with for most of her working life. She loved the dales altogether. On the other hand she did not love, rather she admired, the gritstone peaks; of which there were outcrops even as far south as she'd landed, black rocks jutting up out of farming land. At weekends, always, they were dotted from top to bottom with the bodies of brightly dressed climbers, whose vertiginous skills Grace envied.

The little valley she'd come to, though within the gritstone, and still stone wall country, was different again, not like anything she'd imagined. Most Derbyshire houses were set gracelessly across hillsides, it seemed to her, in the full blast of the wind and weather. Her cottage, on the other hand, the stone heart of it seventeenth century, not only sheltered under a hill, it stood at the gates of a park surrounding an undistinguished eighteenth century mansion now used as a school, overlooking an artificial lake; the whole site so gracefully landscaped, with its cedar tree and tall chestnuts, it almost appeared southern. "This delightful spot" the estate agent's brochure had called it; not inaccurately for once.

The eighteenth century brick front of the cottage itself was lit, like the brick front of the once matching, now much extended house opposite, by a "three-part Venetian window, with a half moon Diocletian window over," according to the same brochure. Grace did not care what the windows were called; she'd just liked the place at first sight. In particular she liked the three-arched window and the half-moon shaped one over, which was the window of her bedroom. Since it was this, not the neighbours, that had drawn her to the place, she was disconcerted later, drinking in the pub down on the main road, to discover that she had inadvertently landed herself in what was thought of in these parts as a middle-class ghetto.

"'S a pound a puff oop at Tendersley, in't it?" one man said looking over his glass at her, sideways. Grace did not answer, just glowered at Terry; meaning by the glower, "Take that smirk off your face." Terry in fact was smiling from incomprehension mainly; he still hadn't got the hang of the local accent, any more than some locals had got the hang of his. (Grace's Somerset burr, he'd noticed, not only sounded much less out of place, but appeared the more pronounced, time passing.)

School was a pisshole mostly. You'd've thought I'd learn something in eleven years, wouldn't you, apart from how to piss sir about — but I didn't. Except for reading an' that; some of my mates couldn't even read proper; they stopped bothering about anything much, back in the juniors; I bothered a bit till around my second year at the comprehensive when I realised there weren't going to be no job at the end of it, so tell me the use of all that woodwork and metalwork — not that we got to make much except bookends — *bookends* — and ashtrays — let alone all those exams we weren't never going to take. Thick as two planks I am, never passed an exam in my life, never wanted to take one. That school were as glad to see the back of me as I was to see the back of it. The things Reg and Grace taught me, about her furnace and that, about what the heat does to glass, what cold does, what glass does to just about everything, seemed like the first things I learned in my life that I saw the point of.

Heat comes first then. Heat's the first problem. Enough heat to melt the glass 's going to melt most other substances you can think of — so what you going to make your pot out of then, what you put your glass into? — even you get stuff stands the heat, it's not going to stand the glass, necessarily. You can't believe how glass eats things when it's hot and melted, miles worse than heat does. That's the second problem. I'd never have believed it, only I had to help clean the glass out the bottom of the furnace sometimes. Which is a bad job, I tell you, hot, heavy, dead boring altogether. But you have to do it, if you don't want your furnace eaten. Trouble is, the glass gets spilled out of the glass pot — the crucible — when you work it. The bricks it spills on at the bottom of the furnace, hold the heat OK, that's what they're there for, at the same time the dripping glass worming its way into 'em, day in, day out, they end up full of holes, like bleeding cheese.

So this is what you got to do to clean it. You open up the hole at the bottom while the furnace is still hot, let the old glass pour into a bucket, scraping out any what won't pour of itself. Then you put new bricks in place of the ones with holes in. I nicked an old brick once and took it home. It looks fucking weird, not just holey like I said, like cheese, but with glass all over, blue an' green glass, smeared and shiny. The glass ain't blue an' green when you blow it, why's it turn blue an' green down there, I'd like to know?

This new furnace we're making Grace designed herself; I seen the plans, they're brilliant, don't ask me where she learned it. Inside this time, instead of brick, we're using cast cement, plus a couple of inches of fibre blanket, because cement heats up a whole lot better. There's still red bricks on the outside though, to keep the heat in, also white ones, all those damn bricks have got to be sawn to size before we get to build the bugger; plus there's getting on for six hundred pounds of cement to mix and chuck in moulds to make the round sections for the middle. It'll be knackering work, I'm not looking forward to it. Though it will be better'n hanging about the way we are at present — Grace's shirty most of the time, and the studio feels all creepy and dead when we go down there; like a house that ain't yet lived in.

So what we do now is sort out her house; or rather I do mainly. The kitchen's done now and the front room, as well she don't fancy the wallpaper upstairs, I'm painting that over. She don't seem to fancy my company these days much, neither. Mostly she just throws this load at me — God help me if I don't do it proper — and takes off in Reg's old Escort (she sold her own car after he died) walking the country or something. If she don't want me walking with her, it's no skin off my nose, I tell you. There's more than enough country round here already, I'm not looking for no extra. Nothing but bloody birds (and not the kind I'm after) and tractors, and odd tarts on horses, and more people walking, with maps in plastic cases like they don't know where they're going, with neat little packs an' hefty boots an' anoraks, do they think our hill's Annapurna, or even the North Pole?

The dilatory suppliers of Grace's materials had much to answer for. Who knows, had she not had less to do at this time than at any time in her life, had she not for the first time she could remember been wandering aimlessly inside her head and out, she might have started taking the smell of cooking for granted; might not have imagined, let alone bothered to listen for, the rattle of pans when there was no one in the kitchen to rattle them. Might never have caught the sound of that thick voice mocking her. It grew more verbose as the days went on, sometimes taunting, sometimes crooning, almost always talking, so softly, in such indecipherable accents, it might have been talking to itself not Grace. But she did hear, could not for all her walking, her attempts to escape it, keep herself from listening. And though in time she would have stopped listening if she could, things had gone too far by then; it was too late, she could not do it.

Would not know thisen, would thi, dozzie, to see t'cot when I wor tenant. Wor a right ratchelly patch to one side, a wood on t'other, nor no road before to tek thi feet. Wor'nt a road in this stony country not cross and irksome, not to 'oss, nor foot, nor carriage. T' wood worn't no use to us neither, did we seek to tek coneys for us dinner, they fetched laws in from Derby to vex us. An' if I wor to brangle on't — I wor ever accused of being a branglesome woman — they know who done taught me, wor I not fetched to learn my letters at big house along of mi lonely little lady? I may tell thi who wor t'quicker of us two; t'w'ren't her, t'mardy lass, mi dozzie. Her with the house to her name an' oll the money, that oll the men of her family wor after, an' me wi' now't to mine. Her wi' her fancy dishes to table, her boyled fowl an' patty, me wi' stewed leak and coney sometimes, and then glad to get it, without I or mine mun eat up stone of t'earth to mek us bread like most men in these stony parts.

What's good of letters to one mun seek a bite o' dinner from t'earth, they kep' ask mi? But they con't tek mi letters away, con they, if they have mi for a witch 'an wish t' hangman hissen on mi do I but use mi noddle t' set food in t' mouths of mi family. Nor mi wenches nor mi lads could have said that I stinted 'em, even young wench, t' babby, one drove me to mony a sluffet. She wor not so green as cabbage-looking, that one, I tell thi, liike that lad here of thi'n, dozzie; got out of wedlock, wor he? Wor better for thi, dozzie. 'Twere better to keep out of wedlock, even gets thi some man con minger, con get thi bread besides his'n; WEDLOCK, I say thee, is PADLOCK.

Grace never heard the voice outside the house. That was another reason for her long walks. But not the only one — it was a long time since she had last, whether on horse or foot, roamed any piece of country freely; it appeared she had missed such old freedoms, without ever knowing it. Even so it seemed perverse, if not unkind almost, the way this flintier land, its fields hemmed by drystone walls rather than the hedges she had grown up with, made her ache, for the first time in years, for the red earth, the more generous, swelling, not to say female, lines of her homeland, West Somerset.

"Her" her mother had always called that country, she remembered; never "it" let alone "he". "Her's too shy to put up her veil," she'd say on misty days, or, at another time, in sourer weather, "Her's sulking this morning;" or, on just such days, in just such a season as the one Grace now spent roaming the Derbyshire hills, watching the new foliage soften its stony angles and wondering, amazedly, when she'd last watched a changing season so closely, "Her's getting her spring coat on at last." Grace may have escaped the smell of cooking when she left the cottage behind her; she may have escaped the unsought, unwelcomed, inexplicable voice of the "branglesome" woman; but she could not escape this softer, frailer voice — cowed she'd once called it — belonging to her mother. Any more than she could escape the unwelcome realisation that it was through the eyes of her mother she had first learned to look at that Somerset countryside; learned to notice what she would otherwise have taken for granted.

All of which made her wonder one day, caught in the twists of Lathkill Dale, its sides as steep and steeper and higher than the sides of her Somerset lanes, not to mention a different colour, not only what she was doing here, but where'd she been, all these years: where she could now be going?

"Thi's got mulligrubs terday. What ails thi?" said the voice in her ear as she set foot once more in her alien kitchen. A question that as usual she did not choose to answer. (Mulligrubs, she presumed, referred to her bad temper, the way she slammed the door and yelled for Terry.) Nevertheless it set her asking the questions of her own that, equally, she preferred not to acknowledge. Not only to whom the voice belonged; and why her kitchen persisted in smelling of food. But why in all this she would keep thinking not just of another ghost, the reputed witch who had insisted on baking her own funeral meats, but of her mother.

Sheep made her think of her, for instance. With all the lambs about you could not help being aware of sheep at this moment — lambs came later in more northern country. Grace's liking for sheep over and above cattle, crude, lumpen creatures in her view, comparatively speaking, was the one thing she had, unequivocally, shared with her mother. Even years later, the day of her father's funeral, when Winifred, sitting in her kitchen (the Rayburn had long since been replaced by an electric stove) told her that she and her husband had sold the flock in order to concentrate on beef (Friesian-Hereford crosses what's more, in place of their father's Red Devons), she found herself exceedingly, unexpectedly, put out.

Winifred didn't notice what she was feeling. Winifred almost never had noticed. A small woman compared to Grace, she might have come from a different country, let alone family. Though she too had feared their father, she'd never had such reason to hate him; she had quite lacked the adamantine will which, in Grace's case, had caused the old man to break against her over and over like a wave against a rocky shore, only to fall back defeated. "Devons aren't profitable," she was saying. "They don't do unless they're suckled. These black and white babies, though, they're another matter. You can take them straight off their mothers and trough-feed 'em from birth."

"Of course," she added, in passing, "being kept inside addles they. They go crazy when you first let 'em out. One of our batches, we put 'em in Baker's, Grace — don't you remember that's the steep field along the lane, hard by Styles? — they careered straight from the top to the bottom and couldn't stop, went straight over the hedge on to a car. The driver didn't half get a shock, the poor fellow. Almost as much as they crazy calves."

"And no wonder," said Grace, "the poor lummocks." (Remembering that story now she was reminded of Terry. She'd seen Terry, always, in similar respects, as wanting.)

Sheep in general, though, lambs in particular, had always aroused in her altogether different feelings. She was amazed, even terrified, to find that they still did.

"You'd make a good shepherd, Grace," her mother had said once, after they'd spent a whole night together, labouring over some difficult births. "You have to be motherly to get along with sheep." A statement that Grace had denied vehemently ever since. Even when feeding her orphan lambs, enjoying the pull of their suck against the bottle, the small wet grasp of their mouths upon her fingers, she had denied it; even when pregnant years later, at least once Jas had gone, she had suppressed the idea so firmly she believed sometimes, between awe and terror, it was her own sheer will had caused her to lose their baby; still now, seeing lambs in Lathkill Dale and elsewhere, she refused to acknowledge in herself the smallest vestige of maternal instinct.

In Grace's new garden, weeds started exploding into life. At the beginning of May, not altogether reluctantly — she'd had enough of walking, also, despite some angry phone calls, the materials for the furnace still had not arrived — she began, dutifully at first, to do something about it. Her mother had been a gardener, of course. Setting trowel and fork into the earth, ruthlessly sifting out weeds which even after all these years she still knew to distinguish from plants, Grace rediscovered the pleasure of having earth between her fingers; the pleasure, indeed, of being able to touch any substance with which she was working. You could not touch hot glass the way she had used to touch, knead, bully, coax the clay for her pots. Jas was right, she thought, when he said a glassblower had to play magician as much as maker; manipulating this product of the earth at a distance, as if he disdained as well as feared it.

One way and another, she felt so cut off from glass at the moment she could not so much as sit down with a pencil to sketch ideas for the new kind of almost geological glass she wanted to make, let alone begin to work out the technical problems involved in it. The only labour she felt fit for was the kind she put in on the long flowerbed outside her kitchen window, crouched till suppertime often, listening to the evening plaint of the rooks from the rookery in the wood across the road — one rook, she noticed, had something wrong with its voice; each attempted caw terminated in a squeak.

It was so dry these days she was having to water the plants already. She could not do as much for the rooks, they were also thirsty, to judge from the corpses she found in the wood. Other corpses were reported by neighbours who stopped sometimes while she was working on the garden and leaned over the wall to exchange the time of day. Their voices made her jump if she was not expecting them; sometimes, momentarily, she mistook them for the other voice, the one that by now had grown so familiar it was like the voice of some garrulous relation you hardly needed to listen to much of the time.

"Where's thi poor wherret?" it kept asking. Had she been willing as yet to answer, she could not have done. It was days before she realised that by the poor wherret was meant Terry; whom she had enough on her conscience these days, the way she kept treating him. Not least she could see he was lonely; she was lonely herself come to that, grateful even for encounters with what at any other time, in almost any other place, would have been, quite certainly, the unwelcome intrusions of her neighbours.

Terry would have been glad enough these days to see anyone, I tell you, butcher, baker, plumber, candlestick maker. Even the kids from the school in the big house next door what cheek me over the wall when the teacher ain't looking are better than nothing. Even the posh neighbours that stop me sometimes to say how do or tell me where they live, as if I was interested, are better'n nothing. What they really want, of course, is to know what we're doing here, why we come, is Grace my mum, or what, but they don't never ask us, they're too polite to be openly nosy.

Only last week Grace got herself invited to the house over the road, the one with the windows like our ones. "For a drink," they says. "To meet your neighbours." By now, of course, we knew the people a bit already. He's the tall thin geezer with a beard, always working in his garden, never mind the weather, always asking us if we'd like a cabbage or two for our dinner. You know, what they call a good neighbour. His wife's the opposite, short and fat, a social worker or something, she told Grace. Bleeding teacher kinds of people anyway; not working-class types like me and mum, like all of the people where I come from. Not like Grace either, come to that, but not for the same reasons. So I don't altogether fancy the idea when Grace says she wants me over the road with her — that's it, though, whether or not I likes it — any more than I fancied the look of the fuckin' booze they're offering. Sherry it was, they could tell it were not my tipple just from the look on my face, they came up instant with some cans of lager. The hard stuff'd've done nicely, they had some, but it weren't for the likes of me, leastways I weren't offered any. Though they were all very polite and friendly. So friendly you'd think that even dolled up in my best jeans and fanciest jacket I made them anxious, as if I had a flick knife concealed around my harmless person.

So did Grace make all the neighbours anxious up to a point, for different reasons. There were blokes in particular couldn't hardly keep their eyes off her, though they pretended not. She wore her jeans like always, don't think I've ever seen her in anything else. But she also had a red silk shirt, and gold dangles in her ears and a huge gold necklace like a Red Indian or something. Among that lot she looked like a Red Indian; or like a dancing-girl in a library. Just different is what I'm trying to tell you. It made them curious you could see. Some of 'em couldn't hardly hold off the questions, what we was here for, and so on. Some of them actually asked some, but shied off as soon as they got no proper answer; not like my mum would have, she'd have gone on and on asking.

Of course there can't have been one really didn't know by now we was setting up a workshop, at the bottom of Cliff Wood. Grace introduced me to one bloke as her assistant. "Assistant at what?" he asked straight out. But didn't give her no time to answer before he goes back to explaining his dog-training techniques. He had a beard and a fucking Scots accent, his old woman, natch, had a kilt and a fucking Derbyshire accent. He said you had to beat dogs at every turn, "Just like you do children. And assistants," he added, leering at me. "That way they know who's master." I think he were just taking the Micky. Grace said just as deadpan she wouldn't know about either, she'd only ever trained horses.

"Horses," the man said, looking much more interested. Pointing his nose in her direction just like one of his dogs. It had gone red at the end I noticed, but then I'd already put him down as a boozer, the amount of whisky he were knocking back. His lady's tipple were tomato juice; the colour of blood halfway to being dried. "Maybe you could find a ride round here, sometime," she offers Grace between sips, as if she was trying to ease things somewhat. Grace shied off that, though; I don't wonder, neither, seeing the way the bugger was looking at her, you'd think he hadn't noticed her properly before and was having second, third and fifth not only thoughts but sly ones.

In a moment we'd been moved on to other people. And still Grace didn't answer no one's half-asked questions. Maybe she would have done if I hadn't stuck so close, but then who else could I talk to in all that lot? Apart from some of 'em being boozers, you wouldn't think they belonged to the same country as me and my mates, as my mum and her mates, come to that. They weren't even the same colour somehow; their faces were pinker; save one woman in pink and purple to match her face, their clothes were much more dim. Perhaps London's another country, though I'd always thought of it just as England. Perhaps all proper towns are. Or perhaps — and that's the most likely — being skint and out of work's another country.

Afterwards I asks Grace why she chose to be so fucking cagey. "There'll be time enough to talk," she says, "once we get working." She said it as if she were afraid we wouldn't get working, not if we talked about it too much first. I hadn't never thought of her till then as superstitious.

She ain't much less cagey when we go down to the pub, I must say. But she is, at the same time, I notice, a whole lot more friendly. A drinker's pub, the man with the beard called the one we go to. And it's true we don't see none of the neighbours there, even the Scots bloke, I daresay they aren't that kind of drinker. Not that we're that kind of drinker either, Grace sees to that. She never has more than a pint or two, and nor do I, the amount she pays me I can't afford to. She gets bleeding cheerful all the same, you could say talkative by her standards. All the men like her. I like her. Once or twice when we walks back up the hill afterwards she links arms with me, even. I like that too; though I don't care to look at her when I can see her, when we are passing one of those yellow street lamps what turn our faces yellow. Sometimes I wonder what's going to happen once we're back at the house. Soon as we're near the door, though, she drops my arm like it burns her; or like I smell bad or something. And in the morning is as tetchy as ever, if not tetchier, so's I can't hardly believe all that friendly chat she's given me a few hours back, about getting the work going any minute, let alone what her arm felt like in mine, walking up the steep hill in the cool of the silent night.

It was not that Grace couldn't see how Terry suffered from her silence and her uncertain temper. Most of her outbursts had nothing to do with the work he was doing around her house, she accepted he was making the best job he could of tasks quite new to him. In such circumstances, the gloss paint he was applying to her kitchen door was hardly likely to be free of brushstrokes. Nor was it his fault that the smell of paint did not drive away the smell of cooking as she had hoped it would, any more than the smell of mint that she brought in on her fingers from the garden drove it away either, let alone drove away the unwelcome voice.

"Ay then, dozzie," it was blethering one day in the garden. "Thi knows how they'd talk of mi, often enough; I stood in the court, before t'judge, I could scarce endure not to mock, when they did name me 'a strong robustuous person of rude brawling carriage.' A scold to be ducked, you con say; though 'twas not as a scold they done try me. Art thi not also a 'strong robustuous person?' Do I not see thi brawl and tratch before that poor tool of thi'n? I do not doubt it is needful. How else may us weak women live, mun we tek no gawm of no one, no man, no boy, no matter how lowly, no matter how high and mighty; no matter he sets himself down at our own hearth. 'Tis better to fend for thissen, to deg thi own garden as I see thi do set to, mi dozzie, even in a year smopple as this 'un. When rain comes to it t'earth will soften, be nesh as thi to thi own infant, to t'mardy green things thi hopes to be rearing to thi food, to t'food of that poor wherret of thi'n."

(Poor wherret? Grace was wondering. What's she on about? What's so interesting about him? If she'd only been half listening till now, she heard the rest all right. With increasing shock and indignation.)

"Is he thi'en, that one or is he not I ask? And if not thi'en, 'tis no older I reckon than ony lad of thi'en might be, did thi but have one. Maybe there is such a lad of thi'en bak in the places where thi coom from? Maybe there's one thi don't choose to have alongside thi. Maybe there's one that died from t'cradle?"

"Maybe there's one that died from t'cradle . . ." It was the last straw just about. Grace hoiked out of the earth, particularly viciously, some harmless, even pretty if rampant, forget-me-not plants. She did not need, she had firmly avoided making till now, the calculation that Terry must, to the day, practically, be the age — had he lived — of the baby she had lost. Never mind any other feelings he roused in her, it made her want, there and then, to go inside and bang his gormless, innocent head — not so green as cabbage-looking, hadn't the voice said? — against the wall he was currently painting. She abandoned the garden. She even went indoors. Fortunately perhaps for Terry, she forgot him as soon as she saw the water lying on the floor before the sink; she had to call the plumber instead, to mend the leak in the pipe underneath it.

Terry was upstairs at the time; at work on Grace's bathroom, quite unaware of how near he'd come to being battered. He didn't even hear the plumber's shabby white van come down the lane and park under the wall opposite the cottage, next to the noticeboard that gave the times of the services at the village church. After a while, though, he did hear the voices in the kitchen. Unable to resist the prospect of another face, another voice — anyone's face, anyone's voice, so long as it was not his own or Grace's — he dumped his brush in the can of white spirit and came downstairs. To find Grace propping up the Aga, and talking, garrulously by her standards, about her migration to Derbyshire and the work she and Terry were proposing — the very things she'd refused to acknowledge to anyone local — to someone visible, from where Terry was standing, only as a backside and pair of legs in baggy blue jeans, jutting out from the cupboard under the sink. Lengths of copper and plastic pipe and an open bag of plumbing tools set neatly alongside his feet made the man's trade clear enough. What was less clear was why this man, in particular, was being handed so freely all their, Terry and Grace's, trade and business.

Nor did Terry find himself reassured, let alone comprehending, when, the leak duly fixed, the pipes and tools were gathered up and the baggy backside was revealed as belonging to a lanky ordinary-looking young man with a wide smile, short gingerish hair above the surprisingly pink and innocent skin that sometimes goes with such a colour, and an equally innocent tendency not to look quite at you while he was talking. By this time Grace seemed to have said all she was going to say about herself and Terry; she was pumping the plumber for local gossip. She *fancies* him, Terry was thinking. How could she fancy a git like this, he asked himself, over and over. She had to fancy him, he assumed, to ask the kind of questions she was asking, one hand laid on the cooler of the Aga lids as she did so; once she reached out a hand and poured more coffee from the pot without even asking the bugger if he wanted it. As if she knew what he wanted, without having to bother to ask.

"You said there were some tales you could tell round these parts. Tell me some then," she was challenging him. "Are there any ghost stories, for instance? If you've lived here all your life." Whatever had come over her? Had his hardheaded gaffer gone crazy, Terry was wondering. But the man glanced at her over his mug, looked thoughtful for a minute, as if the question was, after all, reasonable enough, then shook his head and told her there was no ghost he'd ever heard of.

"Mind you," he added. And he was boasting now, from the tone of it. Trying to make her shiver. "Oop t'hill over there, when me dad wor a lad, he said wor a tree coot down, that wor used for hangings. Hangman's Oak it wor called, he said. And when they coot it down they found an old jar under t'roots, full of silver coin clippings. Wor a hanging job once, clipping edges off coins to melt 'em down for silver, so he tol' me. They would have hung them from that very tree, most liike. If there wor ony ghosts, you'd think, maybe it wor 'em."

At this point Grace turned her head. As if she had not till that moment realised that Terry was standing there, on the steps leading down to the kitchen. It was the only acknowledgment he got. The way she looked at him, moreover, she might never have clapped eyes on him before. A moment later she had turned her head back to where the plumber stood, by the sink now, against the window, the light behind his head making it impossible, effectively, to see the expression on his face. He seemed to have settled himself in. Reaching out to the bottle standing on the table and adding more milk to his mug, he proceeded to sip it very slowly.

Terry, too, had no intention of moving. His standing a little higher than Grace and her plumber his only advantage, he did not propose to give it up, despite his growing fancy, if not longing, for a cup of coffee. Real coffee, he was thinking. What was wrong with Nescaff then? Grace usually made real coffee only at breakfast. And what was she doing telling the bloke all their business that she had refused to tell anyone else? And what was all this talk of ghosts and hangmen?

"Where I come from," Grace was saying, "was a tree called Felon's Oak, that they used to think was used as a gallows. But that was just a story."

"Folks liike such stories. It meks us nights a bit more gruesome. In a pleasant manner of speaking," agreed the plumber. "Very near Taunton was that?" he added. "Liike me Granny's place wor? She that speaks liike you, so's I knew right away you coom from Soomerset."

The awkward way he said this, glancing beyond Grace to where Terry stood glowering down on her, might have been meant both as explanation and apology. Almost certainly Terry imagined such a thing. Why should this pink-skinned young man have thought it necessary to explain himself let alone apologise to Terry, for the fact he and Grace had suddenly become so matey? If anything it fed his jealousy; he felt still more of an outsider compared to those two long-legged, seemingly confident beings, lounging one against the kitchen table, the other against the sink; more puny, not to say scrawnier than ever. He *was* scrawny. Besides being covered in spots. At the same time it fed his determination not to move; let alone leave them alone together.

Now the man was blurting out, as if he and she were old friends, "I con see you're a bit different, Grace. Not liike the other folk oop at Tendersley."

He blushed perceptibly after such daring. Opened his mouth, shut it. Started to gabble, almost incomprehensibly at first, about his wife and his little boy. "He started woking only last week ond when I coom home, he yells out Dad-dad, Dad-dad," he was saying; Grace, though, thinking about Terry, hardly heard him.

The fact was that not for a single moment had she actually been oblivious of Terry. Even standing with her back to the boy she was aware of him in every sense; more aware than she had ever been. Because of what the ghost voice had said, partly. But still more because of her having taken in at once, even at such a brief glance, the nature of the boy's feelings. His jealousy, in particular, had startled her immeasurably. Also alarmed, disconcerted, annoyed, and intrigued her. Intrigued her more really than the man in front of her. Whose chief interest to her, at the moment, lay in the fact that the ghost voice was objecting to him so strongly.

"What's the good of 'un to thi, dozzie," it was urging. "Get 'un gone, liike I tell thi," it was saying, in one way and another, over and over. As usual Grace made no answer. But she had no intention of obeying it; of telling the plumber to get gone. Not given the feelings he was rousing in her; undeniably lascivious feelings — Terry had been right about that. The plumber's long legs in their tight but not too tight jeans — she liked to be aware of a man's sex but not to have it, as it were, thrown in her face — outlined against the white china of the sink; the dent in his chin; his rather long neck, with its prominent Adam's apple, supporting both the dented chin and his very ordinary but pleasing smile, revealing slightly crooked teeth — made her realise how long it was — since well before Reg died in fact — since she'd last had a man in her bed.

Probably the man fancied her, too. In fact she was almost sure he did. She seemed to read his lust like a book. "I can see you're different from t'other people oop at Tendersley," he had said, if that wasn't chatting her up, what was? She could see just how it would be with such a well-maintained and handsome lad, in some pub on a Saturday night. And afterwards — especially afterwards. But this was not a pub. And there was no simple after, a fact he now made quite clear.

This was his afternoon off, he was saying; he had come simply as a favour to a new neighbour. The sun burned through the little ginger-gold hairs on his arms where the short white sleeves of his sports shirt ended. On his left breast was embroidered a small green laurel wreath. How, under her sink, among old cloths, buckets, spiders, goodness knows what, had he stayed so clean and white, Grace was wondering, relinquishing him at that moment without a struggle, for a number of reasons; starting with the fact he was married and had a little boy who called him "Dad, dad, dad"; going on to the probability that he was, down to his blue and white scuffed training shoes, much too innocent for her, or ought to be. Ending with the wholly practical matter — perhaps this was the one carried most weight — that good plumbers were not worth driving away for such entertaining but irrelevant reasons.

And besides, if she did persuade this plumber to render her a few extra services, how to explain the lengthy presence of his van outside her house? Given her own rural upbringing, Grace knew too well how quickly such things got around. (This was another reason she had been, till now, so cagey with her neighbours.)

Then, of course, there was the problem of Terry. It came to her at this moment, almost for the first time, that in due course it might be as well to find other lodgings for Terry; together with an altogether surprising feeling of dismay, even loss at such a prospect.

"What do I owe you then, Paul?" she asked the plumber firmly. And having paid the ludicrously small sum — by London standards — he demanded, almost hustled him and his bag to the door. "Coll me op ony time you need," he was assuring her. "Onything. Onytime. No job'd be ony trouble for a Soomerset lady." I bet it wouldn't, Terry thought sourly. I bet it wouldn't. An' what kind of job would you be meaning, I wonder? 'S a good thing I'm around. Never mind if Grace thinks it isn't.

Maybe Grace did or maybe Grace didn't. Probably, as usual, she hardly knew herself. Any more than she knew what drove her later. Whether it was the thoughts roused in her by the plumber's visit, or a new determination to defy the ghostly voice in her head (she did not like, was determined to cast down the triumph with which it had murmured, as she dismissed the plumber, "Thi's coom to thi senses, then, did I not say thi would?") or whether, even, it was Terry's likeness to one of Winifred's lost calves, or, much more likely, the unsought and desperate tenderness aroused in her by all those fieldsful of gangly lambs; or, more likely still, the look she had been so startled — and angry — and touched — and intrigued — to observe in the boy while he was standing on the kitchen steps.

What was certain was that this was the first night that she did not push Terry away when they came back arm in arm from the pub, neither outside the door nor inside it. Having turned the key in the lock, she then, to his unutterable joy and amazement — the clock on the wall said a quarter to eleven, leaving the pub at ten they must have dawdled up the hill — took him in her arms and kissed him. Thereafter, to his still greater joy and amazement, she led him upstairs and into her double bed. Where, bit by bit — in this as in other things he turned out a good, not to say deft learner — she taught him how to please not only her but himself. (He did not please the woman in her head, on the other hand, she chuntered on all night about it. So confounded as well as put out, it seemed, she was back to Wedlock is Padlock, more or less. As if turning Terry's lust to the use of her own, Grace thought, had anything to do with Wedlock.)

So much, all the same, for the poor wherret, "Not so green as cabbage looking," as her ghost had put it; Terry wouldn't be so green, it was clear, by the time she'd finished with him. Assuming the ghost, if it was a ghost, had lived here, had *she* never had a man beneath this roof? Grace wondered in passing.

Chapter Four

"It may be melted but 'twill never be calcined . . ."

Well then, all you buggers out there, that's it. I did it. Honest to God I did it. And how. And how. Zap. Bam. Pow . . . *Whoopee* . . . If this is fucking, I like it. Never mind the tart's old enough to be my mum. And if you don't like it, why should I give a monkey's, you can stuff it up your arse for all I care. At the same time it ain't quite what I expected. It's better in some ways, more than my mates ever let on in all their bragging; in a few other sodding ways it's less. I mean what's left in the morning beyond a great silly grin like what I woke up with; what the look of her wiped off, straight. Since it seemed like it said she wished it never happened. Or didn't believe it really had. Not so you'd've noticed, anyhow.

Even now, because of that, I can't stare her straight out, can I? Though I sneak my eyes sideways at her. The times she catches me she stares *me* straight out. Like I'd know for sure in the end what colour her eyes are. Like nothing ever happened and how dare I think it? It makes me so fucking angry I want to grab her by the tits, sometimes, have her there and then, show her. How I did. How I were boss. Except I'm not boss. And it weren't me made her randy, it were that bleeding plumber. And after weren't no one to hand but bloody Terry.

Which is all wrong, ain't it, it should be the feller what calls the tune. It's like she's the feller here, and I'm the bleeding woman. But in the end, when it comes to it, I'm not complaining, I'm not going to say no, am I. No matter what, it was — is — blooming marvellous. She's blooming marvellous.

And I can't wait one moment to get stuck in again. Though the way she is this morning chance'd be a fine thing, that's certain.

How old *is* Grace, I wonder? I never asked before. I didn't need to. Suppose she's old enough to be my mother, what's it matter? I bet none of my mates ever fucked anyone that classy. I daresay some of those nosy neighbours still think she's my mum. Let them think, I know she's not, all right. I fuck her, don't I, little do they know. Though I'd shout it up and down all these bleeding hills if I dared to. And I'm blowed if I'll think it were the plumber turned her on. It weren't the plumber's name she screamed out when she came. Nor mine, come to that. Oh God, oh God I were shouting, that made two of us. Even though the way she looks at me this morning she dares me to believe it. But I do. We did. Oh yeah, we bloody did. And she liked it. And I liked it. So stuff it all you buggers out there, just stuff it.

Not that it seems to have cut much ice with her, Grace — Grace — I can hardly use her name to her face any more — I find myself saying er . . . Grace . . . er . . . what's got into me then? She ain't no different from usual. She's spent half this morning on the blower, chasing up the suppliers what haven't sent the stuff for the furnace. At dinnertime she goes out, not saying where she's going, taking the Escort. She's not gone long. Comes back with a whole load of groceries she dumps on the kitchen table, pretty sour she's looking, muttering something about it were time I learned to drive. Whoopee again. She's not only learning me to fuck, she's going to learn me to drive, who'm I to stop her?

She frigged about in the garden all afternoon while I finished off the bathroom. Later I went out and walked through the wood over the road. I ain't used to it yet. Woods make me feel creepy, like there was some psycho lurking, waiting to get you, as per some video nasty. Though it's an OK wood, really. At least I suppose it is; new green leaves spiking up through the dead leaves along the track and over my head, branches still bare enough to see the birds in. They sing so sweet some of 'em. The only bird I can remember listening to before was my Nan's canary when I were just a kid, I always did like it.

Still I'm glad to be out of the wood, thinking of the psychos. You have to go past a house and garden then turn sharp left on to New Lane and come back up and over and down Prior's Hill, past fields full of sheep and lambs. Not only I didn't listen to birds before, I don't remember seeing no sheep, ever. Let alone lambs, except on my plate the rare times mum got round to cooking us a joint for Sunday dinner. "Hey Sunday dinner," I call over the gate, natch the lambs don't take no notice. I end up feeling a right git when some old bird comes along and catches me at it.

You can see a long way from here, at the top of the hill. Right across the valley to the other side. There's a great thing on a kind of cliff there, like Nelson's column. They put a light on it at night that flashes on and off. To warn planes, or something. But what's a thing like Nelson's column doing here, I ask you? It's hot in the sun. I take my jacket off. It's all right, the country, I begin to think, eyeing some little yellow flowers — just so long as you can see a house or two around you. There's plenty of houses on the other side, grey little houses, stretching up the hill and over, and one or two here, a bit down the hill, all of them's grey also. They build stone houses in these parts, not like London. It's all right just so long as you don't start thinking you're alone in the green world, bar some nutter skulking behind a tree what's got your number.

I turn right at the bottom of the hill and down Pigg Lane through the wood to Grace's cottage at the bottom. I can smell cooking from the road, even. Course, that kitchen smells of cooking always, anyone'd think there was a ghost in there, joke, I don't think. But this ain't no ghost. This is Grace. I can't hardly believe it when I go in and find her. She's got a cookery book open on the table, the sink's piled high with dishes and she's crashing and thumping about like she hated the day she was born, let alone all this, so why the hell's she's doing it, I'm asking. I don't fancy the look of her meantime. If I've learned anything it's when to keep out of the gaffer's way. So I creep upstairs, and lay down on my bed that last night I didn't sleep on. Fact is I didn't sleep much at all, I weren't given the chance to, cuddling up to her after and between like I never cuddled up to anyone, not wanting to miss one bit of it, not one moment. She can't've slept much either, come to think of it. Maybe that's why she's so shirty this evening.

I'm asleep before I know it. Wake so much later that the sun's got down behind the bare trees in the wood and is shining into my eyes. I hear Grace yelling; bellowing rather; Concorde's no louder. "Supper," 's what she's yelling. And I go down to find the table set out posh like, and Grace red-faced and with her hair on end, worse than a day at her furnace. She's made us a fantastic nosh up. Fantastic after what we normally gets, I mean, the bacon and eggs and sausages I cook, or else fish and chips from the chippy down Matlock Bath, the only place round here with life in it, where there's even bikers with studs and leather jackets, like some of my mates in London. Plus a flash arcade or two with fruit machines and that, along of the boozers. Not that I get the chance to hang around there much. (You can always hitch a lift home, says Grace all nasty, when I lag behind her. Maybe I will one day. Too right I'm going to.)

I like the kitchen here. It's cosy at night with the Aga. Even though it's me what's been lumbered with getting the coal in, filling it, getting the ash out, morning and night, I don't mind. The Aga's like the furnace in the glasshouse, it makes the place alive. There's a dresser on the opposite wall with plates and cups on, also some odds and sods Grace picked up once, old stones, for instance. Oh, and a big dish she told me she'd made herself when she were more or less my age; a greenish thing, with a great horned sheep's head in the middle that glares out like it hates me and the world likewise. I rate the glass higher; there's all kinds of pieces what slipped a bit, what weren't quite right; goblet's got too big a foot, for instance, or the stem ain't straight, or the knop's uneven. I don't mind that. I like those bits more than most. You understand the glass better for 'em. They're like guys you know aren't quite straight, yet can't help liking all the better.

On the wall next to the dresser there's a huge plate hanging. Grace made that too in the time she was still a potter. It's got two little figures in the middle and a great tree and all round the edge in great letters, MATRIMONIAL BLISS. It's some kind of sick joke, if you ask me, putting it up there like that. As if everyone don't know Grace's feller upped and left her all those years ago, before I were born even. What's she want to look at it then for, except to mock herself, me too most likely? And what do I know of matrimonial bliss, except it weren't my mum's fancy. Nor my dad's neither, the way he fucked off and left us. Or maybe it were just mum and me he didn't fancy.

All the same, I still like this kitchen. I like the lovely nosh-up even better — steak and kidney pie, full of onions and mushrooms and that. I tasted better pastry a few times, but that don't mean I'm complaining. Tonight it's no wonder the bleeding kitchen smells of cooking.

Apart from the pie, there's a sweeter stink, spicier, from the baked apples she gives us for afters. She's put nuts and raisins in the middle — who learned her that I wonder? My mum never learned it.

We drink a few jars also. I'm beginning to feel randy when Grace jumps to her feet and says ever so sweetly, "Well, Terry, I did the cooking, your job's the washing up." Which I don't hold against her; not that there haven't been plenty of times I've cooked and washed up both, not that there ain't more than enough of these dishes for two of us. Grace is neat in most things, but not in cooking; I'm a bit pissed-off when I see just how many pots she's piled up in the sink. Grace stays sweet as nohow; she's shy you'd even say if you didn't know her; all of a sudden she says, her voice high and sweet, "Don't forget to lock the doors and turn the lights off, Terry, before you come up. I'm tired. I'm off to bed." She don't seem to be inviting me to bed, neither. And even if she is, what can I do about it, up to the elbows in soap suds?

She has a bath. You can hear everything down here, the floors are that thin, unlike the walls are. She's got the radio on, from the sound of the voices I can tell she's listening to the news. The speed I do all those dishes I'm going to make the Guinness Book of Records. Whereas it looks like Grace is going to take her time — I'm wiping the last plate, and she's still not left the bathroom. My hopes are up now, I start feeling randier than ever. Then I remember there's still the fucking Aga. I do that quick and quicker; don't even bother to remove the ashes, just jam the new coal in, it won't do no harm for once, or so I think. I'm halfway up the stairs when I hear the door of her bedroom shutting loudly, like she wants to be sure I hear it. She even turns her light off straight away which I can tell because I turn the light off in the hall to make certain. I try knocking on her door once or twice; getting no answer I don't dare take it no further, I slink off to my room instead, feeling a right proper charley the way I'd been thinking, hoping, assuming, more or less.

In the morning of course the Aga's out because I didn't clear it. The way Grace goes on it seems more likely she'll give me the sack than let me make it with her even one more time, let alone several. Then the stuff for the furnace turns up. After that we don't stop working for a single second.

Grace had meant to take Terry into her bed that night, if out of simple affection. Perhaps the affection was the problem; was why she didn't. Perhaps she was not used to such warm and simple feelings, except to Reg before he died, and they had never resulted in anything. Not that she was prepared to consider it as a problem; merely woke up wondering vaguely what could have got into her to make her behave the way she did.

Over the next few days, though, having started building the furnace, they were both too tired to think of sex. Grace, however, noted, with approval — she was not aware of noting it before — the effects of the hard physical labour on Terry. How his muscles were harder and his shoulders broader, for instance. How much more fluently and easily his body moved. When he first came to her, she thought, his hands and feet and head had looked like a job lot, too big for the rest of him. His bones as raw as if there was hardly skin and flesh enough to cover them, he had flopped and jerked like a puppet worked by a novice.

He's still not John Travolta exactly, she concluded. But he would do. He would have to. Which just might, perversely, have been one more reason for keeping her distance from him. With still greater perversity she did after all, in due course, between irritation, weariness, and simple need, stop teasing both of them and summon him to bed again, offhandedly.

I hate her sometimes, he thinks. She's a right cunt, she is. What am I doing here with such a bitch, I wonder. Bitch is about right, too. She treats me like a dog; no, worse than a dog. A bitch don't take no notice of the dog between times, the dog don't want to know her anyway; but I want Grace; and how I want her; never mind how much I wish I didn't, seeing what she does to me; seeing the way I grovel to her, like I had no pride, no nothing.

I'm knackered most of the time, that's half the trouble. It's hard work what we're doing. It's taken us a whole week to make the curved moulds for the central section that goes on top of the fire bricks on the floor. It'll take another week to do the casting, that means mixing the six hundred pounds of cement bag by bag; plus another week fitting the bits together. The last thing will be to fit and adjust the burner. We're likely to have trouble with that. It's got to work in two phases, one for the old lehr, one for the furnace. Back in London, at Reg's place, we had an electronic thermostat, someone had to go in twice a night to check it; she was even letting me do that sometimes, towards the end. The burner she's got for here, though, is hand adjusted. Grace has worked out the setting already — she's got plenty of mates in the business to tell her. It's fitting it all together, she says, that's more likely to cause problems.

She'll get it right in the end of course. She's clever. I never thought a bird could know the things she knows, let alone do them; I never thought I could, come to that, let alone understand what I were doing. But I do understand this more or less. Just as I see now how the furnace is going to work. It's neat and it's simple, I love it. I can't wait till we get the crucible in and set the whole thing going.

They had odd days off from the furnace, of course. Usually because they had run out of materials, not because it ever occurred to Grace that either of them should rest. On those days she did not walk the country; nor did she do the garden. Instead she sat at the table in her room with her note-book; making rough designs for future work; rough calculations of how, possibly, given that the bulkier pieces would need longer annealing times, different settings for the lehr, how she was going to set about it. Some time ago, after her trip to the States, she had bought a book on kiln firing of glass. She had lost interest in it as soon as she learned that the processes it described were almost as slow and cumbersome as those she had discarded when she gave up ceramics for her nimbler glasshouse arts. But now she dug it out again. She went to the second-hand book shop in Cromford in search of geological text-books. These, too, she pored over whenever she had a spare moment.

In her head, all the time, ran a conversation she'd had years ago, with Jas, about a sculptor. She wished it wouldn't. It put a clearer picture into her head than had been there in years, of Jas with his then flowing hair and Indian shirts and Indian silk scarves; the guru look he had cultivated just before he left her. This man, this sculptor, Jas had said, hadn't been interested in creating obviously man-made objects. He wanted only to make things that looked as if they could have been discovered rather than made. "Natural artefacts," he said. "Man-made nature. Objets made to be trouvé. Objets gotten with the body rather than designed with the brain."

By that stage of their relationship Grace had ceased to be dazzled by Jas' loquacity. She regarded most such talk as not only pretentious but arrogant. The more arrogant, if not intolerable, when Jas proceeded to pat, with a kind of patronage which she was to find almost the hardest thing to remember, let alone forgive, in the time after he left (she could even, at times, have blamed on it the death of her baby) her newly pregnant belly. "That's like wanting to be God," she had said, disapprovingly. "Got it in one, Gracie," mocked Jas. Who used mockery at this time as one means of distancing himself from her. Determined not to give him the satisfaction of thinking she noticed such a tactic, she merely nodded. And he went on — almost pleading with her now — "So what's wrong with that? Doesn't all creation make us like God? Don't we sit there like any god at the beginning of any creation, saying I am lonely, I want to make a world? Isn't that why we do it?"

"You may," Grace said. "*I* don't." Why *should* she want to be like God? she was thinking. She hated God; or thought she did. It was still the one emotion in her powerful enough to set beside her love for Jas. Which was another thing Jas mocked in her. "My live-in Barbara Cartland," he said, though not without pleasure that he could rouse in such a woman feelings of what she had, once, and only once, broken her reticence to swear to him was everlasting love.

Twenty years on, though, Grace no longer hated God. Or perhaps she did not call what she hated God. And even if she did hate Him, what better revenge could there be than taking over His function? She, too, these days, sought to make her pieces look God-made; that is, earth made; as if they had not been wrought with human hands, but rather, like the substances from which they were fashioned, arrived intact either from earth's actual bowels or at the least from its exposed surface. If she only knew how to. But she did not. She knew only her dissatisfaction with the opaque black bowls she had been making before Reg died; but which now, even knowing how they sold, she did not think she could bear to .

All she knew how to make, it seemed, was her furnace. Which she did gladly; much more gladly than she had ever expected. Though her motives, her reasons for building it herself had seemed practical and financial, she had come to recognise other more significant motives. She would have made the very bricks herself, she thought, if she could have; would have forged the metal for the ties that were to hold them together. Heavy as much of the work was — heaving hodsful of brick, humping cement-filled moulds, made her fear sometimes for the more delicate bones of her craftswoman's hands — she could not resent it, seeing how it gave, would give her, a still more intimate contact with the substance of her working. Such an intimate contact in fact, there were even times she could have wished she was working on her furnace alone. For all the effort was so backbreaking; for all it would have taken her still longer.

Perhaps that was the whole trouble. Perhaps she treated Terry the way she did, because in the end she was jealous; because she did not actually want him there, sharing the work with her. It was as if she had taken him into her bed to make him part of herself; and so fit to join her in this act of intimate if hard labour. In other words her desire for him was more than a matter of him being young and available, and also, as she had become aware, distressingly vulnerable. More than his being quite unlike any of the other boys she had had working for her. None of whom had aroused her maternal feelings; none of whom had been allowed to satisfy her body.

But then none of those other boys had she seen, potentially, as a rival. Green, crude, untutored as he was, Terry had talent, she could see. She almost always had seen it, even sometimes feared it. Suppose in time it equalled, even surpassed her own? Observing the hungry look with which he took in all she could tell him, the uncomplaining way in which he tackled the backbreaking, weary work, she saw the true obsession in him. Terrified, those times she could have wished him out of sight and out of mind. Even though at the same time, she could not have borne for him to be anywhere but with her. Pehaps that was why his gaucheness so irritated her. Why, at times, she found herself torturing him the way she did.

She could and did actually hurt him, one way or another. One night after a particularly hard day she had, without warning as usual, invited him into her bed; only to grow impatient because, not only was he tired and slow to arousal, he was also clumsy in his attempts to arouse her. "I thought I'd managed to teach you something," she said. "But I needn't have bothered. Anyone would think you were making bread not love. You clumsy little oaf," she added, a moment or so later. At that she had actually, literally, kicked him out of bed. He lay on the cold floor beside her for a moment, weeping; and then got up and stumbled back in the dark to his own room.

Neither slept much after. He lay in his bed seething with shame and hurt. She, in hers, was devoured by her own ambivalence. Not only the ambivalence between guilt and anger; more her ambivalence concerning him, which she resented the more because at this time, she told herself, she needed all her energy for her furnace. Next morning, seeing how heavy-eyed he looked, how he sulked and avoided her, she wanted first to take him in her arms, then to strike him for making her feel she wanted to. They were mixing cement at this point and casting it in sections to form the central part of the furnace. As they manhandled one of the moulds they had just filled, Terry misheard a muttered instruction; when his end dropped, Grace could not hold the mould alone. It fell to the ground between them and broke.

Grace stared at it for a moment. Defiantly, without apology for once, Terry stared back at her. It was difficult to know which of them first launched themselves at the other. Maybe it was simultaneous. In both cases they went like animals, without words; almost without sounds apart from some grunts and later from a few particularly loud cries. He went for her legs and body, kicking and punching; she grabbed him by the hair; grappled at his face. Before long, they were rolling among sacks of cement on the stone floor, their hair, their bodies dusted over, the taste of it in their mouths, the fine grit penetrating every orifice. When Terry felt some in his eyes, he was too blinded by rage to do more than blink it out; he was hardly even aware of the pain it caused him. By then cement was mixed in with all of their secretions. Having snatched off the necessary garments, they were not only fighting, they were fucking, grunting and yelling, hating each other; and so all the more desirous.

For the first time if not the last, Grace looked at Terry that night, both coolly and unkindly, and suggested finding lodgings for him in the village. She did not want her neighbours to start talking about them, she said. If they were not talking about them already.

Yet, only a moment later she was inviting him into her bed. He almost drew back. She, almost, urged him. And in the end, as he was bound to, he acceded. They were too tired, now, to take it physically any further. Not that it mattered. In other senses they took it further than ever. Lying all night wrapped in each other's arms, in the most profound of slumbers. Waking in the morning to find themselves still enfolded, not only by each other, but by a feeling of ease and peace that the day dissipated gradually as it was bound to, but which, in the meantime, kept them both safe, at home, relieved, even, in a sense, enchanted.

Oh mi dozzie, I seen thi working down there, thi's a witch amn't thi? And never had a thought how's enough to mek men fear thi, meddling with such things? Not that it stopped mi. Did not stop mi for one minute. What have us women? Do we have looks, that's all we may have. Do we have money and marry, the man teks it off of us, as the fine one she wed took it off my young lady. Have we wit we dursen't use it, without we have money. Us poor women keep us tongues to ussens; only rich ladies con afford to be witty. Beauty's the only power we dare hold open to t' world, the rest we mun hold behind us doors, secret. As thi hold thi fire secret, down in that deep wood. Oh yes, I see, I know it. Did I not mek a secret fire to myself, and did I not that way hope to bring food to my young ones?

It was the first time in almost two weeks' working Grace had heard the voice. Or maybe she had heard but not noticed. Or maybe it was simply — and this she recognised as most likely — its owner had not yet found the way down here, to the glasshouse. Or at least, as her words suggested, she had not yet found a way of making herself felt there. Not yet anyway. Maybe, whoever she was, whatever she wanted, wherever she came from, she hadn't even tried. Maybe she had, cunningly, held her tongue waiting for the right moment — this moment — to reassert her presence. It was true that the most brutish part of the work had been finished at long last. The moulds were all cast. Now, towards the end of May, the furnace was within reach of completion.

The sun, unlike the sour smoke from the dump, hardly penetrated the stone shed at the bottom of the wood that Grace had had converted into her glasshouse. All the same, they only had to step out of the door to be aware of the coming of summer round them. When they first began working on the furnace the sun had fallen delicately and gently through new leaves on to the path down through the wood. By the time they finished it, even the tardy ash trees were covered in leaves. The white spikes of flowers on the horse chestnuts in the park by the house were already turning brown at the edges, while the amazing blue mist of the bluebells in the wood over the road which had appeared quite suddenly from nowhere, it seemed to Terry, was almost as suddenly fading. The sweet chestnuts in the garden opposite had no flowers that he could see. But they gave off a scent that embarrassed him in some way, made him feel almost randy; perhaps because, if anything, it reminded him of his own semen. As for the little willow tree against the wall at the bottom of Grace's garden, it had begun to shed its seeds profusely. The seed heads withering, the fine down carried them everywhere; they lay in drifts on the little lawn, floated in at every open door and window. He was forever sweeping up the down with the ash from the Aga. Why had he never noticed before that there were so many different kinds of trees behaving in such different ways, he wondered? Even if he had, he had never taken them in before the way he did this year; sometimes almost ecstatically; sometimes with feelings that were nearer terror.

He might have been more terrified still if he'd known how

Grace was responding to them. It is true she took the habits of the trees more for granted than he did. But the line of the hill opposite, the one on which there had been reputed to be hangings, made such a sweet curve sometimes in the morning and the evening light, the new green on the hills she saw across the valleys as they walked to their wood across the park was so lively, so inviting, she found herself not only weary but wholly defenceless sometimes; as if longing to bury both her mind and her body in the landscape, the same way Terry, unthinkingly, buried himself in her; not only fucking, very nearly suckling from her also.

It rained three nights in succession towards the end of the month. The paths, rock hard before, remained dry enough, but the drip of the leaves on his head, on the new curled fists of the bracken, while they were making their way down to the glasshouse each morning, filled Terry with foreboding. Not least because, the end of the work in sight, the furnace just about ready to be lit, he and Grace had grown suddenly, unaccountably, happy. As if he had just invented, at the most only seen in a nightmare, the way things had been between them less than a week earlier.

The third afternoon the furnace was done, finally. When they had set the crucible inside, when she had got the burner going, Grace produced a bottle of vodka. Terry had not drunk vodka before; he did not like the taste now much, let alone its fiery choke at the back of his throat. But he liked what it did to him. So, it seemed, did Grace. She put her arms round him. Then withdrew them so hurriedly he thought he was being rejected as usual. But she was not rejecting him, not this time. Instead she went to a cupboard in the corner of the room, and lifting out the bag containing the precious tools that Reg had used the whole of his working life ceremonially presented them to him.

"Spare the rod; his or thissen? They wor saying ollus do no good to thi child. Thi man child, partickler. Don' say me I give thi no warnings, dozzie." For once the voice spoke in sorrow rather than anger, just as Grace and Terry were arriving back at the cottage. Most likely, thought Grace, she was about her cunning habits. Either way, as usual, she took no notice of such warnings, assuming they were warnings. Unless it could be said that they hardened a resolve which had been growing in her since Terry had taken the tools from her, to take the celebration further; to make a whole evening of it; she started at once by setting out to cook a meal for them.

She'd no time to shop, of course, they would have to make do with what she could find in the cupboard; the result was some kind of fish pie made out of tinned tuna fish, potatoes and eggs. When it was almost ready Grace opened a bottle of red wine, and having handed Terry a glass, had him setting the table with a ceremony that he was not used to, that she had never demanded of him till now.

"Get some candles out," she told him. There's no candlesticks, though. You'll have to stick them up on saucers." They had only had candles in her father's house at Christmas, and then only ordinary white, domestic candles. But she had always liked them, whether they burned in candlesticks or not. Her mother's mostly unused candlestick had been silver-plated; a present for her and Grace's father's unimaginable wedding. Her mother too had liked candles. Would no doubt have lit them more often in a less barren, graceless household than the one she had been permitted to keep, thought Grace, almost tenderly. The voice, meanwhile, wreathed its way into her nose and thinking along with the good smells from the food. It was thick with approval; maybe it liked her cooking, Grace thought wrily, more than she liked its cooking. Assuming it had something to do with the smell of food in the house; increasingly she thought it must have. Come to think of it, she had noticed the smell less recently. Or maybe she had just been too busy.

She did not take in, though, much of what it was saying. In any case it ceased as soon as she went upstairs. When she came down again, the long gold rings in her ears, the necklace about her neck picked up little glitters from the candles Terry had already lit for their meal. Has she togged herself up just for me, he was wondering, noticing, with as much alarm as pleasure, and not just because he'd never thought to change his clothes, that she had donned her red silk shirt. What's she playing at? he wondered. More apprehensive than he had been for days, he wished he had a can of beer between his hands, instead of the glass of wine she gave him.

When the fish pie had been devoured, they ate young rhubarb that Grace's neighbour had brought over from his garden opposite, the ginger crumble mixture on top one Grace remembered her mother making. This time, the effort she had made cooking seemed much less alien. Between the wine and his full stomach, the at first wary Terry was soon so soothed that he ceased to regret his beer. He was even happy, remembering the gift of Reg's tools with an urgent gratitude and pleasure that had not been vouschsafed him in the moment of receiving them. He actually thought — he dared think — that she, too, was happy. Or rather, even more amazingly, he took it for granted that she was. About tomorrow he did not think. Why should he?

Grace did not chase him to the sink this evening. They set the dishes in together, then she came and stood behind him; after a moment laid her cheek to his head, stroked his cheek with her left hand; cradled his head against her. Through the darkened window behind them, at the roots of the sky, a faint, deep glow still lingered. "In two days, Terry," Grace was saying — *she* hadn't forgotten tomorrow, but Terry, his head laid against her red silk breast forgave her — never before had he heard her speak Somerset so broadly, — "In two days us can put in the cullet; the day after see to they witches; make the witch's piece. You've heard tell, haven't you, Terry, of the witch's piece? The one us must set on the furnace to keep they darn witches away?"

The table was lit only by burnt-down candles. In the face of the growing darkness Grace had closed the doors but not bothered to switch on the lights. At the sudden pounding on the door they might even have thought it was the witches come already, come too soon, before they'd had time to make their piece.

But it was no witch. The pounding paused for a moment.

When it started again, Grace motioned Terry to get up. He pulled the door open to find, towering over him, or at least seeming to do so, a tall man in jeans and cowboy boots and with a big belly on him, whom Grace looked at blankly, as if she had never seen him before, or thought she hadn't. The man cleared his throat in such a way you could have assumed that he, too, was taken aback. Yet when he spoke, at last, in what seemed to be an American accent, he did not appear to feel himself a stranger.

"Well, Gracie," he said. "Well, Gracie. Didn't I tell you I'd turn up like a bad penny? And here I am, large as life; and larger." (Here he patted his belly.) "Well, Gracie? After all these years aren't you going to say hullo?"

"Not as long as you call me Gracie. I always told you not to," she replied, to Terry's amazement. To his still greater amazement — and horror — she pulled him back to his chair and set him down. The fingers of her left hand began digging into his left shoulder. The fingers of her right tenderly, abstractedly, ruffled through his hair; she was once more cradling his head against her. What was she muttering, he wondered, trying, discreetly, to jerk himself away; he assumed, of course, it was her muttering the almost inaudible words that came from above him, though it sounded almost too deep to be her voice. Wedlock, something. Wedlock? Matrimony? It did not matter. Between shock and anger, pique and embarrassment, he knew suddenly and all too clearly, staring at this tall stranger, who he was.

Chapter Five

"It gives fusion to other metals and softens them . . ."

Twenty years ago . . . oh my God. Twenty years ago, between Grace and Reg and the glass, what more could I have wanted? Nothing. That was the problem. It wasn't too little, it was too much. And when the baby started coming — I felt like — Hephaestus was it? — so much for a classical education — the one caught in a golden net with Aphrodite and wanting out, from fear of being caught, probably; I don't know what else. I still don't understand. All I know — and knew — was I wanted out.

I liked the glass though; how I liked the glass. Also, still more, I liked Reg. He didn't deserve what I did to them. Nor did Grace come to that, but though she was the one that was pregnant, in some ways I worried more about Reg. Grace knew how to look after herself, like all my women. You could say that's the one thing they have — need to have — in common. At the same time it's part of the problem. Take Grace, for instance. She gave me everything in most senses — not least her virginity — yet in the end I never quite had her. I knows it sounds crazy, but the fact she didn't even bleed then drove me crazy. Though had she let me have her all ways round, I daresay that'd have got me in the end also; the fact is I'm not only a shit, I'm perverse with it.

And then there was this about Grace. She wasn't witty. She wasn't fun. She didn't know how to make me laugh. The way she took everything so seriously, she was more like a Russian than an Englishwoman. It's fascinated me, if you like. I never met anyone like it, before or since. But I couldn't take it; not all day and every day. Not in my bed each night. It was like being forever on Olympus, like being a brother Karamazov, with never a chance to play Bertie Wooster. I got to long for some lustful and all too human courtesan. Who made love like it were fun, and not always like we were erupting volcanoes. Or worse still, when she didn't feel like it, or I didn't, like struggling, dormant volcanoes.

It was no good trying to explain any of this to Grace. She just shrugged her shoulders, as if it didn't matter. Or else as if it was yet another of those iridescent bubbles she saw me as blowing round her; gazing at me open-eyed, mesmerised even, the same way she gazed at Reg's furnace; at the molten glass. Oh yes, she liked the glass, right from the beginning. I thought she'd get to work it in the end. In that sense you could say I did her a favour by getting up and going.

Like I said, I was sorry about Reg. I know what he was hoping; that was another problem. I was not sure I wanted to spend the rest of my life the way he'd spent his. Clearly he expected I would, and I see his point. I saw his point. It worked between him and me, you might even say I loved him, and I missed him after. Grace was my gift to him, in a way. Never mind Reg's views on women, he was a clever old codger. He'd've seen what was in her. More than likely he would have settled for her baby had she had it. As I might have done, who knows. It was only when I heard Grace had lost it, I followed my actress to California. And except for a week here or there to do some work, I never came back, not till now, after I heard about Reg. And Reg's money. Which should all have been mine, though I'm the last person to say I deserved, let alone deserve it.

It was through my actress I got into films. In Hollywood no less, in a small way in the beginning. I'd always played about with cameras, including movie cameras. And it was a good time for it, the late sixties, lots of small new companies, everything happening, all the more if you happened to have an English accent. I got in with a guy who followed the music around, Stones, Jimi Hendrix, you name it, we filmed their lives, their groupies, their concerts, the riots in the arena, not just the music making; that was the time of the 'Nam protests and flower power, before Manson came along and everyone got scared and disillusion took over. It was a fantastic time I tell you. Even afterwards there was still money in commercials. Betweenwhiles I wandered about a bit. Down in the south-west mostly, round Santa Fe before the rich guys got there. Round the reservations. I even wrote a guide book to camping in the reservations. I liked Indian country the moment I saw it. New Mexico, Northern Arizona aren't just monumental, they're open yet self-contained in a way that reminded me of Gracie.

I never imagined myself running back to Grace, of course, not then. But I did go back to LA. And I did get married. Not to the actress, she'd long got the hell out, to a smart and pretty girl, called Nancy, a movie secretary, who said she liked my British accent. Trouble was she was so smart she had me tied up and parcelled before I knew it. But I was older then. I wasn't so hot at running. In a way, too, I'd had enough of running. And besides I liked the kids she insisted on us having.

Nancy said Hollywood was no place for kids, which it wasn't, so we bought a plot of land out in Santa Monica, just up the hill from Venice Beach, and built us a neat little house with a back-yard she soon had me digging and planting. When I'd had enough of domestic merriment I'd take my camera and get down to the beach among the freaks and bodybuilders and pretend I was one of them. As I still was at heart; never mind my neat house and smart wife and cute kids and my more or less regular job, that by now we hardly needed. Not only Nancy knew how to use her own talents, commercially, almost as soon as our kids were born, she knew how to use their talents also; she had them straight out in the studios making money from baby-food commercials. (She'd've had them coining it before if she could. I once heard her trying to persuade a pal of mine that a film of her giving birth to our second would make a great puff for some maternity hospital or other.)

But if the kids were earning twice as much as me, that wasn't why I left. Maybe Nancy did hold the reins tight, not to say knotted, but she was clever enough not to show it more obviously than she had to. And she kept on letting me think I could make her laugh — sometimes she made *me* laugh, even. No, what finished me, even before I heard that Reg had died, was that house at Santa Monica. We'd built on an ant heap, if you can believe it. Before we knew, the ants were in everything. They got in the icebox and the food processor. They marched out of every drawer and closet and cornflake packet we opened. They got into bed with us, their little feet scurried all over from one end of the night to the other. I'd soon had enough of it, and so had Nancy. We called in the vermin man, sprayed this stuff and that, put out little pots of poison in places the kids couldn't get at. For all the good it did we might as well not have bothered.

It's true what they say, ants in your pants mean you're itchy and restless. When the news came about Reg, that was enough, I scarpered. Didn't I say I was an A1 shit? Of course I miss my kids, but I don't miss Nancy. About her I don't even feel guilty, she's another survivor. I daresay she'll ditch the ants, too, in the end, get the hell out of that nice little house up the hill from Venice Beach. You could say I will have done her a favour, setting them a good example. Well you could see it like that; Nancy, I guess, won't.

So I came to look for Grace. All it took finding her, apart from a ride on a couple of trains, was the exercise of my charm on my mother, plus a few adverse comments from her on my belly. So what did I expect I'd find then, walking up that hill in the dark? Not what I found certainly. The only thing I didn't expect was what I found. Of course I hadn't thought Grace'd kill the fatted calf exactly. But I hadn't expected she'd look so wonderfully barbaric, by the light of those candles, with that gold stuff dripping from her. Not after twenty whole years. Like a Giacometti figure, all legs and shoulders. Or like one of those archaic Greek statues, the kind with the geometric formality which is so much more satisfactory than the later, classical stuff, no matter how lifelike the drapery. And still with that slight female voice of hers, which had always seemed strange coming out of that body and now seemed even stranger.

It was like seeing her for the first time. I *was* seeing her for the first time; in spite of that damn plate hanging, the one she made after we got married. MATRIMONIAL BLISS. I ask you. What could she be thinking of? And worse still the sheep's head on the dresser. The first time I saw that dish I knew what an artist she could be. At the same time I hated it. It scared the shit out of me that ram's head, it always did, from the beginning.

And worst of all that bloody boy. And her clutching him. Like he was her boy, our boy; the one that died inside her — he must have been about the same age; but the opposite of pretty. More like half-made, spotty, awkward; like a badly plucked game bird, with the stubble on his neck. He couldn't even take his liquor, he had great blotches on his cheeks from the plonk she was feeding him. I'd've taken him by the scruff of the neck if I could and hurled him outside on the instant, I don't know why I didn't. Sure, it wouldn't have been politic. And was, I admit, at this point, none of my damn business.

What Grace seemed to see looming in the doorway, that evening, was more a three dimensional shape than a person; the candles did not so much light Jas as transform him into a mass of shifting, illuminated shadows. A big man certainly. Fattish; his belly outspanning his jeans. Above his check shirt was a broad, even moonlike face, the mouth in it small enough to make her think, as he moved a little further into the room, that she had seen such a mouth before; a long time before. Just as then, too, she found herself wondering why a mouth so ungenerous in its proportions could in some inappropriate way so engage her.

The Man in the Moon Came Down Too Soon and Found his Way to Norwich, she recited to herself, to avert her sense of panic. (Was it Norwich the man found his way to, she'd used to wonder, when her mother recited the rhyme, only because it had to rhyme with the porridge he burned his mouth on?) The curly hair, shorter now and receding in the front, made the face so exceedingly round it seemed more like the Man in the Moon's than ever. He had these little white teeth in his little mouth. He was smiling and smiling at her. He was saying something — she hardly knew what, but his voice was the same as ever, in spite of the exaggerated Californian that had replaced the faintly Cockney accent he used to affect when she first knew him. It reminded her as she had never hoped to be reminded of the roller coaster of feeling on which he had kept her travelling, up hill and down, in no more control of it, of him, of herself, than she'd been of the running river into which she'd fallen once as a child and nearly drowned.

"Don't you remember me, Gracie? Don't you remember?" How long, exactly, was it since anyone called her Gracie? But she was stronger now. She saw no reason to let him reach her. He was ugly, she thought, for all his jeans and high-heeled boots. He had gone to seed. What had she ever seen in him, she wondered, and found herself able, for the moment, conscientiously, to despise him.

"Don't dare," she repeated, clutching the boy, stroking his hair, as if she loved him. "Don't *dare* to call me Gracie."

So Terry doesn't get to Grace's room, does he, let alone her bed. He sleeps in the back room, all on his lonesome, and pretty cheated he feels too, after all that come-on and build-up.

Not to mention I lie awake half the night listening to see if that git decides to look for his oats and come upstairs, 'stead of staying in the front room where she puts him. Why didn't she give him his cards on the spot, I wanted to know, why didn't she just tell him to get lost? But she didn't. She let him stay. And gave him what was left of our nosh too, and he made out he was so bleeding grateful the smarmy git, with his disc-jockey American accent, he did all the washing-up later. For which I should have been grateful, I daresay. But I weren't. For two pins I'd have smashed MATRIMONIAL BLISS in his fucking face. I saw him look at it all mocking like. How dare he? What's he doing then turning up out of nowhere like a bad penny? Grace don't want him. No more than I do. How can she want him, after what he done her? Anyways, she's my lover now, look at the way she were touching me up when he came in. If he hadn't come I'd have been right in there for sure, the way she were going on. Instead of lying here, picking up every creak and rustle, just in case he tries something. And remembering what I hates to remember, that never mind he's fat and her thin, both of them broader on top and narrower at the bottom, they're alike a bit, some of the same shape and nature.

Grace also lay awake, also all too conscious of Jas in the room below her. Unlike Terry she did not fear his coming, not tonight at least. She knew, still, that Jas was altogether subtler; cleverer; assuming that what he was after — she assumed he was after something — included herself. This did not mean to say she was ignorant these days about the effect she had on men. She had exploited that often enough, when it suited her, when she needed physical release. Had she not been accused by some of those she'd had — not as many as you might expect, her work gave her too little time — of treating them as men more usually treated women? It was an accusation which could make her laugh, wrily, at times, not least because there was, she knew, a certain amount of truth in it. She could even find it in herself to feel sorry for the used-up males she threw out. Though she always answered their complaints coolly. "Then the biter's bit, then," she might say, with as little emotion, seemingly, as she'd used to show when her father despatched the lambs she had reared so lovingly to the abattoir in Taunton. It was the way of things, she knew, she wasn't a tough farmer's daughter for nothing.

I lie awake for a long while. In due course, there's the damn voice again, that sits in my head the way it might as well be her own, chuntering and muttering so fussily, I think she must be moithered as I am by the presence of Jas down below. "As if I don't know your views on wedlock," I say wearily. Which at least stops her going on about Jas. Or even Terry, this time.

Though maybe I'd rather she went on about Jas or Terry. It's disgusting what she says. Not that I don't wonder if I didn't bring it on myself this time, daring to answer her back.

Do thi know how 'tis to be stroong oop by t'neck till thi be dead, mi dozzie? Thi and oll thi yoong ones? I'll say thi doesna'. They don' string men oop such ways now, I hearsen. Well then, I'll tell thi how it was direckly, donna wittle.
 They tek us out one morning, an' we know we're to coom a cropper, had not the judge at the assizes done order us be scragged, till we be dead. With oll folks glegging us, so's they con know not to do as we had been doing of. Liike I say they tek us out. Hangman wor reight keggy-honded, he tek his time about it, fixing them ropes about us necks, that wor fixed in morning about t' tree. Wor oll standing on wagons, wor we; but they held me back, I had to gleg what wor done to mi sons and dotters, the ones I borned. Must I not see oll theirn chokin an' twitchin an' pissin' theyssens, theirn tongues out their gobs, their gospin an' greetin, their cheeks liike torning to blue, their great ommocks twitchin in the air, liike a dance at a wedding, only this wor a dead wedding, death hissen being the bridegroom. Then wor mi turn. Did they string mi oop, drive wagon off mi, wos mi donglin an dancin, mi tongue stretchin, mi breath gooin an' gosping — had mi hands fixed behiind mi, coouldn't get 'em to ease mi. It tek an age to die, it did seem liike; by now I needed to die, liike it wor a long drink; wor it a keen morning, wor it hollin down, the while, it don rained oll t' morning long that we wor a-dying. Wor thi ever choked, dozzie, did they stretch thi neck for thi in fun or meaning? Wor no pleasure I tell thi; tho' I'm a dead 'un afore rain clears; not afore time, tho. Art thi 'arkin, just how 'twas, dozzie? Art thi 'arkin?

"Yes, I am harking," I answered. Why *hadn't* I thought to answer her back before, I wondered? finding I could use the sound of my own voice, inside the head that she'd stolen from me, to hide the sounds that accompanied this nasty recital; sounds like people choking to death horribly and slowly; and like other people enjoying the awful sight.

If she thought she could rattle me so easily, she hadn't reckoned on what I'd been brought up to. Didn't my precious lambs each year go to slaughter? Hadn't I been made to watch, once or twice, when he slaughtered one of mum's hand-reared pigs? All the way through the voice's describing her awful fate — or what it wanted me to think was her awful fate — it could be she just wanted to shock me — I threw back at it my memories, of the pigs' fearful squealing, for instance, when they perceived what was to be done, don't tell me they didn't know, why else did they squeal so? Their carcasses were hung upside down after, the blood draining from their slit throats no more or less sadly than the light drained from their eyes when the knife went in.

Not that I expected such things to shock her. I just wanted to demonstrate that I too had seen blood shed.

"Who *are* you?" I asked. "Who are you?" And "Did you live in this house once? Then when did you live here? Did you ever speak to anyone before me?"

"Of course I got no answers; I did not expect any. I had to try to work out some answers for myself. The agent said some of the house dated from the seventeenth century; maybe the voice was of that time — not that history has ever been my strong point. Assuming its owner had lived here, as seemed most likely, it wouldn't be earlier anyway. What else did I know concerning ghosts? Nothing I thought, coolly, falling at last into a sleep full of the terrors I'd managed to keep at bay till now, but seemingly couldn't hold at bay any longer. "Con't flee mi, dozzie, not liike that," the voice was saying. "Con't flee mi."

In some senses Jas' coming made no difference to either Terry or Grace. They had work to do and that was that; with infinite relief they did it. If Jas wanted to help out sometime, that was entirely a matter for him. As yet, though, he made no sign of any such thing.

It was another four days before they started making glass. It had taken all of three days to heat the furnace and check the burner. On the third night they put the raw material — the batch — and the broken glass — the cullet — in the crucible. In the morning, at last, it was ready for them to use.

Terry waited then, curious, for Grace to make the witch's piece. But she did not make it. Maybe it had only been a joke, he decided. Maybe she had simply forgotten the necessity. Maybe it wasn't a necessity really, just worn-out tradition. It did not mean enough to him, certainly, to make him consider reminding her. Especially given his relief that Jas, though continuing to hang around the cottage, did not, as yet, make an appearance in the glasshouse. No doubt he was playing it carefully, thought Terry in cynical moments. Or maybe he really wasn't interested in anything except a free bed from Grace, the lazy sod.

Mostly, though, he did not reflect on Jas' motives. He did not even ponder, except in passing, the still greater mystery, why Grace had not got shot of Jas straight off, as he would have expected. All he could think of these days was that the glasshouse was alive at long last, its great heart roaring and burning; that he was back doing what he had come to know and love doing best: making glass. He hadn't realised how much he'd missed it. He and Grace had not, it seemed, lost one single little step in their choreography. It almost seemed as if the three months without it had not happened. He had not even forgotten what hard, hot work glass was; particularly now, with the summer almost in. For the moment, though, he did not the least mind it. Why should he care what Jas was doing either? Let him lie around in the garden the whole day long if he wanted, it was all the same to him. It was enough to have to face the man later, over the dinner. For though no one had asked him to, Jas had taken to cooking their dinner; these days they came back to find cooking smells entirely of now and mortal. Terry would sooner have smelled ghost smells, had fish and chips every night, or even cold beetroot and vinegar, if it meant sharing Grace's bed again now and then, rather than lying on his own, listening out for the sound of her ex-husband creeping upstairs to find her.

Not that he had heard him yet. Far from it. It was he, Terry, whom Grace laid down one evening in front of the furnace which he had only that moment, on her orders, closed up for the night, and had fuck her, heartily.

He was hungry afterwards. "Let's hope the nosh'll be cooked through tonight," he said, as, rather later than usual, they locked the glasshouse door and set out up the hill. "Jas don't seem to have got the hang of that stove yet, do he? If he had, he'd have cooked those chops right last night, they wouldn't have turned out raw when we dug our knives in." He had been triumphant at the time. Now, though, the smell of Grace still on his hands, the thought of any meal was welcome; at least it was till they were almost home — the reek of burning pizza didn't even have the decency to wait till they were inside the door; it flaunted itself; it came halfway up the lane to meet them.

Perhaps I should come clean as to part of my motive for coming back. It wasn't just the bloody ants. Reg's money had something to do with it. I saw no way to the bread directly — a will's a will, unless, occasionally, you're a relation with a legitimate grievance regarding undue influence or some such, and no relations of Reg made any complaint. Maybe he had no relations. Nor would they have got far with any suspicions they did have, Grace must have been the last person on earth to guess what Reg intended. As for me, I'm no relation. My only hope of getting at anything of Reg's was through her, my ex-wife, through Grace.

But it wasn't only the bucks, you understand, when it came to it, or what bucks there were. Even though twenty years ago I walked out on the old guy, what I wanted, I think, in some obscure way, was a piece of Reg.

Curiosity's another thing. Don't most of us start being curious, around the age I am, about some of the things and some of the people we invested a bit in? I'm curious for one. Maybe more obsessionally than most, for some reason.

Above all I'm restless, that's my problem. The surprise is

not so much that I keep on wandering but that I have stayed so long in some places. I'm restless now. God knows why Grace doesn't throw me out. It doesn't look to me like she's usually so tolerant, nor does it look like it's lack of will exactly. As for why I keep my arse here when there seems so little in it for me after all this time — the only thing I know for sure is because it bugs that bloody youth.

Which isn't the point and don't I know it? It never was the point. Though I told Grace I loved her more than once or twice — not my usual style, I tell you.

She hasn't changed much. The jeans she wears all the time might be the same ones she always used to. If she looks still more elemental, like some kind of human landscape, she always did look potentially like that, there always was that terrifying ruthlessness of hers; not unkind, just certain. At the same time you could, then, reach out and touch her. When you planted something of yours in her soil, there was a chance that it might grow, if not in a way I was capable of predicting. Could you still touch her maybe, something might grow from that touch. The problem is how to touch her. It's not just me. I couldn't blame her for holding out against me, after what happened. She has grown a skin — a gloss — a layer of glass, if you like — against the whole world it seems, behind which she sits these days, smiling, not at all sweetly, not enigmatically, or defiantly, or like someone used to smiling; simply smiling. The worst thing being that if you accused her of it, she genuinely wouldn't know what you were on about; what you meant.

I keep thinking of a definition of glass I read years ago. "Glass won't rot, rust, perish, decay," it goes — something like that — "but it can be broken." And that's it. That's the worst of it. She is invulnerable behind that glass, OK. But if it could be broken, God help whoever did it; man, woman or baby. God help me if *I* did. I'm not going to try. That's why I don't apply my usual winning charms and just get on with it. Why I sit here like a lemon, saying nuffin, doing the cooking, for Chrissake. I did say, I suppose, that that's what I've landed up doing. Not that I'm such hot stuff as I used to be, that bloody stove burns stuff to a frazzle one day, and leaves it half-cooked the next. If I wasn't a rational being, I'd say the damn thing was bewitched.

Next time that boy smirks at me for it, I'll knock his block off. He gets smugger daily. Probably because he doesn't seem to bounce off that glaze Grace has set about herself, he good as vaporises through it. I could swear sometimes they're both looking out at me from inside, jeering. Worse, they took that damn stove inside with them. If I didn't know it wasn't possible, I'd say Grace had fixed the bastard herself, just to show me. Whatever's wrong with the food she never says anything. The little schmuck, Terry, makes up for it, though, grinning all over his spotty little face. He had a field day last night with those bloody — in every sense — pork chops. Tonight he's still happier, that stove having got the better of me altogether. I made pizza the way I used to for my kids — I'd even made the dough — after ten minutes in the oven it wasn't just burned at the edges it was charred right the way through; inedible, damn it. Terry's beside himself with joy, plus he keeps looking at me smugly as if he knows something I don't.

None of it, of course, draws one single word from Grace. She just gets in the car and drives off to get fish and chips (which is one thing that in California, I tell you, I did not find myself missing). She won't let either of us go with her. That leaves the yob and me staring at each other. If he's going to live till moning I'm going to have to go outside right now and dig his grave or something, else he won't bloody live till midnight, let alone morning.

It was June already, and light till late. Driving to the chip shop in Matlock Bath, Grace saw what she had been too busy to notice, that the lambs in the fields had mostly lost their pathos; no longer skinny and lively, they were not only fat with wool, they moved ponderously like their mothers. Also that the trees had lost their early freshness; that the swifts were darting low round the red walls — glowing redder in the powdery evening light — of Arkwright's factory as if they had appropriated the summer with no reference to herself.

Why didn't she tell Jas to go, she was wondering, as usual, as she stood in a queue amid the steamy, neon-lit, wholly urban drama of the chip shop. She wanted to. Had he come to her in London, she would have told him. But things were different here. "I told you dozzie," the voice in her head was saying. What had it told her? — for once Grace was hardly listening, certainly not bothering to answer. It had not even occurred to her to wonder yet that the voice was speaking to her here — till now she had never heard it speak away from the cottage. As she walked out of the shop, clutching her hot and greasy parcel, she was observing instead, almost in horror, with none of her former acceptance of such things, the relentlessness of these long light evenings; of the harsh greens of summer. Perhaps the leaves were of all things the most relentless, because withdrawn each year and then repeated. The frowning rock walls of the gorge, on the other hand, behind and above her, would not, once eroded, come back the way they were, not ever.

In my head, still, the voice goes on murmuring. "Stay with me, dozzie," it seems to be saying. "Mun us trust ussens only. Niver reckon on they men."

"Get lost," I tell it, "I heard this damned foolishness a time or two too often. And I don't even know your name." This time, to my astonishment, she answers; meekly. "Betsy is my name." She so surprises me, it's only now, when I get into the car and close the door, I realise how strange it is that she continues keeping me company. What on earth does she make of the car, let alone the chip shop, I wonder?

The smell of the chip shop makes me hungry. The same, if fainter, smell wafting up from the hot newspaper-wrapped parcel on the seat soon gets too much for me altogether; I scrabble open a corner one-handed, and take a chip or two. Though their greasy crispness is pleasing, I feel at least as gratified by Betsy's unremitting presence. I am even exhilarated by it. "Teking vittles back to men," she is complaining.

"What's good of a man, but to get thee babbies on thi, gobble oop thi vittles. I lost mi man young, it's good to say, were ever greetin' and had no nerve to fend for the babbies the way I fended, dozzie." — "How you do go on," I break in. "Men aren't all bad, whatever you say. Dozzie. Dozzie." I don't believe a word I'm saying. It is just for argument's sake. I daresay she knows it the way I throw back my head and laugh out loud. "Ah, dozzie," she says again. As for me I could even admit in this moment, with this land laid out all round me, in this melting evening light, how I would miss my unseen companion if she went away entirely. How, for the most part — give or take those things she tells me that I'd much sooner she didn't — I've come to look for her inexplicable presence; how I regret it sometimes when she leaves me.

It has even occurred to me lately, that maybe such tetchy, inconsequential, affectionate banter is how it can be when women friends get together. Not that I'd ever known it. Unlike my sister Winifred, I never had — never felt the lack of — female friends. Nor had the time or inclination to seek out feminist groups or movements. If I've worked out my life, if I've succeeded without benefit of groups or movements, why can't the rest of them do it?

I am acquainted with some women of course, but professionally, only. Most of them being glassblowers, gender does not come into it; what I respect — or don't respect — is the quality of their work. Gender, on the other hand, I am beginning to understand, dimly, has everything to do with the way Betsy and I talk together. Even driving up the hill I am wondering if we aren't in collusion of some kind. If we aren't both of us equally responsible in some way I am unable to fathom for the stove's maverick behaviour?

We are over the brow of the hill now; coming down the wooded lane towards the cottage I can see, beyond, the slope where the gallows tree stood, according to the plumber's father. Where the woman was hung, presumably, if she was hung, and why should she claim it if she wasn't? But what was she hung for? Witchcraft? I don't know, and I hardly want to. All I do know, which is more than enough of injustice, is that such as she and I used to be hung freely, if not for witchcraft, for crimes as little as stealing a crust of bread or poaching a coney.

"Back to the men — what do we be needing wi a man?" she screeches as I open the door into the kitchen. "Shut up," I admonish her. "You've made that point already. Dozzie." Even so, laughing to myself in a way that excludes bloody men of all ages — I can't help it, if, like any ewe or heifer, I enjoy being tupped sometimes — I dump the still warm, even greasier parcel down on the table in front of the ravenous Terry — Jas seemed to have disappeared somewhere — and wonder, for the first time in my life, why I'd always seen myself as getting on better with men than women.

"A maid'd do thi bidding sooner. Why never tek a maid to aid thi?" Betsy is asking, seeing with her ghostly eye no doubt, as I do, the way my ugly boy gasps for my culinary and other favours. Why did I never take on a girl, I wonder?

The smile Grace gave Jas when he appeared through the other door was almost provocative; as if someone else was doing the smiling. Returning it, irritably, he concluded he should stop all this nonsense, should just walk into her room one night and have her; or, alternatively, get up and leave her. What good reason did he have for hanging about? Terry, meanwhile, glancing surreptitiously between their faces and seeing collusion of another kind from the one Grace had been thinking of, dolloped ketchup angrily on his share of the battered fish, as an afterthought added vinegar. Bloody Grace never remembered to put vinegar on in the shop, she never got pickled onions either unless he was there to remind her. None of which stopped him gobbling the already tepid food straight out of the paper. Then, his fingers still greasy, he went and walked alone in the darkening wood, longing for the first time for days for London and his mates, if not his bloody mother. What was he doing here for God's sake, he, too, asked himself over and over, forgetting how he loved his glass, why didn't he up and off next morning? Not even the image of making love to Grace in front of the furnace could comfort him. If anything, it made him feel still gloomier than ever.

But of course he did not up and off. Next morning he was down in the glasshouse with Grace, wielding the punty. How *could* he escape her? — the little bottles that he worked on at odd moments were improving all the time.

Grace had their working time well organised by now. Four days a week were spent between Reg's eighteenth century lines and doing the administration; sorting out orders and VAT, typing receipts and invoices on the old typewriter she had inherited, like everything else, from Reg. The fifth day — and the weekend, if necessary, she did more administration, also worked on her own and Terry's one-offs. She did not make many of her cloud bowls to Terry's regret, no more than necessary to fulfil the orders still coming in. Instead she played around with fusing rods of plain and coloured glass in the lehr, starting it up from cold, then letting it cool down much more slowly than she did when annealing blown glass; letting it go over a whole weekend sometimes, as when they'd made paperweights, instead of just one night. (The thicker the glass not only the longer it had to be annealed, the more difficult it was to get the timing right.)

The delicate stability of glass had always intrigued her. In her case, though, for practical rather than intellectual, let alone philosophical reasons; none of Jas' psychological, social, even political analogies made any sense to her whatever. Reg, of course, had exploded his Rupert's drops for her benefit. But they were the crude end of the matter only. Even in glass cooled slowly you could, she knew all too well, get the balance wrong, leaving its substance unstable, liable to crack eventually, if not to explode at a touch. She wasn't sure even now if she was getting it right, she told Terry; what she really needed was some kind of strain viewer so she could check the internal stresses in each hunk of glass she worked on.

It was all Greek to him. He knew what you had to do with blown glass, how you set the lehr for that. Like Reg, like the old glassblowers, he was happy enough to gauge the whole thing by feel and eye and experience, putting the thicker pieces, for instance, where they would cool more slowly than the thinner. Secure enough in his own expertise these days to make such judgments, he watched with bafflement and even impatience Grace's forays to the glasshouse to check progress, the copious notes she made in a red school exercise book bought especially for the purpose. He couldn't see the point of any of it. And said so.

Today, however, Grace herself seemed impatient with it. She started experimenting with blown glass again, refining her cloud vases into ones more like flame ones; blowing some of these directly into moulds, so that they came out square or oblong, not rounded, fluted instead of smooth. None of them were what she was looking for, but at least they were saleable objects. What she had forgotten — she had never used to forget such things, Terry thought — was that they were running out of glass; a delivery of cullet which should have arrived two days ago, had not yet done so. Before the afternoon was over, the glass that came up from the bottom of the crucible was almost unusable, at least for blowing.

Grace did not know quite what — apart from simple frustration — had put the idea into her head, any more than Terry did. Seeing her go outside and return with a bucketful of sand from the heap the builders had left, he thought she must have gone quite crazy. He thought her even crazier — seeing his face, she went on with it in some ways just to vex him — when she picked up a shallow tray from a corner, filled it with sand, damped the sand down thoroughly, and made a firm hand print in it. Into this she proceeded to pour some of the mucky glass from the bottom of the crucible. When it had hardened sufficiently, she took the hand shape out and put in the lehr with the rest of the day's output. "It won't anneal properly," she said to Terry. "But it may give me an idea or two. It's time I had some."

After that he helped her close up the furnace. But she did not then, as sometimes, stay behind, making drawings, writing up her notebooks. Instead she walked back up through the wood with him. Halfway up, at a point where the bracken was beginning to elongate itself and thicken, she took his arm, to his surprise, and drew him off the path.

No doubt she felt him flinch. "Don't you want to?" she

asked him. "I know it's hot." "You mean here?" he said to stall her. "Where else, dozzie?" She had never before enticed him in such a thick, crooning voice; a voice not the least like her normal one. It might almost have been another speaking. She had never, in fact, needed to entice him. Even now, he did not know how to refuse her. As uneasy as he felt, hot and sticky as he felt — as she felt after their day before the furnace — he remembered last night's episode, and finding himself beginning to be aroused, let her draw him down amid the new bracken.

It was the first time he had made love in the open air. Having started his sex life in more comfort than most, it was only now perhaps he realised how fortunate he had been, compared to those who had to make do with alleyways and canal banks and the backs of ancient bangers. Used to Grace's double bed, he found disporting himself in this place not only uncomfortable but embarrassing. There were insects wandering on his exposed flesh; when Grace insisted on laying him down on his back and riding him, clods of earth and twigs ground into his back and legs and buttocks. He closed his eyes to avoid hers, not so much because he did not recognise the expression in them — he was used to not recognising that — but because he could not bear the sense that he was not only literally but actually being ridden. That no matter how he struggled, she had him fast; that it was only with her consent that he would be able to rise to his feet again, ever.

Hearing voices in the distance, he wanted to move very badly. The voices getting nearer he twisted this way and that, his eyes wide open to the painful youth of green bracken fronds, of the surprisingly juicy grasses, in which he caught and did not want to catch the little gold and emerald glitters. Trapped the way he was by the surprisingly white yet strong flesh of Grace's two long legs, the image he had of them, exposed, half naked to the world, made him groan with embarrassment and terror. Not just one or two people were coming from the sound of it, but several. He and Grace could hardly avoid being seen, he thought, they were only a yard or two off the path. If not, the way Grace was behaving they would be heard, for certain. He would not even have put it past her to be drawing attention to them. She was giggling now to judge from her grimaces, the rocking of her body. How long could such giggles stay silent? He saw feet already beyond her through the grass and bracken; feet in thick socks and hiking boots. He heard them clattering against the path. The voices rose and fell; they were passing, they were past — no, not quite, two stragglers followed. In a moment they, too, had vanished.

Grace erupted, immediately. The behaviour that had surprised and alarmed Terry, surprised and alarmed her no less. The laughter forcing its way through her was not a release as much as an invasion; it felt as if it belonged to someone else. In a moment she stopped laughing and looked down at Terry almost with pity. His eyes closed, he did not see it. Regretting the normality of the voices he could hear no longer, he was clinging so desperately to the growl of traffic from the road below them, that the wooded walls of the valley magnified and flung up, he'd not even realised she'd stopped laughing. The first thing he knew was when she leaned over, picked up a handful of dampish earth and leaves, squeezed them together, and in a voice so different it had nothing to do with him whatever, said quietly, "How, I wonder?" Then she dropped the earth, climbed to her feet and let him go. He scrambled up at once; in his hurry to make himself decent made a poor job of brushing the earth and leaves and grass, the prickly russet dust of last year's bracken from his backside, enclosing so much of it inside his hastily dragged-up jeans that he itched for the rest of the way.

Grace could not remove these hidden irritations. But she brushed others, twigs and leaves and grasses, almost tenderly, contritely, off the outside of his clothes. An act which no more dispelled his alarm, than it could dispel her own. He was more frightened of her now, than of the wood. The very anger he felt, at the way she had mocked him, added to his fear. The sound of the traffic below was still almost the only thing that proved him real — the itches against his flesh did nothing, he thought, but prove him crazy. And her? She was wondering the same. It was a nightmare that only faded from them slowly as they went up through the wood, not so much arm in arm as like prisoners chained together, to emerge at last, thankfully, on to the open slopes of the park. The bracken here was not yet high enough to hide in. It was all each could do, seeing it, not to burst into cries of relief.

Chapter Six

"Acid juice nor any other thing extract neither colour, taste nor any other quality from it . . ."

We had to wait a day or two longer for the cullet. Not Grace's fault, just that there always have been problems with the supply of cullet, there were in London, nothing odd about that. But it ain't as if there's nothing else we can do while we're waiting. Though it's Friday by now and though we do sometimes take the weekend off, I'm surprised, I'll admit, not so much that Jas suggests going off walking, but that Grace jumps at the offer. The cunning bastard, of course, reckoned among other things on getting her away from yours truly, but Grace wasn't having none of that. Not that she asked me, she just assumed I'd want to go along. In which she were quite mistaken. I don't have no fancy boots for one thing, like the blokes come past the house with their maps and anoraks and gaiters. I don't have no nothing.

But Grace says she don't have no boots either, come to that, and on a dry day which it looks like it's going to be, as usual, trainers will do. So that's that, glare Jas might, he's lumbered with me, off we go all three of us in the old Escort at nine in the morning. The only reason I am going is because I don't fancy the idea of her up there on her own with Jas. Now I see what happened with her and me in that wood, I don't trust her nowhere, no more 'n I trust him, I think, giving his dirty looks back good as I get. Not that Grace seems to notice. At least she pretends she don't notice. Maybe she really don't, for all she's sharper about such things these days, I wonder if Jas sees it.

It was about an hour's drive, on a morning so bright you could hardly see it. We dumped the car by a pub in a place called Hayfield — of course there weren't any hayfields, not so's you'd notice. We'd come over whitish, greenish country; this place had smooth slopes, too, going up, and stone walls; but higher it had great dark edges; this was where Jas said we was going.

It weren't too bad at first. We went up a bit and along, over black earth that sprang under your feet like a bed. Then down a bit towards a lake, what weren't no lake really but a reservoir filling up a concrete basin. Then up again along a stream, for just a bit. Which is where it started to get steep. And hot. I was OK, though, and so was Grace. Which was more than could be said for Jas I were glad to see. He were puffing and blowing, those bloody curls of his sodden sweaty. Just to make him feel better I went up and came down twice. So he'd know it weren't so bad if you weren't paunchy. That had me sweating a bit too, I tell you, but I made sure he wouldn't see it.

We wasn't the only walkers of course, by no means. Being Saturday there were whole families, mum, dad, kids, it set me to wondering how we looked, if people thought we were a family. Which were more than enough to make me puke. Gawd help us, I'd rather my old soak of a dad even than Jas, as for Grace, she's not my bloody mother, she's my lover.

Well, we made the top of that hill in the end. Before we got to the end of it, I wished I'd shown off a good deal less. Even so I was better off than Jas — the way he slipped and slid, grunting and wheezing, the colour his face went, I thought he weren't going to make it. And how, if not, we was going to get him down.

Luckily there weren't any steep bits after that, or hardly. For a good way we walked on the level mostly, on a beat-up yellow path and in and out of rocks, with a cliff to our right and the black bog reaching leftwards.

It weren't a cheerful sight that black bog, worse than Battersea Park in November. The great gleam of the sun made it gloomier if anything. It had deep, winding channels in it, with sand and white stones on their beds but no water. About all that grew apart from what they told me was heather, was things like blobs of cotton on little dried-up stalks. No, Grace says when I asks her, no, she don't find it creepy. Maybe she said it to annoy me. Or maybe to shut me up. Or maybe she did really like it, if so it could of learned me something about her I didn't know till then.

The rest of it was all right. With all that sky above and all that land beneath, we was kings of the whole fucking country. Mind you, it were scary, you didn't have nowhere to hide from so much space, not even in the bog channels. But it didn't matter. It should of made me feel small and weak, fact I felt bigger and stronger. The gloss of the midday sun like blotted out all colours but couldn't, no way, blot out me, yours truly.

I wanted to fuck Grace in one of those hidden channels. I would of, I swear, if Jas hadn't been with us. He'd stopped puffing, the bleeder, now we was on the level. The country putting me off my guard, he and Grace had got together somehow. The way it had me feeling, when I saw them marching on ahead of me, they made a mistake walking along that cliff, I tell you. For two pins I'd've pushed him off: pushed them both off, come to that. Just to bloody show 'em.

But of course I didn't. I walked behind them, meek as you like, not even looking at them folk we was meeting. I'd have liked this place still better without any of the people. The way I was feeling I'd have liked to have been up there without Grace even, by myself, never mind that till now I'd found open country a bit too fucking lonely for comfort.

The cliff turned right after a bit. There was an angle in it, and in the angle a great rock downfall. By rights, according to Grace, there should of been water coming down over that downfall, but there weren't none now, not in this dry season. Though there was a wind still, there always was a wind she said. When there was water, it didn't fall, or hardly, it blew up and back in fine sprays like horse's tails. It was a long enough speech for her; it was like she'd understood something suddenly; or rather, she and fucking Jas understood something suddenly.

We sat down to our dinner then, in sight of where there weren't no water. Seeing the way Grace and Jas had their heads together; seeing that today I was the one by the look of it, not wanted, my teeth felt like Dracula fangs, for biting into flesh rather than cheese sarnies and bananas and Bournville chocolate — Grace always gets plain chocolate, why can't the bugger get us milk, the way I like it?

To sit on a high hill looking out used to be my only pleasure, apart from the horses. I wasn't the only one either, mum would go up the hill behind us, times she'd had more than she could endure to. When we were little, before I took to such things myself, she'd lug me and Winnie with her, calling it a walk or picnic. I daresay it helped her accept the kind of life she was forced to. If she thought it could help me accept it, that was some hope; I wasn't going to.

She'd been not more than seven, probably, eight at the most, the time Grace best remembered and still preferred to forget. They'd come out with the pony, Grace and Winifred taking turns to ride, to pick bilberries ostensibly. There was one place their mother particularly loved, on the other side of Stout's Lane, just before it turned down over towards the Roadborough valley. Having climbed the lane, they had only to traverse a quarter of a mile or so of rough track to reach an unfenced space above the common, from which they could look down across gathered and folded country — an isolated barn set into one fold as if it had grown there — to the Bristol Channel. Beyond, on the far side, lay the mysterious places called Cardiff and Port Talbot. Names and places Grace had never been able to imagine as being real entirely. Not least because, to the naked eye, they weren't there, often, mist and cloud hid them. While at night a light would wink out from somewhere nearby in a sequence she could never quite grasp and never quite wanted to grasp, either.

That day, in that high place, they'd eaten the tea their mother had brought, sitting amid stubby, yellow-green leaved bilberry bushes, with their livid and fiddly fruit — "urts" or "urtles" Grace's mother called them. The stocky dark bay pony, meanwhile, its reins held loosely between Grace's hands, bent its head and cropped the verges of the track, flicking away flies with its bushy tail. It was an awkward-tempered if pretty beast, despite its almost always suspiciously rolling eye; Grace loved it with an overwhelming passion. The cropping sound it made, the swish, swish of its tail, the buzzing of the persistent flies, permeated her memory of that moment; of her mother's half-whispered, barely remembered words (even to her children, the woman spoke always in doubt and apology). Waving her hand at the widespread land, its reds hidden just now by the yellowing corn, the bleached greens of late summer, she said, as she often did in one way or another, "Isn't her beautiful, Gracie? Can there be any more handsome sight in the world than her laid out resting so comfortable and easy?"

"Why do you always say such barmy things?" asked Grace, turning her head away. Her resentment, even fury, was all the deeper, because she had at last, if only briefly, seen what her mother meant; seen the land as so female, she had been able to pick out the woman's thighs and head and belly. To this day she wasn't willing to admit that it was this moment, this perception, first set her towards being an artist. What if it did show you could transform what you saw into an image of something else, and then — as followed naturally in due course — recreate that image in your own way and in whatever material you chose to? She was damned if she was going to thank her mother for it.

So why do I keep thinking of mum these days, when I least want it? I wonder. Sitting on what seems even on a summer day, a much unkinder hill than that one, I open my mouth hardly knowing I am going to; I find myself trying to tell Jas what she made me see. Though all that comes out is, "My mother liked hills. She used to take us for walks up on the Brendons," Jas looks astonished just the same. Even when we were young and I thought he loved me, I wouldn't say a word about any of my family; or the places I had come from; not one single word. I wouldn't even invite them to our wedding. (Not that dad would have agreed to let them come if I had done. I don't think so.)

So what makes me try to talk about them now, now I don't love, rather I hate him? Looking at him blankly, as if the white-out of the land, of the sun, has so blinded me I can't even be quite sure who I am speaking to, I go so far as to add, my voice almost inaudible, "My mother died you know, Jas. Also my father."

And all the time I am thinking; why has he let himself go? My father never did, not till the end of his life. He was always a fine figure of a man. It seems like an insult in some ways. A reflection on me for having loved him. Sometimes I am almost glad that the child he fathered on me didn't survive either.

In any case why is he still here with me? Why do I talk to him about mum, for God's sake? In London I wouldn't have let him stay under my roof a single instant. He is like a stray dog on my doorstep, I chuck a grudging bone only to find him, a moment later, sitting under my kitchen table, wagging his tail at me. I cannot think how it happened. Unless it's the same as it was once, when he could make me so against my own will. Or unless I pity him in some way, and he knows how to use my pity.

Even in the beginning, I distrusted his cleverness and feared it; it showed him at ease with the world as I never could be, nor my mum and dad either. Because of him I began to look on them, without compassion, as two orphans, one ranting, one shivering, clinging together against the raging storm. (It's how I still remember they in a way, though I'd just as soon I didn't.)

Grace jumped to her feet. She would have walked with Terry then, if Jas had let her. But Terry was too busy sulking, chucking stones over the cliff and at the sound of each bounce imagining it was her bones breaking, or Jas', to oust Jas from the place he again assumed as of right. Nor would Jas be shaken off it. What's more he'd taken it into his head to tell Grace about some of the different kinds of landscapes he'd encountered on his travels; how they'd compared with this one. If he had intended to soften her, dissolve her suspicions, he couldn't have done better. He carried himself away also.

His American inflections growing less perceptible by the minute, he made her, too, yearn for mesas and canyons — for spaces in which this seemingly huge one could be fitted a hundred times over. Made her want to weep with frustration for what she was after in her work and had not yet succeeded in getting.

(In a little while Jas almost, but not quite, started to put his arm about his ex-wife, Terry's lover; the glowering Terry might have been a hundred miles away; he spoke to Grace now, only.)

"I was in an earthquake once, in California. You look at this land, Gracie, you think it's so static, everlasting; you think nothing can shift it. But you don't think it any more, once you experience one of those things. Any more than you imagine glass stays the same substance, once you've melted some in your furnace; once you've brought it out all glowing and felt you understood the nature of matter. Then you feel you're really a magician. Until the earth shifts that is, you feel it. Then, understanding or not, you realise you aren't. That you're just a flea on the back of an elephant that's shrugging its shoulders and catching you in its wrinkles. Maybe you'd like such a feeling, Gracie, but I can't say that I liked it. I was scared as Moses, so would anyone be, that had any sense left them. Not because the house might fall about your ears, for Chrissake, that's the least of it, what the hell is dying? It's the power of the thing that gets you. Even the little jabs, the playful ones, make damn sure you know it's powerful. That's what you want to get at in your work, isn't it, Gracie, what Ruskin would have called the awe-full, ineffable moment; the sheer power of the substance you're working with; or rather of the place it came from. What's the sense of making anything unless at some point you catch it?"

At that moment, on her feet once more, walking, close to Jas but not touching him, not wanting to touch him, Grace might have been back before the popping gas fire of her bed-sittingroom in Jas' mother's house, fired, among other things, to catch what she'd always tried to, chasing after the will o' the wisp of the deep soul thing inside her; something that for a time, more than twenty years ago, she had been mistaken enough to see in Jas also; and very nearly, for a brief while, in Jas only.

(As for Terry, his eyes the sharpened eyes of the jealous child or lover, he was asking himself one minute, why in fuck's name don't she tell him to get stuffed? The next he was giving himself his own answer: because whether she knows it or not, she don't want to, do she? She don't bloody want to.)

As for Jas — if he had not yet won — of course he had not yet demanded — right of entry to Grace's bed — he had won right of entry to her studio; which was in a way still better. He knew it. This was maybe why, when they had at last stumbled, weary and aching, from the hills, he did not just insist on drinking in the pub by which they had left the car, but in practically every other pub they passed on the way back to the cottage. He bought Terry, too, drink for drink; they got drunk together, if for different reasons. Ending the trip, in the last pub they arrived at, with their arms round each other, singing, "My old man's a dustman," to the amazement of their fellow drinkers. Till they were as good as thrown out by the landlord, to be driven home by a tight-lipped and sober Grace who put them both to bed, reflecting as she did so that it was as well she had no cullet; Terry could not have worked in the morning had she wanted to, and Jas would have been no better, if he could still handle a punty, which she doubted, but knew she would shortly discover.

("I told thi so, dozzie. Don' say I didn' warn thi." Maybe it was Betsy said that to me; maybe it wasn't. It wasn't clear to me at all if she was with me that night. If she wasn't I missed her. Yet what else could she have said, and in her most gloating manner — I told you so, don't say I didn't warn you.)

Twenty years I lived in the US of A, and all the time I never stopped being exhilarated by the sheer humming pizazz, brash as it might be.

Which doesn't mean to say I failed to hang on to some

notion of where I came from, never mind I might have thought once that I despised it. Ten percent you could say I even craved for, or if I didn't crave it, had come in time to appreciate its value; and came back for, maybe. Not that I've yet found it.

I didn't just imagine, did I, a kind of innocent decency? What happened to it? Why do things now seem so much nastier and meaner? People like my parents, for instance, who once thought themselves more than decent, are like lying on their backs, winded, don't know what hit them. Most of the rest think nothing any longer of showing how much they hate and despise each other; at least they don't seem to. It's like a glasshouse in which everyone is throwing, or about to start throwing stones. As if they thought there was room to. Or, more likely, as if they didn't care a fuck there wasn't.

And, come to think of it, what was the innocence anyway, what did it consist of, apart from that veneer of eccentricity that the English call character? All very pleasant but spineless, like my mother's sculptures. As lifeless even then, the mid-sixties, as one of those animals she used to keep in the freezer. Or those little ethical dilemmas my lapsed Jew philosopher daddy would insist on posing us at breakfast over his matzos and bacon.

And what was the use of *that* in the face of the seventies; let alone the eighties. Let alone our bourgeois Boadicea in her clean white apron, summoning up Gradgrinds left right and centre from every provincial quarter. Winning elections on mean glories and meaner terrors, sweet harangues, sour circuses and bread (with an increasing inclination to forget about the bread). Democracy in the hands of demagogic tabloids makes you despair of it entirely. The English were the only people who really believed in democracy anyway, at the very moment, usually, they were beating the democratic shit out of some subject people or other, home or abroad. Maybe it's that useless sweetness of belief in something that never a hundred percent existed I miss so badly; though, all through my grass-fazed youth, I despised it, and still do to the extent I can see Her Patronage has her uses, that the whole damn place really needed stirring up. Overweight fagend I may be, yet in some parodic way I'm her new man exactly, hopping on my bike — I'm still waiting for the Audi — taking my profits exactly where I find them. (Who cares if I grind the faces of the poor in passing, isn't it their own fault they're poor in the first place? Take schmuck Terry, for instance.)

So no, I'm not about to cut out the rotten patches, if you ask me. If I cut out the rotten patches, what for Chrissake's left? Well, one thing is left, I tell you: Grace is what's left and always has been. Provided she can stand the heat in the kitchen; and doesn't let herself get basted. That's why at times I used to hate her, even while we were still married. Why I hated her today, walking past that almost comfortingly blatant stink of corruption, that dump next to her glasshouse. Hated her when I saw her working. For what she was and is. For what I didn't know how to be, short of I let her teach me. And I wasn't going to have that, not for a minute. Not bloody likely.

I was jealous I suppose; the moment I clapped eyes on her in front of that furnace. When I saw what it was I'd been looking for I wanted to run a thousand miles. Not least because it was me made it. She wouldn't have been a glassblower if it hadn't been for me. She'd have been a damn good potter I daresay, but that's by no means the same thing, I tell you.

She was so clumsy the times she used to work with me. But she's not clumsy now. By no means. And if I'd always thought of her as a witch of some kind, I'd always said that glassmen in general were magic. In a manner of speaking.

She didn't see me at first that morning I came down, after the cullet arrived and she and Terry started working. Maybe it was coming in out of that steaming wasteland that did it. That made the sight of her have the effect on me it did. Or maybe it was just the fact I hadn't seen anyone blowing glass for twenty years and never known till then how much I'd missed it. I revelled in everything, even my hatred of Grace. The smell, the noise, the poised yet almost off-hand concentration; the very choreography — the only problem being that the bloody brat, Terry, was Grace's dancing partner. (Never mind it was my own fault I wasn't. Never mind that I wouldn't have wanted, if I'm honest, to spend twenty years handing her the punty; having her hand me the punty.) He was such an oafish little cuss I was surprised to see him so skilful. Though I shouldn't have been surprised; Grace wouldn't have brought him up here if he hadn't been any good at it. His activities in her bed — I don't doubt, the way he glares at me, he got into her bed — are beside the point.

They were making a set of goblets that morning. Always an awkward business, don't I remember from my time with Reg. Just to get six matching you might make ten, twelve, on a bad day fourteen. I didn't distract them, I was glad to see. They did it in ten this morning, not at all bad going.

Don't ask me what I felt about it. Did I feel I'd wasted my time, fat slob that I now was, seeing where Grace had got to in all these years, seeing what I had to set against it? No I did not exactly. Which is not to say that as the morning went on I didn't start itching to get my hands on an iron or something. At the same time as being shit-scared that Grace might actually suggest it. I didn't entirely trust her not to. She'd have known as well as I do that you can't be twenty years out of this business without losing at least three-quarters of your skill. It was not something I fancied demonstrating under the nose of bloody Terry. So I left before there got to be any danger of it, spending the rest of the day flat out in her neglected garden — it didn't look as if anyone had touched it for weeks, but it's not my garden, I wasn't going to let the sight of the guy across the road mowing his lawn make me feel bad about it; as it was I was assaulted by the sound of his blue-smoking motor and later, towards evening, by the chanting from the bloody rooks just up the hill. I wonder if Grace ever noticed there's one bird with a cracked voice, different from the rest. Or if she realises, yet, that the stink that hangs around, when the wind blows from behind us, comes from the piggery up there and not from her septic tank.

Not that I think she imagines for one moment I'm as cool and humble as I play it. She couldn't be that stupid. But so I still make myself out to be down at the glasshouse. I don't so much as touch even a punty. The nearest I get to the glass while they're working is spraying those bloody pink pads of newspaper with water — God knows why the FT's so much better for the purpose than the Times or the Guardian; but it always was and still is, seemingly.

In betweenwhiles I go and look at the stuff Grace has set out on the shelves at the back of the workshop. Seconds mostly. The good stuff is all packed and ready to go. I know because I packed it, that's one thing I can do. In the middle of the shelf I saw this hand one day; her right hand. Only it was made of glass. When I asked her why, she couldn't or wouldn't tell me. She merely shook her head; leaving me searching for evidence of her hand in the glass one. If it lacked the patterns of her skin — how could you catch in glass the patterns of someone's skin? — it was, all the same, almost like a limb she'd sloughed off. A lizard sloughs its tail doesn't it, only to grow another? I looked suspiciously at her right hand, I tell you — it didn't look like a new-grown hand; it looked as worn and sinewy as her left. But if the glass hand on the shelf was a third one, whose in God's name was it?

(I never caught myself having such crazy thoughts in California. But then in California I never got to watch my ex-wife blowing glass and fucking minors.)

And so it goes on. And on. Some days I come out of that place so dazed and blinking, I can't stand the thought of that stone cottage, all I want is the pub. I'd take Grace along too, if I could, with or without her it's better than watching schmuck Terry glaring at me over burnt chops or underdone spaghetti. I daresay he understands as I do that there's been a kind of shift somewhere, since that day on the High Peak. Grace is much less wary; lets me pull the words up over her head and scarcely takes a glance behind her. Whereas Terry, given half a chance, would bash me over the head with a blowing iron; a hot one preferably; the hotter the better. I can tease him I discover by being quite deferential; bowing, as it were, to his skills while they remain superior. If he's more suspicious of me by the day it's nothing to the way I am suspicious. Ugly little runt that he may be, I know I can't discount him. Which is why, I daresay,

I blew my top the way I did when I found out whose tools he was using.

I didn't need telling that Grace had my tools. I assumed it. She nodded when I asked her. It was around lunchtime, these hot days the glasshouse is almost intolerable by noon. Grace had been talking of starting early — at six o'clock or so — and finishing at midday. But she hadn't yet got round to it, maybe it would have been better if she had, we wouldn't all of us have been so scratchy and sweating. It made *me* sweat, and all I'd been doing was manning the phone and tidying up. I went on sweating while I asked my question even though we'd stopped for a break and were sitting under the trees on the opposite side of the track, knocking back cans of lager.

Grace said she was too hot to eat, but Terry was laying into some mini pork pies he'd brought down with him from the cottage. When I leaned over and took one he glared at me but said nothing. He had taken his shirt off. His chest was white and thin, almost hollow under the pectorals, the rib bones lined themselves up so pathetically, even crookedly, so meanly, it looked as if I could crack them one-handed without thinking. I nearly did crack them. Not just because I was imagining those ribs lying against Grace's. But because almost off-handedly, after telling me what happened to my tools, she answered the question I hadn't yet dared ask her, "I gave Terry Reg's."

"Reg's tools?"

"She weren't going to give me Reg's trousers were she?" said the boy triumphantly. And then he cringed; as I turned, the sweat dripping off my forehead; as I leaned over him — but I was hardly seeing him then, those easily broken bones, that bruisable skull, those closeable-up eyes. I was seeing Reg. Whom I hadn't seen and chosen not to. Whom I'd abandoned twenty years ago, which was the real crime, more than abandoning my wife and stillborn child.

"Do you want your tools back then?" Grace said reasonably; as if none of this meant anything. Maybe it didn't. She pulled the ring off another can of beer, thought better of handing it over, started tipping its contents down her throat.

And nothing happened. Not yet. There were three people sitting in a wood near a rubbish dump, opposite a stone hut converted into a glasshouse, the heat of it shimmering in the air that breathed out from its open door. They were drinking beer and eating mini porks. The youngest of them was shifting dapples of sun on his bare white skin as if he meant to and knew what he was doing. It was midsummer already and intolerably hot. Not as hot as California, of course, but hot enough even for one used to California, given that the people were talking about someone dead more than a year and about the tools of his trade. Which the man, Jas, quite unreasonably, thought should have been kept for him. Grace could keep hers that had been mine, but Reg's belong to me, he was thinking. Even though he hadn't touched a tool in twenty years.

He could have killed both his companions in that moment; Reg suddenly seemed like the only person he'd ever loved. Whom he'd murdered, in a manner of speaking. But all he did, sweating in his plaid cowboy's shirt, a band around his head to keep the sweat falling into his eyes, all he did, his mouth pursed to a button, Grace noticed, was chuck beer cans into the rubbish dump; one, two, three empties, clinking. Followed by a full can, with a deathly thud. A fact both she and Terry noted — but neither of them said; though Terry opened his mouth and shut it; and never took his eyes off Jas as, with the desperate anxiety of someone who knew what deprivation meant, he seized the last full one, pulled the ring off, lifted it to his lips.

Afterwards Terry put his shirt on feeling himself too exposed, somehow, too vulnerable otherwise; too bloody right he was exposed, thought Jas, evilly. So evilly, he even scared himself. He lumbered to his feet and without another word left them to it and went back to the house. Not caring tuppence for the heat, he weeded the garden all afternoon, weeping. Or maybe the wetness down his face was only sweat. When, later, the rooks started up as usual — he was flat on his back then, there was going to be no Jas-cooked supper that night — he decided he would have got the one with the broken voice if he could, once he had it between his hands he'd wring its bloody neck. He would even have climbed the trees to get it, if that seemed practical, which it was not, since birds can fly and this poor, arrogant sod, he thought, had never thought he needed to learn to.

Chapter Seven

"Cold and wet disunites and breaks it, especially if the liquors be saltish and the glass suddenly heated . . ."

Where did you go to then? First you pester me so as I can't not notice, when I get used to you and get to like your voice, suddenly you're not there, there's not so much as a whiff of rabbit, let alone beefsteak, can't you even be bothered these days to spoil our supper? What am I supposed to think? That I made you up? That you never existed? That we've all been driven crazy by something straight out of my head?

Them's plenty words for thi, dozzie. When did thi ever speak so to me nor ony other? Ond only to chid me, I notice. Ond only to mind I wor not with thi which is not so certain. Who's to say thi worna' minding? That I spok' thi constant and thi never howd me? With that man of yours, that gobby slob, con not so much bek a pie but he chars it. Woren't mi not speaking. Woren't mi went away. Woren't first to go in mi life, neither, that one did be mi friend, she swore she would be ollus, till she waited on a man and of a sudden I wor no one. Mi little lady, the one with her I larned mi letters, she wor my friend when we wor childer, woren't she? But soon as us were grown I wor just a serving wench, she had her man, much good it did her. Wor not he and they, her cousins, brangling over that wor hers, did these same cousins not break down door of t' chamber to steal will that proved her heir, did not her man, her husband, wound one of 'em near death to defend what wor but hissen by wedlock; wor she not called murderess by her cousins for it? I tell thi, had been better for her to do what I said, stayed alongside mi, her dozzie, to tek no man to husband to her.

(To which my reaction was that none of it had anything to do with me. Maybe I *was* looking for something from Betsy. But no, it wasn't this.)

Working with glass ain't so bloody good in summer. It makes me think what the bloke that worked with Grace before me said about the glasshouse: that working in such heat was like being in hell.

If I sweat, of course, it's nothing to what Jas does. Sweat pours off him, tho' all he does is sit on the blower and clear up a bit after us. Play it ever so humble he does, and never takes his eyes off me, especially since the day he heard it was Reg's tools I was using. But he's not going to have them. Any more than he's going to have Grace if I can help it — when he's not staring at me he's staring at her, the great lecher, bleeding great spider licking his chops, just waiting to catch her.

Grace sweats a bit too in this weather, but not like we do. She seems to shrivel in the heat the way a joint of meat does in the oven, sweating out its juices. By midday, most of these days, even she'll have had enough, we close up the furnace and set the lehr, then crawl back up through the wood for which these days I'm grateful, even in this weather it's danker and cooler. Back home I grab a pie or sarnie and sleep the rest of the day. I sleep upstairs. Jas, more often than not, slumps in front of the telly, snoring with his mouth open, and the sound turned up loud, to keep me awake, I expects. It's fucking tennis at the moment, give me snooker any day. John McEnroe swearing is the only thing worth watching in tennis. I wish Jas could see himself the way I see him if I go downstairs some time, the beer can parked on his bare belly, the damp on his forehead, his open mouth, his putrid tonsils.

I suppose Grace sleeps on some days. Others I know for certain she goes back down to her glasshouse. Even in this heat she can't seem to keep away. Like a cat minding its kittens. Like she's trying to work something out and don't know how to. What's me and Jas to her such times? She don't take a blind bit of notice.

Of course when she do take notice, it's Jas she notices. It's like they're plotting something. Not sex. It's too hot for sex. It must be. All the same she's in with him somehow, she's been in with him since that day on Kinderscout. It makes me feel lonelier than ever. Here in all this heat I want houses not trees, I'm thinking. Even those bloody blue spikes of the flowers outside the kitchen window seem to be getting at me somehow. Everything's getting at me. When those rooks fly about in the evening making their stupid racket, I can't help hearing the one that Jas pointed out went squeak instead of caw, I might think it funny if it didn't cheese me off so, if I didn't feel it was just making that noise to bug me. I can't stand all those hot, empty fields, neither, the ones alongside the lane down to the main road, I can't stand the little hills, here, there everywhere, the way they lie against each other there's no rhyme or reason, they shut me in and leave me open at the same time.

I tell you what I want then, simple as a goal from Kerry Dixon, first home match of the season. I want people. I want streets. I want houses. I want London. Now. Now. Now. I want it.

Matlock Bath's the nearest I can get. I go down to the pub of an evening with Grace and Jas, when I scarper I bet they don't notice. She could be my soak of a mother for all I care these fucking days. I hitch a lift along the road sometimes. Or, if there is one, I catch the train that stops at places between Derby and Matlock, I spend the rest of the evening in the boozers and the two arcades, pulling at the handles of the fruit machines or playing Sky Raiders, wondering now and then when Grace's going to learn me driving like she promised. Even more when I have to get back along the road and there ain't no train, no nothing.

There's bike boys around some evenings. Though I'm glad to see them, they remind me of London, I keep well clear. It's not just that the ones here talk different from the ones in London. All bike boys are foreign somehow. They're bigger than anyone else or seem it; I think it's the gear, mainly, all those steel studs and leather shoulders, like with King Kong you play it careful, not that this lot are Hell's Angels, exactly. The ones I see in London, some of them mates of my mates, aren't such bad geezers underneath, even if they look fucking weirdos. This lot talk quite normal to the geezer behind the bar, for instance, like they're good mates of his, why shouldn't they be? Aside from the fact of having to shout, the first thing they always do when they come in is put on the juke box, sixties rock stuff and a bit of punk, mostly. Till they go they don't leave it off one minute: I look at them a bit envious, sometimes. I wouldn't mind being a bike boy myself, if it weren't that a bike needs more loot than I've ever grafted. Also they're into death a lot more than I am. "It'd be a great way to die, go under a bus doing a ton, great," says one of them in my hearing. Nor he don't seem to be kidding.

He's a big bloke this one; perhaps the biggest. He's a bit different from the rest, much cleaner and shinier. That's one thing about these blokes mostly, like my mum says they're not too in with the soap and water, bollocks to you, mum, I've seen you pick worse ones. They got long hair 'n all, this guy's ain't short exactly but shorter — it's curly and sticks up on top, giving him the look like he's biggest and tallest. Dave they call him. There's a little blonde tart, too, clings to him all evening like a gnat to an elephant, he don't look like a guy needs to take notice of no one. He takes no notice of me for one thing no more than the rest do. They don't give no aggro neither. They fill up the whole place, or seem to, I sit in my corner, letting them smash me out of my senses that's all, if they but knew it. Like Grace's furnace does in one way, like her humming glasshouse. Though their metal feels a lot less lethal to someone who comes from where I do, and who's got trouble right now with a furnace and a glasshouse. And in particular with the people what work at the furnace.

The third night I see them, in the pub opposite Lover's Walk, I'm on the fruit machine; three pineapples come up the moment they walk in. And I don't just win 50p, do I, I seem to have hit the jackpot; the stuff comes pouring out, with an almighty crash and clatter. I could have done without it at that moment. Not only the place goes fucking silent, the whole lot of bike boys come and stand round me, they've not even put on the juke box. While I'm picking up the coins, shoving them in my pocket, the big one, Dave, the clean one, leans on his elbows on top of the machine. "Looks like you con afford to buy me a pint, lad, don' it?" says he, winking.

Though he don't actually say it nasty, I can't say I trust him. I'm afraid the rest of them are going to push their luck also, in fact it's like I'm Dave's property all of a sudden; they make out they've lost interest.

"What'll it be then?" says I, lively as I'm able. "A pint of bitter?" I don't hear Dave's reply, the juke box's off again; but I can guess it, the cosy way he shouts at the barmen. His tart's not with him this time, could be he needs a new interest, he don't go to talk bikes with his mates anyway; I seem to be tonight's flavour. Maybe it's because I come lucky, my pockets are still jingling with silver; maybe he thinks my luck's going to rub off. As if all the tattoos on him ain't enough luck already. (He's a skull and crossbones on his chest, for instance, you can see when he unzips his leathers; it matches the skull and crossbones in studs on the back of his jacket.)

With all that noise, he puts his mouth to my ear to talk to me; it's a bit intimate to my mind, I hope convenience is all there is to it. "Yow from London then?" he asks in his foreign, Nottingham accent. "What yow doin' round here then?" The beer doing its job nicely, I proceed to feel a bit less chicken; put my mouth to his ear this time; get a lipful of his one gold earring.

"Glassblowing? What's that?" he asks, even dishing me out a Woodbine. Anyone'd have thought I was a bleeding bird the way he is nudging me, if it's just another way of taking the michael I'm getting too pissed to care a monkey's. He don't seem to mean much harm by it. He even buys me a pint, for all the loot that's still loading down my pocket, burning a hole in it. I feel happier now, less lonely, than I've felt in a month of Sundays. Why should I care he's one of those great swaggering blokes, the kind more often than not get all the gravy, the kind I wish at the bottom of the sea usually, but sometimes want to follow there, or anywhere else they got in mind, that they might need some numbskull like me to come running after. His great wide grinning face is a bit like Jas' even, except his lips are bigger and wider, and his hair a whole lot longer. He's got an amulet hanging on his chest over the skull and crossbones, and a great signet ring on one finger. Trying to keep my end up when he says he's a fitter and turner, I tell him more about Grace, about the glasshouse in Cliff woods and the kind of work we do there. I'm boasting a bit, of course; but I seem to have impressed him; he's listening to me keenly, pushing his earring closer.

It ain't so long, of course, before it's, "Time, gentlemen, please." But I stop hating the landlord for it when Dave asks if I'd like a ride with him and his mates somewhere.

Would I like a ride somewhere? By this time I'd ride to the moon with any of 'em. The bottom of Grace's hill would do, I tell him, if he and his mates are going my way, which they are, it turns out they're en route to the M1 to give the bikes a bit of open. What's more they've a helmet to spare, that's why they'll take me. (They aren't going to risk being done by the old Bill for the likes of me, not bloody likely.) So there's me then next minute, clutching the back of the bloke a bit like Jas, that I could have hated often enough, but love in that moment. The hefty studs of his jacket, marking me for life by the feel of it, the hair coming out from under the back of his helmet giving me a mouthful if I don't keep my head turned sideways, are the least of what I could have put up with from him this evening. Not that I care about nothing, I'm pissed as a newt, not just on beer, neither, on the talk, the blare of the juke box, the flashing and dashing and clatter of the machines that grab your money. I've forgotten not wanting to go under a bus doing a ton, I'm flying along in the dark on the back of a BMW not caring a fuck how Dave's showing off a bit, maybe trying to scare me, with his fancy corners around this bend and that one. He has us near laying to the road once or twice, but I'm not scared in the slightest. He can have me under a bus I'm thinking, any time he wants it, if that's what it feels like.

A week later King Dave and his mates are back in Matlock

Bath. But it's a different evening. I'm in the arcade this time not the boozer, bombarding myself with green and purple ray gun flashes, all the same when he recognises me at once and comes straight over, I'm chuffed, I think I've made it, he don't think of me as a foreigner no longer. But there ain't no jackpot tonight; it ain't my luck he's after, I get no mouthfuls of his gold earring, let alone the offer of a pint at the boozer, though thinking it would be friendly, I offer to take him for one I can't hardly afford to, being skint this evening.

No. It's not my luck he's wanting; it's Grace he's after, all the gen I can give him. Where exactly she hangs out, for instance, where she — what you call it, lad — blows? — her glass. Sounds a right interesting place, he tells me — well that's the gist of it, I can't pin his Nottingham language. "S'pose yow an' me an' the lads go along and tek a look?" He's not looking at me as he says that. Like hell we can, I am thinking. I'm not drunk now, I find I only half like the bloke this evening with his fat smiling lip and his uppity gold earring. And maybe I didn't trust him, any more than I trust myself. The way he puts out a hand to set off the ray guns I've paid the use of, he don't mean me to trust him. Could be he does take an interest, does want to take a look at what goes on in a glasshouse. But even looks can lead to something a bit more than you bargained for. So I don't take his fags. I don't tell him nothing. I'm afraid it might turn him nasty, his great mates likewise, in their studs and hair and beat-up leather. But the mates take no notice. After a bit Dave himself loses interest, drifts back towards them, is part of that same nation, its cowskin and metal armour, its fag smoke, its rev ups. The next moment the same blonde girl I seen with him the first time is hanging herself on to his arm like's she just one more item of clothing. She has a short little leather skirt, she has a neat little butt, not the kind I've ever had the use of, like I says that sort of bloke gets the gravy usually, neat little butts go for hunky fat-lipped geezers. Isn't clear now if he goes for her or not, it don't matter in the slightest, they all go out a moment later, I hear the bikes roaring, then taking off, then fading. That's the end of that.

The arcade feels empty after. The flashes from the machines turn its corners seedy and hellish — so much for space invaders. I think of going for a beer, but ain't in a mood for the boozer neither. There isn't a train, I try hitching a lift, don't get one. It's not the first time I've had to walk that spooky road home, I can't say I ever liked it.

It ain't closing time yet. The next boozer I pass I blow all the loot I'm left with on two pints and a whisky chaser. It don't do me no good. I feel pissed much sooner than happy. My feet aching and aching, I find myself bloody weeping, at the same time I'm shaking my fist and shouting at all the fuckers who pass me — looking back now, thinking what I must have looked like, I can't blame them not wanting to take me.

When I make the cottage at last, it's one o'clock in the morning, not that I care a monkey's who hears me crashing about in the bathroom. Tonight, I think, I'm not going to bloody sleep on my ownsome; bold as you like — I'm still pissed besides pissed off — I march into Grace's room, and climb into her bed; that I never dared to before when she don't ask me. She's asleep, she's also warm, too warm for me this weather. We're both sweating like pigs when I throw my leg over. She don't wake up. Or at least she pretends not to. She goes on pretending what's more, the whole time I'm at it. Maybe she don't care, one way or the other. Maybe she thinks I'm Jas, her lawful husband. Maybe I'm just some brat to be ignored, till he learns when he's not wanted. She makes no sound, whether or not she likes it. Me, I'm remembering Jas downstairs now, so I don't use me voice much either, for all I'd like to shout, so he knows good and certain. Not that I make a good job of what I'm doing. Part way through, what with all that booze I don't even think I'm going to make it. And when I do finally make it, I want to cry like a baby. Of course I don't. But nor do I stay all night the way I used to. I retrieve my limp cock from her, I creep out of there so fast you'd think I was ashamed, mostly. And go back to my own bed. And feel lonely, not triumphant.

Nothing is said in the morning. I might as well have dreamed it. Only I know I didn't. I've got a head like a drum, beating and beating, soon as we open the furnace it gets worse than ever. The third piece Grace makes, I drop off the punty. I could have cried then too. But again of course I didn't, not bloody likely, seeing the way Jas is grinning. He's another gravy grabber, ain't he. Christ how I hate him.

Did he think I was asleep? Then he's even stupider than I thought him. And even if I had been, I'd have known when I woke up, the stink he left behind him. Such sex seems like old marriage. Perhaps I'm lucky I never got the chance to explore it.

Not that I cared — or care — a damn, really. Any response seems beyond me at the moment. All I want is Betsy's voice which doesn't come and I don't understand why it doesn't. I'm lost without it, in places I'm not used to getting lost in; in places where I once used to be capable of standing up solo.

This afternoon, for instance, I closed the glasshouse after Terry dropped the piece off the punty. It was too hot to work; too hot to do anything — which didn't stop me feeling restless, hot or not I took myself off around lunchtime. I wasn't meaning to go far; up through the wood, perhaps, then up the track opposite, past Knob Farm, and its herd of red and white Ayrshires that I always like the look of, never mind my father only went in for beef, his Devons. What would he have thought, I wonder, of the hotchpotch of breeds round these parts — black Angus, Friesian/Hereford crosses, even some fancy French ones. There were wild raspberries in the hedges, I'd picked one idly, when I heard some man shouting; it took a moment before I realised it was me he was shouting at. The farmer it had to be; a stout man, not a fine figure like my father, in tweed cap and boiler suit, his face red and nasty with the heat of the midday sun. "Tek your thieving hands off mi property." I could hardly believe my ears when I understood what he was saying. "Tek your thieving hands off mi property. You people think you con tek anything. And you'll be sorry. I just sprayed those hedges, you'll be out in a rash, your belly'll be aching 'fore you know it."

If anyone's used to bad-tempered farmers I am. If anyone knows how to answer them, I do. But maybe I'm only used to ones in my family. Or maybe it's so long ago I have forgotten. Or maybe it's Betsy I need these days to fuel my tongue. Or if not my tongue, the dignity to cut my gaze right through him. He's fat and hot and sweating in that blue boiler suit of his, there's no reason for him to faze me, even if he is claiming wild raspberries as private property. I don't need to look at my hands to know I'm not coming out in a rash; nor am I expecting bellyache this evening. But I look at them all the same and he sees me looking, to that extent he has me. As I have him, to get him shouting such pointless threats so loudly. I say nothing and walk on past, which I can do quite safely, this is a public right of way, the kind I stick to up here, though back home in Somerset I used to go where I wanted.

I talk to Betsy again then, but she doesn't answer. It's the sleepy time of the day, maybe that's the trouble; God knows why I came out alone in the midday sun. I cut down the track into the valley that sits sideways above the Derwent valley, I go along under the wood for a bit and then up through and out of it, below the hill where often they run horses — palominos usually, too pretty by half in my opinion — there are no palominos today, no nothing. But when I head back across the field, still on the footpath, I see something much rarer, if not exactly uncommon. That is a hare gets up under my feet, so near I imagine I hear its feet drumming as it streaks off sideways, ears streaming behind it, across the meadow.

After all these years I remember enough to know hares don't usually let you get that close. Not a yard or so on I stop and turn back suddenly. It's a hay field, cut and cleared already, but with wisps and trails of hay left along the lines of the cutting and baling — when I bend down and turn some of it, I find the leverets almost at once. I feel twelve years old again, such a thing has never happened; I'd blame Betsy or thank her, if only Betsy were here, but she isn't. Say she allows it, it's a wonder of the world — say she doesn't allow it, I still dare have this, for now, as a wonder of the world. All three babies together would fit into the palm of my hand. They have fur, their eyes are open, their quivering ears laid back at the same angle as their fleeing mother's. They're three nuts in one shell, each flank, each thigh, each head, is moulded to another's. Each flank falls and rises, each eye is liquid, still and yet shifting.

I would put out a finger and stroke their fur with its miniature brindling, if only I dared to; if it wouldn't stop their dam coming back to them. Else I could pick them all up in my hand, I could crush the life out of them — seeing what my glass is still lacking, will always lack, I am with Betsy again, almost I want to crush them. (The only sentient life I give my glass comes from my breath when I'm blowing. Of which there is no preserving.) I love them. I *hate* them.

Betsy where are you? Is wedlock only what you tell me?

Even my kitchen does not smell of food these days unless I've cooked it or Jas has cooked it or Terry has cooked it. This heat bodes no good. There are storms coming. The blue of the delphiniums is like flames not water. It's so many years since I saw them supplant peonies and poppies, since I saw peonies supplant tulips and wallflowers, the way they did in my mother's garden. I find I do not like it. I pick one small blue trumpet and crush it between my fingers. The mood I'm in I can almost feel the crunch of its petal bones, as, under their fur wrapping, I would have felt the bones of the leverets splinter within my fingers.

At night I still don't hear Betsy. Unless it is she that keeps stuffing my head with a silence as ominous as heat. There's bound to be a storm sometime — it is so hot the moon burns like silver in the crucible of a smith. But there's no sign of it at the moment. I sleep for a little and wake from a dream in which my throat is full of molten glass that I wanted to vomit up and couldn't.

The next night, the sky having thickened all day, the weather broke, just as they had been expecting. The attack that came, though, was much less violent than they'd assumed it must be; the hub of its fury remained a good twenty miles away. Near Buxton, for instance, a man had been struck by lightning, but here they suffered no such problems. Of course it had rained hard enough — some delphiniums had been flattened. There was also a damp patch on one wall where a gutter had overflowed. Refusing all Jas' offers of help, Grace borrowed a ladder from across the road and cleared it.

I took a lot of trouble over Gracie's garden, as over Nancy's, even though gardens have never been my line exactly. In this case you could say, perhaps, that to occupy myself in mindless digging seemed my one salvation; working in the glasshouse itself was driving me crazy. It was taking for ever to pick up my old skills. I don't remember it taking nearly so long to learn them. Or maybe it did; maybe it took longer, the difference being, one I didn't expect like I do now to be instantly expert, two I was not trying first time round to show some spavined youth I was as good as he was. Not that I gave Terry much chance to see I wasn't. I practised when he was not there mostly, other times I played unobtrusive. Not that he appeared to notice, when he and Grace are in full flight, both of them take me for granted. Which is of all things the most insulting. I'd have given up working with them altogether if it wasn't that the glass itself had, once again, grabbed me by the short and curlies. I'd forgotten precisely how the heat worked on it, for instance. Reg and Ruskin got it wrong in some ways. Or rather sold it a bit short, it's not just ductility and translucence you can — and should — give it, you should also try sometimes for the movement and colour of the molten substance. I wonder if Ruskin ever did see glass blown in Venice? I think he must have. Last week I discovered on a shelf at Gracie's, Johnny R's collected works in Reg's Everyman edition. I spent hours with *The Stones of Venice*, but didn't find any glassblowers, just got myself high on his prose style, the way I always used to.

I like Grace's fire pieces precisely because they get at the nature of the molten substance. And if I'm less taken with her present yen for geology, that hasn't stopped me helping her out once or twice, when Terry's not there for some reason.

Not that she seems to notice it's Jas not Terry assisting. With me as with him these days she confines herself to silence.

As for her garden. It's a bugger in a way, being on three levels. There's a flat bit under the wall; then a raised sloping bit, with a rockery at the top, under a wall covered in honeysuckle that scented the whole cottage all night when it was out, making me feel good and randy. Above that's another bit, run wild in the course of this summer. Grass and weeds are a foot high, there's some raspberry bushes that haven't fruited. You could grow vegetables up there, I told her, she just shrugged a bit and said there was nothing to stop me planting vegetables if I wanted. Because of the heatwave, the ground was rock hard at the time, I didn't bother to take her up on it.

The day after the storm, though, reckoning on the soil being easier, I dug most of the morning, and most of the afternoon. It was hot work, for all it had turned so much cooler, and I took my shirt off, revealing my beer gut, not that there was anyone to see it.

Terry and Grace were working later today than they had been. (Another effect of the change of weather.) When they walked down the road towards me at seven o'clock, they looked glum to my eye, though preoccupied rather than angry. Spurred on, I dug the harder. And all at once yelled, making them both jump, neither of them had seen me up there, any more than I'd seen, till this moment, the rounded earthenware vessel my spade just bit on.

I knew what its contents were, though, the moment I saw them, even if I had only seen such things before locked into glass cases. My spade had knocked the top off the jar; the frail metal fingernails tarnished and dull, none looking like they were silver, spilled out on the earth where I had been digging. My fingers covered in earth, salt sweat dripping off me, I put every one of them I could lay my hands on back where it came from, before I charged, jar in hand, down the steps to meet the others.

Even Terry managed to address a word — two words — to me, for once. "What's them?" he asked, looking at my naked belly, which I admit these days is freaksville, more Venice Beach than Malibu. Grace said nothing. She averted her eyes from my belly. She put a hand inside the pot, let the clippings slip through her fingers; one, of the same dimensions, clung to her forefinger briefly, making me wonder for the first time what she had done with the wedding ring I gave her. She'd've sold it if she'd any sense. But I half hoped she hadn't.

I always have been a fund of useless information. My mother was heard to cry out once from her family's bosom, "What have I done, why am I condemned to life with three fools and a knowall?" (No prizes for guessing the name of the knowall.) Now I wiped the drops of sweat from my forehead, smiled at my ex-wife nicely, and said, in answer to Terry, whom I did not look at, "They're coin clippings. They used to clip off the edges of coins and melt them down for the silver. It was a capital offence at one time. By which I mean if they caught them they strung them up. They topped them." Grace did not look impressed. She looked funny, inasmuch as Gracie can ever be said to look such a thing as funny. (Alternatively she never looks anything else but funny.) She didn't say anything. Nor did Terry. He was too busy clutching at his neck, making choking noises. For two cents I could have strung *him* up, on the spot, gratis.

Jas did not go to the glasshouse on the next day either. He went to Matlock. Another item from his fund of useless information was that such finds were treasure trove and ought to be handed over to some local museum or police station. He did not inform Grace of this, however. Nor did he go to any museum or police station, he had some better ideas for her treasure trove, and if he could still find them after all these years, the odd shady friend in London. What he went in search of was information. It took one telephone call after Grace and Terry left for the glasshouse to establish the whereabouts of the county archive. To the archive, accordingly, he drove himself in Grace's car, which she wasn't after all using, and which used, after all, to be Reg's.

It wasn't the Bodleian, exactly, the Matlock archive. Just one barnlike room turned into narrower rooms by rows of iron shelving. Today it was presided over by a woman in a lemon-coloured dress who, to judge from the apprehensive expression on her face when she took in Jas' high-heeled cowboy boots, buckled belt and Hands Off Nicaragua t-shirt, hadn't encountered anyone like him lately among her regular local historians.

She had an Afro haircut above round glasses, and though the dress wasn't Jeanne Moreau, exactly — more like early Julie Christie, Jas gauged it — she had a very good figure. More than a good figure. Under her pleasant but rather indeterminate features, and her equally indeterminate Saxon colouring, was the body no more and no less of a Venus de Milo. The anomaly intrigued him; even if it was not what he had come for. Seventeenth-century Timbersley was what he had come for. (The origins of the cottage being seventeenth century, that seemed the most likely date of the clippings.) But surveying the crammed shelves — the boxes of local government papers, the albums of newspaper clippings and photo-copied documents — the original stuff, the librarian told him a little mournfully, was in Derby; tatty books published in the early twentieth or late nineteenth century on local antiquities and history, stacks of even tattier pamphlets by amateur historians, on such matters as well-dressings, farming customs, local ghosts, children's rhymes and dialect usage — he did not know where to start looking.

The lemon-yellow librarian with the body of Venus de Milo appeared more than ready, fortunately, to scour the index drawers with him. "It's the summer holidays, of course," she explained, as if trying to justify any apparent underemployment. Whether it was Jas' smile, his assumption of helplessness, the soft, slightly exaggerated Californian he used to set out his needs, or whether it was her own enthusiasm for her sources which eased, even in time removed her suspicion of him, would be hard to say. But removed it was; and quickly. Before long every relevant document, album or pamphlet, every stained volume, was laid out before them on one of the long library tables. There wasn't much to find, of course; but what there was they found it.

Jas himself, for instance, came across a newspaper cutting about another jar of coin clippings dug up around 1850, from under the roots of a fallen tree behind a house which sounded suspiciously like the house opposite Grace's. This find dated from the seventeenth century; it was then, according to the newspaper report, that extra penalties — branding for instance — had been slapped on coin-clippers, one of whom, it suggested, had then decided that discretion was the better part of valour and hidden his booty. (Nothing was said about hanging; Jas remained certain death had been one more penalty.)

The librarian, meanwhile, unearthed a nineteenth century report of a seventeenth century lawsuit, concerning the big house next to Grace's cottage and its heiress. The men of the woman's family had objected to a female inheriting, thereby passing the whole property on to the family into which she'd married.

"And how could she help that?" whispered the librarian indignantly. "How could she help that? 'Everything'," she recited in a flat voice, as if it was something she'd learned by heart, "'everything owned by a married woman automatically became the property of her husband.' I'd never like to have got married myself if it wor the same these days. Would you?" she asked Jas earnestly. Looking up at him from time to time with a gaze so ingenuous it was almost intimate, she went on to read aloud to him how these same men had incited brawls, tried to steal the will under cover of them and, when that failed, accused the woman of hiding other wills, and worse still, of consorting with criminals and witches.

"Doesn't it sound just like Dallas?" she hissed excitedly; before proceeding to dig out yet more juicy lawsuits concerning the injustices perpetrated by this same rich family when they enclosed their park behind walls and wouldn't let the local peasants in even to catch conies.

"Conies are rabbits, you know," she explained. "It's in the bible, you know. Conies. Fancy not letting them tek rabbits. Ond they never had enough to eat. Of course I'm working-class myself. And my husband. He's a policeman. All the injustices mek my blood boil." (A budding socialist then also, as well as a feminist, thought Jas, enjoying it.) "*Conies*," she was saying, wiping her spectacles.

"Yeah." Jas stood back a bit, and looked at her intently. He assumed that, unlike his wife Nancy, the librarian would not interpret anything he said as patronising; leaning his arm on the table as if it was his own, he quoted, very softly, "'The hills are refuge for the wild goats. And the rocks for the conies'." "Con you recite *all* the psalms by heart?" she asked. And smiled as if she not only accepted him, she thought she had found a soulmate. "Which part of America do you coom from?" she enquired aloud — she was even forgetting now, to preserve the silence of the library. "We do get Americans in here sometimes, you know, looking for their English ancestors."

Jas chose not to disabue her. The way he stationed himself now the librarian stood so close to him, peering down at the book from which she had been reading, that his bare forearm was almost touching the tender gooseflesh on her upper arm, below the reach of the lemon-yellow sleeve; a fact that disturbed him in ways he found both pleasant and unpleasant. He was not used to such open displays of white skin. White skin on California women confined to undersides and crannies intimate enough to escape the sun, it made her seem more naked in her lemon-yellow dress than those golden girls had ever seemed in their minimal bikinis. Was the frisson he felt desire or more nearly terror? In his arrogant youth he'd always despised rather than desired, would have died rather than been seen with women like this one. She wasn't even young, he thought; and only passably pretty. Yet the elemental force of her body — combined with her apology and awkwardness — did she really not understand the nature of such flesh? — affected him deeply. He even liked her Afro hairstyle; who cared if it was ten years out of date?

To calm himself, he considered Ruskin; who apparently preferred the bodies of women to be like children's without so much as a trace of pubic hair; whereas he, Jas, preferred proof of their owners being adult; like Grace for instance. You couldn't think Grace was any younger than she was. Yet he still couldn't get near her he realised; realised also, perhaps for the first time in the proximity of the lemon-yellow woman, the extent to which that unassailable distance, not to say alienation, was beginning to anger and frustrate him. He considered inviting the librarian for a drink. What he wanted still more was to embrace her. As if she realised the danger, she moved away slightly. Either because of that or the thought of her policeman husband (though the actual marital status of his women had never much concerned Jas, experience had taught him that the status and nature of their men was another matter), he hesitated a little before taking the matter on; had only moved one fraction nearer, fortunately, when another librarian, a stately lady, also spectacled, dressed in what, to his quick glance, looked like a check tablecloth, as if materialised before them.

If the Venus librarian had not yet appreciated before the senses her seemingly unconscious flirtation had aroused in Jas, she appreciated them now. Her eyes speeding other ways she seemed, quite suddenly, to have concluded him as dubious as she'd first thought him. Her skin, no longer white but pink — she was the first woman he'd ever encountered who blushed from the neck both upwards and downwards, setting him to eye her with frank, and this time quite unlecherous fascination — she asked in a loud voice if he would be interested in some pamphlets on local dialects. Not the least abashed himself, merely curious, Jas took pity on her. To demonstrate her innocence in face of her disapproving colleague was all he could do for her, he thought, almost wistfully; he accepted the pamphlets she handed him as if they were, truly, the one service he'd asked for.

He read the pamphlets even. He took some of the words he discovered home — after all she had no other words to give him — together with a local folk story he'd come across in a book full of damp-stained pages about a woman who lived in a glasshouse; together with some takeaway tandoori and a dozen cans of beer. The story would keep, he thought, for the appropriate, vicious moment; woman in a glasshouse was exactly how, after the encounter with his library Venus, he felt like describing Grace. The words on the other hand need not wait, he intended producing them with the beer and tandoori; words, he thought, in the end, being better to eat than most things.

Grace and Terry weren't back, of course; it was barely five o'clock when he reached the cottage lying under the bleached August light that he'd forgotten was so different from the light in other months. The moment they did come, around seven, by which time he'd devoured most of the food and was halfway through the beer, he stood up at the kitchen table, and proceeded to demonstrate his grasp of Derbyshire. "I was smopple as a carrot," he said, "till I got me stuck into this local ale. I wor rit clammed till I gan stodgin' mi 'odge. Who's a mardy boy then, Terry, so nesh he looks like he needs his mam still; who's not so green as cabbage-looking, surely."

Terry hardly picked up a single word. Has the bloke finally gone bonkers, he was thinking, almost wishing that he had. (He got enough sense of the last bit, however, to know he was being mocked. And to resent it.)

Grace was another matter. There was no way to describe how she looked; how Jas had never imagined her looking, not for a minute; even the day he'd left her, he would not have expected her face to show anything like this. It was an archetype of shock; fixed like the death mask of someone who'd not realised till the moment of death what death was; let alone known that it was coming. She was a stone woman. Or, from another angle, a stone fury. Glass did not come into it, poor Johnny Ruskin wouldn't have liked her now, Jas thought, any more than he liked the head at the side of the church of Santa Maria Formosa. "Huge, inhuman and monstrous," he'd read, only yesterday. "Leering in bestial degradation — too foul to be beheld for more than an instant." (This was, as a matter of fact, a description Grace might have been equally ready to apply to him, in the horror with which she had heard Jas pulling the words as if out of her own head.) Jas, meanwhile, was thinking, Ruskin and I differ on the subject of the grotesque; I *like* it.

I might as well have raped Grace, he decided, not simply spoken. This was not how she'd looked when he took her virginity; fucked her for the first time. Nor how she'd looked when he returned from the dead that evening, when, clad in red silk like the lethal poppy, she'd cradled Terry's head against her and stared straight back at him standing at the cottage door. Now, not just in hate, though that was part of it, he felt — Grace, appalled, felt it also — that she revealed herself absolutely. And yet, and this had always been what doomed them, he did not, he realised, understand the language Grace spoke in; did not understand, as he felt he had understood with the Venus de Milo woman, what exactly she was revealing.

"Did I not tell thi, dozzie, of men, to have none o' them? Did I not tell thi, they'll have the soul out of us heads, soon as look on us? Soon as they 'gin snuzzling arter, they tek us youth, we'm done for. Ah' they'll tek all the cob we earn to, tek it out o' us very gobs, they will, out o' the gobs of us young 'uns. Which is why I tol' thi to keep to thissen, to bash on oll chaps, not t' moither thiself with scrating and fearin', just bash on 'em till they be gone or going.

"Do thi' be thinking I left the siller for a man to find, 'twas not so. Shame on thi for thinking. Is thi'n, doz. As my words be mine, an' mind thi mark it ollus."

I have no answer. The fury is hers and mine. It was not the voice I'd been missing and seeking. It was her voice and it was another's. Her words meant nothing, to me or her. What was meant was not in her words or in mine. Though I kept on asking, "Did they hang you for it? For the silver?" Not expecting any answers. All there was between us was this rage and hate, boiling.

Grace came down first the next morning. Before she'd even got to the kitchen she smelled food; burnt food once more. Though there was no means of burning. Once again — this was the next thing she noticed — the Aga was out.

But there was worse, she found, when at last she could bring herself to take her eyes across the kitchen. Staring first at the empty wall, and then, shifting her gaze downwards, at the littered floor, she assumed this was, precisely, what she'd been so reluctant to discover. The thing was of course in smithereens — yet how could it be, no one having heard anything? Jas had not heard, though he heard her gasp — gasp not cry — on the instant, and emerged from where he slept in the front room. And trod on the debris barefoot, and swore, the sound of what he trod on louder than the sounds Grace had made. But not as loud as his voice, when the splinter pierced his foot and there was blood on the floor and on the splinter of earthenware.

Everything on the dresser, of course, was still as it should have been, apart from the usual trash that finds its way on to such things, pens, clothes pegs, tubes of glue, nails, paper-clips, elastic bands, bills, envelopes, having been swept off it, as if by the fury of the other's fall; leaving the pebbles Grace had collected, leaving the rejected glasses, each of them still, in its perfect unbalance or distortion, whole more or less; leaving the ram's head, its eye glaring on everything, alone in its glory.

Whereas Matrimony . . . It could not simply have fallen just like that, though they were all afterwards to maintain it must have, because how could they bear to acknowledge what else might have happened? If it had simply fallen — and things do just fall off walls, sometimes — nails work their way out of plaster, string breaks, fastenings unfasten — it would not have been in such smithereens. Someone both tall and strong might, rather, have raised it above their head and smashed it down with all their strength. They — whoever it was — might have jumped on the pieces afterwards. There was something actually vindictive about the way not a letter remained whole, let alone a flower, a tree, a beast, a heart, a lover's knot, everything with which Grace had decorated it, after some seventeenth century earthenware plates in the Victoria and Albert. Both felt and frivolous, sentimental and mocking — Jas had been almost hopeful for their marriage when he had first seen it — the plate was not like anything else she had ever made. But now some of it was dust. None of it was much more than splinters.

"Shit," Jas said, staring at his bloodied feet. "Shit. Shit. Shit." (When he caught sight of the whole, triumphant ram's head still sitting on the shelf, he wanted to throw that down also, in some kind of unjustified, irrelevant revenge for the other.)

"Blimey," said Terry when he appeared a moment later. "*Fu*-cking hell. Who done that?"

Chapter Eight

"When melted 'tis tenacious and sticks together . . ."

Was it you, dozzie, was it me?

Wor I, dozzie, wor thi?

Does it matter?

If thi would have it so, it matters.

I run my life my own way. I always have. My sleep and my dreams are my own. Even my ghosts are. Or were.

Who tells thi they are not still, dozzie? Not I, for certain.

I tell myself, dozzie. I am not you yet. However you may have it.

Yet, dozzie? Thi wor allus me; in the heart and soul thi reks it.

I am not. I am Grace. I come from Somerset.

Then I wor not thi. Wor Betsy. Wor Derbyshire. What's the difference?

There is a difference still. I feel it.

If there is a difference still, will not be. Sithi.

In the light of all this I remember still more kindly the lemon-yellow woman. The absolute terrifying fleshliness of that white skin incites me all the more, because there are times I get the impression that Grace's flesh isn't flesh at all but metal. And because, just a little, she reminds me of the first girl I fell in love with when I was fifteen. A soft girl; an innocent girl she seemed to me, at the same time a perfect Leda; I'd been obsessed with the myth of Leda and the swan, since I saw the picture — by Titian was it? I don't know for sure, only that my father showed me.

This girl used to walk one side of a canal somewhere near where we lived. That was where I saw her. I'd walk the other side, hungering for her. At the same time I felt as grateful for that space of water between us as she must have felt, surely, had she known not only how I imagined her but how, in the light of this, I imagined myself; as Zeus, no less — I always was a boy with big ideas, maybe to make up for my small — at the time I feared it — cock — my great white wings and beak bearing down on her, invading slowly but fiercely, and then afterwards soaring upwards and away, looking down as I did so, feasting on the sight of her opened body, her face, weeping yet enraptured, her dark hair spread about her.

Which isn't to say I ever actually saw her anything but dressed in a school hat and gingham dress. I used to smile at her, she used to pretend she hadn't seen me smile. Though I don't think she feared me. She wouldn't have kept right on coming if she feared me; as she did keep coming. Came the day, though, I showed off too carelessly, fell in the canal in my new school blazer, and in fracturing the oily smoothness of the water, fractured my illusions also; hers too by the look of it, by the way she laughed at me. So much, you could say, for Zeus and Leda. From that moment the encounters ceased abruptly. It was, somehow, the first of my disillusions. The next girl I fancied I fucked stupid from the first minute.

So what am I to think happened, yesterday morning? Something did, for sure. It's amazing the amount of blood can pour from such a little wound. Even though all the gory splinters of Matrimony have been swept up and thrown into the garbage, I've still got a wound on my foot to prove it.

It had to be Grace, of course, who was responsible in some way or other. But then how come I never heard that plate hit the floor? I was plastered all right the night before, but not that plastered. Maybe it wasn't her, it was Terry? At my crazier moments I even suspect myself, maybe I went sleepwalking, God knows my subconscious could have its reasons for wanton destruction. I also, which may or may not be preferable, remember what the archivist said about the woman in the hall, the heiress, consorting with criminals and witches. Such demonic — by which do I just mean inexplicable? — fury stinks of more than merely metaphoric witches. Or it stinks of poltergeist — maybe that's more likely; of some uneasy, vindictive spirit, belonging to one or other of us. How should I know which? The way things are, we're all unclean, restless spirits. Which has me asking myself why I don't get my arse the hell out, from today if not yesterday.

It's not advice I listen to more than briefly. The situation has its intriguing aspects, and Jas never was one to pass by a good story. Besides, where would I get my arse to that's any better? (I've bread to be going on with, but that's about the limit to present scenarios.) Not to mention that I have my uses, Gracie's not such a fool that she can't see it. She's no business woman, for instance; if I can't get my glass right, one thing I can do is start selling hers for her. She may not have to worry too much about bread now, after what Reg left, but it won't be for much longer. In this business you can never stop, you can never take anything — let alone sales — for granted. It's the nearest thing to a challenge I came across lately. Unless that dish, that dust, those splinters, the blood that poured out of my foot were a challenge of some kind; like, confront me if you dare. Which I guess I do dare; put not only on my guard but on my mettle.

Grace never used to scare me the way she does now sometimes. That day in the wood when she made me screw her I thought she was a bloody witch, I thought so again when I came down to the kitchen and saw that plate on the floor. Matrimony. It wasn't I ever liked it, let alone minded it going — it was just the way it was done; vicious. No other word for it. I thought it was her done it somehow. Course I know she couldn't of, not really. But who else could it be? Not that any of us said, then or later; we just looked at each other like we thought it was an accident. I don't think. I don't think Jas thought it was no fucking accident, neither. And maybe, like me, he suspects it had to be her fault too, after, when for all the times I'd done it before we couldn't get the fucking Aga lighted, nohow.

Of course she'd gone off to the glasshouse before we began trying to. But when she came back in the evening she lights the bugger just like that. And I tells you this also, for free, that the smell didn't go away, ever, not the whole day long, there was still a smell of burning, all the time the stove were cold. How can there be burning when there ain't nothing to burn with? Anyone'd think, what with that and the smell of food where there is none, we had a ghost of some kind. If not a witch. I don't like it. Now and then I think if I'd any other hole to go to, I would go to it, but I haven't. Back to mum for instance? Or hang around the arcades with the rent boys, hoping for that kind of bed? Thanks for bloody nothing. I'd jump in the furnace, I tell you, sooner than go creeping back to mum.

Besides, I kep' my respect for Grace in spite of everything. All the more, funnily, because I fuck her. She taught me everything I know, in bed and out of it, I don't forget it even when I hate her. Even finding that plate on the floor, seeing her face, reminded me; at the same time as, still stronger, it made me want to run.

But I don't run do I, knowing Grace's ways — the same way I know the ways of glass, and for the same reason — because she learned me. If I'd run I'd lose the both of them, the way Jas lost them. I don't forget how clumsy he is still, how he's forgotten all the feel and timing. With me that's not fucking well going to happen.

Of course he's learned the glass again bit by bit. I wish he hadn't. At the same time things are a bit different like, since Matrimony got broken. Like we all needed to work together, not to be friends so much as to keep an eye on each other. Grace and me to watch Jas; Jas and me to watch Grace; Jas and Grace to watch yours truly; never mind we hate each other, we still get on a bit, these days, with a glower or two for good measure.

I haven't been to Matlock Bath lately, to meet up with Dave and co. I don't feel like going nowhere. It's even a relief sometimes when Jas and Grace piss off and leave me to it. The excuse is — as if I cared any longer — they go to look at old mines or something. That's holes in the ground to you or me, mister, sooner them than me, if you don't mind. I'll keep my fucking head above earth at all times, I tell you.

As far as glass goes, things are better 'n before, don't know why it should be — maybe it's just not so hot, means we can work normal hours and so on. Fact is, we're not only turning out good stuff, we're selling it also. Jas has got it worked out, he's a good salesman I give him, with his little white smile and smarmy look, with his fake American accent. Grace 'n me, we don't say much to the people what come to see us, we just keep right on working. They come because he's put leaflets up in hotels and places, and in the Tourist Office at Matlock Bath. Also they turn up by chance, because they happen to be walking past the glasshouse. There's more walkers than ever these days, in the middle of the summer holidays.

These droppers in don't buy the good stuff, of course — the expensive stuff Jas palms off on the fancy shops and dealers — mostly they buy the glass from the seconds table; the little bowls sprayed with iridescent stuff, for instance, that Jas is making us turn out for quick sales like these ones. But whatever they buy — and Jas is pretty good at getting them to feel uncomfortable, not to say mean, if they don't buy nothing after watching us working — whatever rubbish they hit on, he wraps it up as careful as if they'd bought the Crown Jewels off him, smiling his little smile and stashing the dough away in the big cashbox he bought us. One or two of them sniff, I notice, going out the door — one geezer even says like he's puzzled — "I can't quite understand it? Does glassmaking always smell like cooking?"

Nor were he as barmy as he sounded. I've caught a whiff or two myself at the odd moment. Once I could have fucking sworn it was the smell of bacon.

This be stone country, this be, and inside the stone be metal country, there ollus wor metals here and men gettin' 'em and being driven mad in t' gettin' and smeltin', if not getting their backs broke, coughing up blood, sieving at a standing buddle. Thi smelt thi metal by magic, seems to me; I don't see no coal nor bellows, as I wor using to burn down my metals — not that my metal coom from Derbyshire or onywhere liike it. The old parson that done teach me and mi young lady us letters, he wor saying much times that silver coom from far over t' sea. Could be he spek true. Certain I got no Derby metals, not lead, the smell of which con drive strong men crazy, nor cawk, nor toadstone, nor Blue John or ony other metal what's got here under earth; mi metal I got from clipping t'head of monarch. Didn't wish him no disrespeck. It 'un wor a man liike ony other, a rider on t' bellies 'o women, still he wor king, worn't he? — for that I'll gi' him mi curtsey, con I not afford to, since I'm bound to clip him after. As for thi, dozzie, from where did'st thi fetch thi metals? Did fetch 'em by magic means? Did thi find 'em so? If magic's t'means thi know ter fetch 'em, there's no man con hold thi, certain.

On impulse Grace accompanied Jas when he took the leaflets he'd had printed to stick up in the Tourist Office next to the Mining Museum at Matlock Bath. She had never even realised there was a Mining Museum at Matlock Bath. She resented the fact, though she did not say so, that it was he who had told her about it. This was one reason perhaps, aside from her being distressed by the museum as soon as she went in, that she felt maddened by his company from start to finish.

I thought my life used to be hard — but the lives of these people . . . All the pumps for taking out water, the information sheets concerning soughs and levels, rakes and scrins, flats and pikes, can't hide the fact that what they did, day in, day out, (and night in, night out, good as, in winter they'd never have got to see the light of day) was sheer bloody slavery, nothing else; not to say exploitation. Men and women. What's it say here? "Crushing ore to 'peasy' fragments was done by women." The sight of those tools, bucking iron, cobbing hammer, spade and shove, gad and wedge, noggers and kibbles, makes my bones ache in sympathy, remembering how it used to be for me, even if I never did anything to make me cough blood, the way some of those had to. What does Jas know? Standing there with a smile on his moon face, reciting all the names like poetry.

He's on to the names of mines now. Bacchus Pipe and Bacon Rake; Balls Eye Sough and Crimbo Vein; Hillocks Mine and Gank Hole. What does he know about it? Oh yes I can believe they were mining lead here before the Romans. Oh yes, I know all the roughly fenced holes you see around are the remains of mines. Oh yes I know that if you're not careful you can fall down a hole in this country and never come out. But so what? Even if he always did understand how to work with his body, unlike some of those art school gits, I doubt if he understands the real meaning, the worst of it. What's his family, then, painters, academics, judges? He's probably the first for generations, if not ever, that's got to work with his hands; not to speak of his lungs and muscles. As I stare at picks and hammers, drills and pig lead moulds, harmless enough looking now no one has to pull their guts out using them, the very thought of it makes me burn with anger.

Even now, he cannot see it. Though he's given up reciting names and so forth, he still keeps flashing his little white teeth, he still can't stop talking. Dark satanic mills he says. Lead mines and spinning jennies, Josiah Sedley and Richard Arkwright. Luddites and Malthus and Jeremy Bentham. Little sweeps crying 'weep, 'weep, 'weep. What does he know of child labour? I've got eyes. I can see Arkwright's red mills along the valley, the ones taken over by English Sewing. Working in them twelve hours a day was bad enough, but not as bad as being bent double, up to the knees in water, hacking away with a pickaxe from six in the morning till seven at night, a hundred feet under.

Grace was looking at Jas dispassionately now. Set in his older face, his white teeth almost looked false. Like him, she thought; for a moment could have pitied him almost, if she could have borne to. He was not the only one knew how to use words either. Her mother had told stories, for instance, whispering hurriedly when their father was elsewhere. Phrases floated into her mind to set against Jas': "What big teeth you have, grandmother" the most insistent. She wouldn't call Jas a wolf exactly. Even though she imagined very well the grandmother's white frilly cap about his round face, at the thought of it laughed out loud. "What big teeth you have, grandmother." She wished he was a wolf in a way. You should know where you were with a wolf. Whereas she never, even now, in the dim room upstairs at the Matlock Mining Museum, surrounded by redundant tools in glass cases, and prints of workers using the very tools, knew where she was with Jas exactly. She thought she never would. But did not consider for one moment that the reason for this might be herself, not Jas.

For once in that museum, standing alongside a wagon for hauling rock that used to be harnessed to people, I did know what Grace was thinking. She always had despised my non-manually working family; her views begin and end in class distinctions like everyone else's in this bloody country. Who said snobs come only from the upper classes? Maybe they started it, but the Graces of this world are good learners. How dare she assume that only people like her understand the meaning of all these instruments of slavery. In any case it's old hat. She's out of date.

"Take my mother, for instance," I say out loud. Grace looks at me as if I am crazy, it must seem a complete non sequitur to her. "There my mother was last winter sometime, getting on for seventy now, and arthritic, and looks it, trying to get a taxi on a wet evening. Being absolutely prevented by two fit young men patrolling the street to right and left. 'So sorry, Madam,' says one of them, leaping into the taxi they've succeeded in grabbing. 'So sorry, Madam. It's called survival of the fittest.'

"Survival of the fittest," I say, "that's the motto for these days, Gracie. Not the innate superiority of one class over another, by virtue of blood or labour. It can also be called

'Nature red in tooth and claw.' It also used to be called, with some moral equivocation, by my mother's old nanny — oh yes I know, Gracie, our having had an old nanny in the family is a sign of our moral degeneracy as against good working people like yourselves who didn't — it used to be called by her 'Looking After Number One'. An axiom I've spent my life living up to as I'm sure you've noticed, not that I didn't comfort myself till recently with the thought of my chivalrous countrymen continuing to behave a whole lot better. What do you think, Gracie?"

But Grace as usual says nothing. Looks at me with the same blank, masklike expression as she always used to, the only difference being that it's not so adoring; and that I note in its obstinacy an element of the purely childish. Did she stare back at her father like that, I wonder. Did her bloody-minded silence drive him crazy also? She continues to say nothing, even when I point out, accurately, that she is as good an example of "Look After Number One" as I am; if not better. Though my chief hope from this crude abuse is to get some feedback from her, none, of course, is forthcoming.

I should have learned by now. Such a policy's self-defeating. But I have not learned anything, it seems. To the extent that over the supper table I start on her again, this time in front of Terry. Once again I disguise attack as information; after all, apart from a dose of Derbyshire dialect, I've still not passed on the results of my Matlock researches. I bypass, wilfully, the social and legal material; the conies, for instance, and the other pot of coin clippings (Grace having shown no more interest in the origins of the pot found in her garden than she's shown these last six weeks in anything apart from glass). I ignore the likelihood she doesn't want to talk about the things that I increasingly want to — though if anyone should know why she doesn't want to, I should — I don't even get round to telling about the local heiress. I tell her instead the story of the woman in the glasshouse. My intentions in doing so are definitely vicious; I note with pleasure Terry's growing identification between the heroine whose history I am relating and the heroine sitting at the far side of the table Maybe I misjudged him; maybe he's not that stupid.

"Once upon a time," I begin, just as I would have with my kids in Santa Monica, it still seems the best way of starting all such stories. "Once upon a time a woman lived alone in a glasshouse. One day a starving girl came to the door, the woman took her on as a servant, but warned her she always had to be careful, so much the worse for her if she broke so much as a splinter, let alone a pane of glass. The little girl was careful at first, she could see the menace in the warnings, but after a bit she got to know what she was doing so well, the place seemed so homely and familiar, she forgot all the dangers. One day she couldn't be bothered to tiptoe, let alone look where she was going, she was altogether a bit too sassy, ran right round that glassroom like it was someplace else. Then of course she fell over. She fell against a window and broke it.

"'Don't say I didn't warn you,' said her employer all set to drown her in the glassy river that ran past the glass door. But the girl wouldn't have it, too quick for the jealous woman, she pushed her off the bank into the river before the murderess got her, the woman was drowned dead. So now the girl was the owner of the glasshouse; and now she never came out, hid herself against all comers. Now she promised death to anyone who got inside, let alone chipped one splinter off her glasshouse."

There's a long silence when I finish. "Is that the end of the story?" Grace asks, as if she doesn't believe it.

"Of course," I say. "What other end is there?" Thinking of its never-ending nature; the way, generation on generation, the glasshouse is bound to take over.

"I can think of other endings," says Terry, staring at her as if for him, too, now and always, she's half Medusa, half Greta Garbo; desirable but scary.

"I can't see any. What's the point?" she asks. Her voice not uncertain, but, by her standards, not sure of itself either.

"Don't you?" I say. Leaving her to draw her own conclusions. The nature of these conclusions she doesn't, of course, divulge in words, let alone glances. But I know she draws some. Oh yes, she smiles as blankly as usual. Glazed even. Glassy. I am looking at her constantly, but she doesn't seem to notice. Her lack of notice gives me a kind of freedom, it gives me X-ray sight, no I speak wrong, it gives me sight more like a strain viewer, the kind that picks up the hidden flaws in glass when it hasn't been annealed properly. I wouldn't say the stresses in Grace are so finely balanced that she'll burst apart at any moment, yet I can see that they are very finely balanced. I see it in the shift of her eyes, the infinitesimal cracks of the skin that surrounds them, I see it in the way she rises from the table, starts gathering up the dishes; I see it even in the glint of the narrow gold chain at her throat that is her only concession to splendour. With a pity welling up for both of us, of a kind unexpected as painful, I begin to fear that uneasy balance; to hope it won't be me, finally, that breaks it.

Grace had bought a small card of rock samples before leaving the museum. Jas gathered up several pamphlets about local mines and caverns. Two days later he went down to London to see his mother. He tried to take the pot of coin clippings with him; was so surprised by the fury the idea roused in Grace, he gave in quite meekly and went without it. He did, however, intend mentioning the matter to old acquaintances, if he could find them. In the event he didn't even try to find them; having meant to stay down three days, he returned after two. The way Grace nodded at him, she might not have noticed his absence. "I've been looking at some of those pamphlets you bought from the museum," she said. "There's some caves I think of seeing. For the geology. Maybe you'd want to come with me. Terry says he doesn't like caves."

And so it was. They saw caves. If there was one way Jas had not imagined spending August, it was trailing around various Derbyshire caverns behind a succession of bad-joke-a-minute guides and parties of day trippers. And in the company of his ex-wife.

One day, for instance, they stopped making glass early and went to see the Temple Mine at Matlock Bath. Not that there was any guide there, nor much to see, apart from some rusty wagon rails, and a few rather damp, mustard-coloured excavations which you could just about imagine some poor wretch having to crawl into. Seeing Grace stare at them, Jas imagined he was getting the usual silent lecture about the suffering of her ancestors. (She had told him, on the way here, that her mother's family had been Derbyshire miners before moving to the Brendon Hills, he accepted this gave her an interest. But he didn't propose to be brow-beaten thereby, not even by Grace in the orange plastic helmet that was obligatory to all visitors and made her look almost comical to his eyes; part Desperate Dan; part Valkyrie.) In fact she was not thinking of her family at all, merely scouring the rock for dark galena veins; the lead ore.

Another day they took off entirely and went to Castleton. Where the first mine they visited consisted of a long, not very interesting rock tunnel which they traversed sitting at the back of a wooden boat, as far as a pit known as bottomless. (According to the guide, it wasn't.) As if this was not enough they then drove up a green slope, fanged by outcrops of grey rock, to find not one but two caves in which used to be mined a metal Jas had never heard of before called Blue John; this, though, was not what they were after; what they — or at least Grace — was after were the stalagmites and stalactites they found in the second set of caverns. The whole unreality of the expedition was, for Jas, compounded, when they arrived at last amid the usual straggling crowd — they'd had to queue for half an hour to get into this one — at what felt like the guts of the earth, complete with liver and tripes and kidneys, to judge by the oleaginous nature of the white and yellow rock surrounding them, picked out by floodlights for their edification and wonder.

"What's all this about, Gracie?" Jas asked her. "I grant you it's amazing. But why have you decided to come here, suddenly? What's in this for you?"

She looked at him blankly. Shrugged slightly. To her it felt so self-evident as not to be worth saying. "Ideas for my glass, of course. Why else should I go anywhere?"

Up till that point they had followed obediently whenever the party moved on. There were several children in this one; short-haired children in white socks, who stared at Jas in his cowboy boots and little red neckerchief when they weren't staring at the stalactites, or giggling at the guide's jokes. There was not a shadow, a lump, a shape, the guide hadn't turned into some Walt Disneyish character. A shadow was Witch Gretchen ("We had some school-children in here. Of course they colled it after their teacher.") Humped stalagmites in the next cave were the seven dwarves. ("G for ground equals stalagmites, C for ceiling equals stalactites, that's how you con remember which is which," he told the clean children, who may or may not have been listening.)

"You sees that seventh dwarf, one day a man slipped and caught hisself on some tender parts let's say so as not to offend anyone. The way he hunched himself, we colled him the eighth dwarf; Grouchy," the guide went on. The crowd loved it. Jas supposed it was one means of keeping at bay this visceral rock, this all too indecently basic of uncompromising elements that everyone but miners had the sense to stay out of. Claustrophobia suddenly seeming to him the sanest of neuroses, he held Grace back when the rest of the party started following the guide down the steps past the seven dwarves. At the rear trailed an anxious-looking man in a safari jacket, leading a squat but skittish mongol youth of any age between fourteen and forty, who having raised his voice at all possible times to try the echo, now, still, refused to be quietened; he touched each stalagmite dwarf that he could reach, crying, "Go for it," lugubriously, over and over.

Go for it, thought Jas. But what should *he* go for? He knew what he wanted to. It was about time that he did. "How about making your glass to look like this?" he asked Grace; looking up at slimy layers of a grotto, slightly to the side of them, stalactites of different lengths millennially dripping from a surface the shape and texture of which looked, he said, as far as he was concerned, something between the patterns on a baby's matinee jacket, cameo jewellery, and the outside of a suet pudding. Flowstone the guide had called it. (This was altogether, Grace thought, coolly, a much more accurate description.)

"But how could you get *glass* to look like this?" she asked. Seeming as usual, to have taken his question a hundred per cent for real, she did not care to note the other questions in it. Her eyes fixed intently on the grotto before her, she was thinking that what Jas' descriptions entirely missed was the extraordinary time-scale. One stalactite, for instance, was one-and-a-half inches and a thousand years from meeting its stalagmite. A mere blink of geological time she knew; at the same time it felt quite outside her biological understanding.

Jas, meantime, with equal intensity, was examining her face. The cruel floodlight, concealing some features, exaggerating others, made it seem masklike even where it wasn't. In the same way the acoustic of the place arbitrarily, it seemed to him, magnified and blurred both shouts and whispers. She as if floated in her face, his voice. He, when she turned and saw him with his eyes fixed so firmly on her, as if floated in his face, in her own silence.

She did not bother to listen for Betsy's voice. Betsy was not here in this rock stomach with her. Alternatively she was so much here, inside Grace, she did not need to reveal herself any longer. We absorb, Grace thought, with the same gut. Speak, or rather do not speak, with the same voice. We hear with the same ears. She no less than me cannot believe what we are hearing, what Jas is saying, speaking with his face close up to my face; her face.

Go for it, Jas had thought. Once again he seized his moment; grabbed Grace's arm. Taken off guard and balance, she let herself be spun towards him. She could blame Terry if she liked, he was thinking, grimly, but she couldn't, for once, do a damn thing about it. Short of scream. Which she wouldn't, though from the cavern below, the one to which the steps led downwards, they could hear the echoes, still, of other voices.

When was the last time, Jas wondered, he had Grace alone in the dark, give or take the odd floodlight? He was a fool, he supposed to raise such issues now or want to. Suppose the lights were to fail? Suppose all the children were to start screaming? But he could not help it, night after night lately, he'd lain in that room beneath her and called himself a shit for leaving her pregnant. Called himself a shit also for walking out on his Yankee kids. Realised how much he missed them. What keeps me here then, he'd kept wondering all night long, not sleeping. Is it Gracie? Or is it simply the glass that all my life I might have been missing? Or is it Reg — to whom I still owe something; whom I also abandoned; like I seem fated to abandon everyone who cares for me, one way or another.

Go for it, he told himself. Why not. As if that justified what he launched into now, for which there was no justification, let alone pre-planning, whatever Grace might think. She, meanwhile, concluded he did it on purpose. Inasmuch as she concluded anything, torn as she was between shock, outrage and a desperate desire to succumb. (In a sense that Betsy would never allow her, his words might be all she had ever wanted from him.) Jas, on the other hand, was wondering — do I want it? Let alone mean it? Isn't it yet another form of blackmail? For he was not only looking her in the eye, closed as her eye seemed to be against him, he was begging her to forgive him for deserting her in the first place. Begging her to take him back, on any terms she'd have him. As her dogsbody; her apprentice; her husband, whatever way she cared to.

He was a shit he told her, appalled at the thought he might actually mean it. But it wasn't too late to reform, was it?

"You can help me reform, Gracie," he blurted out; pleaded with her; mea culpa, he cried; my fault, mea culpa.

"Of course," she said then, coolly. Loathing his weakness. At the same time yearning for it. "You're not telling me it was my fault?" This being the only thing she felt able to get hold of, that she felt capable of saying.

(The voices and footsteps are rising upwards again, growing nearer, their echo is as hollow as the one I make, still more hurriedly pressing my case. I lay my sins at her feet. I invite her to chastise me, with a blowing iron if she chooses. I say I'll blow glass alongside her for ever; it's sheer fairy tales

I'm telling her, surely? Or sheer desperate determination to hack my way somehow through her impenetrable defences.)

A man in a dark blue t-shirt came into sight now, toiling up the steps ahead of the rest of the party, past the line of yellow stalagmites that reminded Jas more of fungus than of dwarves, merry or dopy. G for ground, he thought, stalagmites, not stalactites, c for ceiling. After which he whispered in her ears — of all things he knew it was the most unforgivable, yet the one he could least resist — or maybe that she could. "We can still have another baby. Surely it isn't too late to?"

(Whatever can I have been reading? I'm as bad as Gracie. Like some fucking princess, waiting for her prince to come. Worse, *begging* him to do so.)

The mongol boy was in sight now, his lips moving as always, the man in the safari jacket holding his arm, bending his head to listen. Behind came the rest of the party, the children touching the stalagmite dwarves as they went past, arguing which was Sleepy and which was Grumpy, in voices ever higher and louder, as though the prospect of leaving the cave was lifting the weight of it from them. If the guide's jokes about their defection were inappropriate also, how was he supposed to know, he couldn't have been more than twenty.

"Well, Grace," Jas said, after. By now they stood looking across a valley so green and smooth apart from its limestone outcrops they could no longer imagine — nor did either want to — the corrugations that lay beneath them.

"Well what?" she asked him.

"You mean you don't ever listen to a word I say?" Indignation was now his tactic. Her eyes though were cool and distant as she said, "Oh yes, I listen."

"Why don't you answer me, then?" he goaded.

"What's the point, when there's nothing to say?" But now it seemed she did have something to say, though in a voice as remote, as slight as ever: almost girlish, in fact. She talked of the ammonites for instance, in one part of the cavern they'd just left, of the wild yellow ruffles that Jas remembered in another, like a cascade of creme brulee, he suggested: flowstone, she again called it. Comparing different kinds of rock, she went on to explain how she'd attempted sedimentary effects in her glass. By fusing laminated sheets, for instance. Jas could hardly believe what he was hearing. Was she playing with him, he wondered. She never used to know how to. But he was not sure of anything any longer. Not having emerged from that great womb, that Hades inside which he had just trapped her. Or inside which she, she understood reluctantly, had trapped him. Or maybe, more accurately, they had with sure aim and gaze just about trapped each other.

"What did they do to you, your mum and dad, to fuck you up so?" he shouted at her in outrage. "Did you love them? Did you ever for one moment love me? Why don't you answer me, damn you?" He did not even feel capable of driving any longer, throwing the car keys at her. She on the other hand felt as if driving was the only thing she could safely do at this moment.

Along the Hope Valley, below the green rise of Mam Tor, they sat in a traffic jam, not speaking, looking at the red berries on the rowan trees. In one field there was haymaking; as there was haymaking just now in the field opposite Grace's cottage.

Jas complained about the traffic. All Grace said was, "It's late for haymaking, August getting on September. Back home us do it in June, July latest." Then she added so very demurely, Jas could not possibly accuse her of teasing, "Wedlock, I've heard said, Jas, is padlock. Didn't you know?" (Grace, he found himself thinking, Gracie, can that be you speaking? Even to her mind, she was not sure if it hadn't been Betsy.)

I went down to the pub that night. Spent the time talking to a guy I'd met before, once or twice. When he mentioned he'd a room to let I took it; moved all my stuff over that same night, plus — with Grace's gracious permission — old Reg's red Ruskin. If Grace thinks it's her fault, she'd be right absolutely. If Terry thinks that leaves things clear for him, let him think it, the little schmuck. And see how he likes it, the mardy boy. If he doesn't know already. How did that phrase go? — not so green as cabbage looking. Though the way I've been carrying on, it applies to me just as well.

And why, by the way, does the glasshouse smell of bacon? And why hasn't Grace made a witch's piece? I only noticed yesterday she hadn't — what would Reg have said, I wonder. Though he wasn't a superstitious man exactly, he always said it was the first thing you had to make, he'd always done it. That leaves me not much option but to make the thing myself. Which I am going to; soonest.

Chapter Nine

"It loses not weight nor substance with the longest most frequent use . . ."

These weren't the first mines I ever saw. I went into a mine once, years ago, up on the Brendons; old iron workings they were. It was just before, I think, I started making things with clay, started wanting to be a potter, but I don't remember exactly, not having, nor wanting, Jas' memory for the past. (Why does he keep on trying to make me remember?)

I was interested in such things then. My teacher gave me a book on the iron mines and the mineral railway that took the ore down to Watchet. I found some levels marked on the map at the end of the book; after yet another of my rows with Dad I rode all the way up to find them. It took me some time; they were buried among brambles, and set in a secret little valley, a cleft so withered and abandoned it made me shiver for who or what I did not know. I tethered my horse near the ruined walls of some cottages, then ventured as far as I dared into the stone and earth tunnel. It seemed sound enough, although propped up in places.

I don't remember much else about it. Except that I walked in water most of the way and had to keep my head bent, being tall already. Except that when it was quite dark, my fear began to release not only the pain of my bruises, but also the fire of my anger. I yelled against Dad who had given me the bruises, but who was too big to hit back in his person. In my younger, nippier days, I'd managed to bite him once or twice; by now, not only the pleasure of hurting him wasn't worth the punishment he'd given me, the taste and texture of his flesh disgusted me even to think of.

My anger grew so much it went beyond yelling; not being able to kill him, I began bruising my own knuckles on the stone walls of the tunnel. Until all of a sudden I felt movement beneath them; closed my fingers on something that fluttered against my palms as I began stumbling towards the light. It stopped fluttering after a while. When I reached air at last and opened up my fist I found two little reddish moths crushed there inside it. They were lifeless by then. I could not have freed they, even had I wanted.

'Tis not t' only question. Can you explain to me, dozzie, how to tell love from hate? Desire from dullness? Wanting from not wanting? Exile from entrance? I used not to think I needed to ask such questions, let alone make such distinctions; Dad never seemed to need to. But now I can't separate design from incoherence. And wonder if there's even a connection.

All I can make — that satisfies me — at the moment, is what I have always made; or variations of it. Which is not to say that I don't try other things. I try many. Fusing different coloured glasses; combing them, half molten, to make patterns; slumping them into moulds made of old pieces of iron left from the nail works that were here previously, into hub caps, engine castings, shapes I form — in casting sand I've ordered up lately — with hunks of stone or wood.

Which is not to say, either, that I don't get some things right. Jas, for instance, has moved out. At the same time he turns out to have his uses — which is entirely up to him, I'm not going to pay him for it. He has fixed me up a strain viewer so I can test the strain in the glass when I've fused it. Technically at least, in other words, I begin to know what I'm doing. A point that is at once everything and nothing; everything, because you get nowhere in this game unless technically you get it right; nothing, because to try everything is to arrive nowhere. To arrive somewhere you have to ride the same road over and over. The way I always have done but don't know how to any longer.

All these techniques are quick compared to the techniques I used as a potter. But all of them are slow compared to the ways I have worked as a glassblower. Only this slowness, it seems to me, redeems some of my impatience; my hither and thithering between one technique and another.

(What good's a man in mi house to mi, his seed's oll I need no other. Oh yes, he's brought his seed, he works with thi, dozzie, this seed hasn't died on mi yet. Nor will. Thissen is padlock enough to keep out wedlock.) Was it loneliness she felt, though, when she closed her furnace each night — she closed it very late sometimes — and came back alone to the cottage? If it was loneliness, she could not or would not name it. Lust was the only thing she was prepared to name, or had been prepared to name for a long time — thi tek thi pleasure, dozzie, she told herself — us be animals, us needs bodily using. Two nights later, not stinting herself, or the boy, she filled them up with booze and then took him to bed again, pulling him over her like a blanket, as if to protect herself from the chilly winds of winter.

I can't say no, can I? Couldn't in the beginning, she got me boozed up on purpose. Thing is I don't want to say no, in some ways it's still bleeding marvellous, nor I haven't managed to pull no other cunt yet, have I, the ones I've tried chatting up in Matlock Bath don't want to know. If I am beginning to hear that Derbyshire's different from Nottingham, none of it sounds anything like the Somerset Grace yells in when we're fucking.

'S funny to think how much I used to like everything she said and did in bed. Now some things make me shudder, I wish she wouldn't. In fact I wish she wouldn't most things, leave aside the actual fucking. Which ain't to say that now I get my cock in her regular, I'm not as jealous of her as ever. Every time she's alongside Jas in the glasshouse, when she's wearing those goggles she's taken to wearing against the glare so's I can't see what her eyes are doing, I think she's leading him on; or maybe he's leading her on; he even hands her an iron with a lecher look. But then he's always got lecher looks; he's after everything in skirts, what's more they'll have him, all the kind that wouldn't have me if I paid 'em. They're fatter than Grace usually. Grace these days is a like a pin man, thinner than ever.

Sometimes — most times — I want to kill him. I'm so fucking jealous of her every single minute, I want to kill her too sometimes when she's with him. It don't matter that often I don't love so much as hate her. Why I hate her is because I want to get away from her; because I can't get away from her.

I don't even want to share her bed more often than not. But every night since Jas left it's as if she can't get enough of it. Sometimes when's she working late down there – with Jas most likely — I don't know, I suspect it — I goes to bed before she comes in; if I think that's going to be my let out for the night, I soon have another think coming. Most times she makes me come to her room. Once or twice, though, she's stayed in mine, that ain't no fun either, there's not enough room for both of us in my bed, not for fucking nor sleeping. For two pins I'd run away, I keep thinking; seemingly there ain't more than one pin available, I don't never do it.

Once, when Grace took me in her bed, I'd get some ace dreams; beautiful *and* sexy. Now what I get from her is nightmares. The same nightmare, often enough. I'm shut in a dark room, hammering at a door, I can't get out; it's just what I remember from when I were a little kid, when me and mum, as usual, were living in a grotty council flat. You can't blame mum for getting cheesed off, living ten floors up in a place like that, piss in the lifts and shit in the basement, damp running down our walls, not to mention having no job, no feller, and a kid kept getting sick. You can't hardly blame her for taking herself off of a bleeding evening, locking me in my room first so I couldn't get out and do myself a mischief.

Of course she never tells me she was going. First thing I know I wake up with an ache in my gut and no one don't come to my yelling. I gets up then, don't I, and goes to the door and find I can't get out nohow, and don't no one still come, no matter how I hammer and bellow.

That's about the first thing I remember in my life, if not the last thing. You wouldn't do it to a dog, leave alone a little kid, what were mum thinking? Except I know what she were thinking. When she comes in at last, I'm slumped on the floor by the door, tears all over, too tired to cry further. "Mum," I calls, feebly, "Mum," but she don't hear me, she's giggling and laughing saying things I couldn't hardly hear neither, in a voice I don't like to remember, though I daresay her fancy man does, the way he were giggling with her. (But then he's never like to hear the way I hear her years later, screaming drunk curses against every man that existed.)

One night, after dreaming that dream, I woke up in Grace's bed crying. She held me like never, she whispered, she even kissed me. Then the next day looked at me like she didn't know me, she ain't never seen me before in her whole life. Daring me to deny it; which of course I didn't.

How can you sleep in the same bed with someone night after night after night, yet still feel so fucking lonely?

Work's the only thing. Or would be if Jas was anywhere other. He's getting a better worker again these days, I give him. He always works with Grace, though. Him and me we don't neither of us get near each other working if we can help it. And when we do have to, when there's no avoiding — it's Grace usually sees that we get together, she does it malicious I'm certain — we're ever so polite, never mind our bleeding teeth are so gritted we can't hardly get them apart after. It's "Yes, Jas," "No Jas"; "Yes, Terry," "No Terry". "Wipe my arse, will you Terry," "Yes certainly, Jas," and "Jas, when you've done that, kiss my cock, Jas." "Yes, of course, Terry." And at the end of that, what do we have for our pains, an ever so beautifully crafted eighteenth century goblet to you, sir, never mind it'll poison any booze what's put inside it, or make it taste of roast pork or frying bacon or black pudding or rabbit stew, all the rest of the things this fucking place stinks of, apart from our mutual loathing.

When I think of those times I thought of pushing Jas off a cliff, or putting arsenic in his coffee, or a live wire in his bare mitt, it seems weird I never thought I don't need such means to top him; I've got him in the lethal glasshouse — how about some sandblasting, Jas — arrrghhh . . . what about this punty for cracking your skull, Jas — zzapp . . . here's some boiling glass for you, Jas — wham . . . I daresay he puts the same ideas my way sometimes, especially now Grace has only me to cook her nice little meals for down in her kitchen; or more like, upstairs in her bed — she feeds me whatever she likes and whether or not I'm hungry; I get a mouthful of splinters, good as. (Don't ground glass kill you, if you eat it? Don't it slice up your gut?)

All those thoughts of topping Jas cheers me up, though, sometimes I even dare cheek him. "Mind your head, Jas," I say, "You ain't got enough hair I couldn't crack it open ever so easy." ("Not as easy as I could crack yours open, cock," he snaps back, "given what isn't in it.") I even dare take the micky about some of those figures he's been friggering when Grace and I aren't around to watch him. Glass bints they are, huge bums, huger knockers tipped with pink glass nipples. Maybe I'd find 'em funny some other place, my mates would like 'em for certain. But I don't find 'em funny here; at least not when Grace is looking.

Not that she's said so much as a word about them, no matter how Jas tries to make her. "Like one of these for your witch's piece, Grace," he says to her one fine morning. "What would Reg say to hear you'd never made a witch's piece? Don't say you're not superstitious." First I don't know what he means by the witch's piece, then I remember Grace saying, months back, how we had to make one. I hadn't thought nothing of it then, why should I, I never heard of no such thing before or after. Nor did I wonder why she hadn't got round to making it. But I wonder now. I also wonder, the sly look he gives us — not just Grace, yours truly — if there aren't quite a few different ways of settling witches; what exactly's Jas up to, I wonder?

I guess I've always had a vulgar streak; more, I've never been ashamed of it, not one minute. I needed vulgarity to survive in my family, what with all that intellect and high art and drinks in the studio. I started in a small way, with Walt Disney and Donald McGill. And if I've moved on a bit since the days I preferred The Beano to Beatrix Potter, my glass ladies must make it clear to all interested parties that despite my progress over the years I never quite lost my taste for pink elephants and large bums.

Not that my parents would call it progress exactly, my willing conversion to creative cynicism. My two brothers and my sister became academics and/or artists, just like them. All I ever did was start at art school, and that didn't last long. I don't even look like the rest of them, they're thin and pale, narrow-faced, weaselly — you'd think I was some kind of changeling with my curly hair and great fat chops. Which doesn't mean they dislike me. They love me. I could talk my mother in particular into doing anything I wanted, I could wind her round my little finger, though none of the others knew how to. Maybe it was because I was the only one took after her crazy Scots family. In some way I'd swear she even liked my vulgarity — even if she didn't, it wouldn't matter.

What I always loved Stateside, why I stayed so long, was the unashamed vulgarity I found there. We Brits may be good at shows, but we're not half as good at the showy. (Look at the way they ride horses in the US of A, can you imagine all that lovely prancing, those lurex jump suits and stetsons, going down well at Wembley?)

Not that we aren't getting better at it in some respects, this side of the Atlantic. I saw something in Watts once, one of the poorest bits of LA — not a green thing in sight, just heat and dust and garbage and peeling wooden houses — that I couldn't have imagined seeing in England. A huge golden billboard, slap in the middle, saying "Wouldn't you rather be in Vegas?" I can imagine something just as sick now, almost anywhere, Liverpool, Glasgow, Wapping, you name it. "The essence of all vulgarity," says Ruskin — I've had a lot more time to read Ruskin lately — "lies in want of sensation." And "Men are forever vulgar, precisely in proportion as they are incapable of sympathy."

Precisely. Isn't that Boadicea of gentility, our very own Selina Smiles, the senile President's Friend, of all people the most gloriously vulgar? Hasn't she — as he also puts it, a way which didn't seem so relevant when, sitting in what Reg called his parlour, twenty odd years ago, I first read that sentence — "Founded an entire science of Political Economy on what she has stated to be the constant instinct of man — the desire to defraud his neighbour." Got it in one, Johnny. Except that in this country now, they call it Get Rich Quick. And Look After Number One. Not to mention Survival Of The Fittest.

Which is all beside the point. What got me on to this subject in the first place was my vulgar glass ladies, which Reg knew all about. But the way he felt about me, I could get away with anything, provided I got my priorities right when we were working together. If I played hookey in my own time, so what, all friggers always play hookey in their spare time. My busty ladies were even my credentials, making up for my poovy accent and art school background. So they were with Grace also, I suspected. Jas on the rampage wasn't exactly her soulmate, didn't exactly remind her of home, but at least it showed I was different from the rest of my family, that she never properly came to terms with all the time she was living in their attic, even if she did end up married to their golden boy.

She couldn't be said to have liked them exactly, my glass-titted floozies; nor my other line, some well-hung wrestlers. Grace hasn't a vulgar streak in her, not of that kind anyway. She was tougher and harder than me, than all my friends and family, tougher and harder than anyone, except Reg, possibly. In some ways she was tougher even than him. She didn't seem to need the kind of relief that I looked for when I'd heard Cosi Fan Tutte once too often, or when I'd airtwisted the stems of more goblets than I could stand to; or when some lover was playing me up (memories of my mocking Leda kept me from being one hundred per cent faithful, even in the beginning); or when Reg was being at his most Reggish.

What I've been working on now is a relief also. Never mind the result's not quite what I expected. My first realisation of what I was getting, the unexpected power of the malevolence, even the primitive terror I had to be harbouring to have produced such a thing so startled me, I botched it and had to start again all over. Which might have lost it; should have lost it in the usual way. But it appeared again, more emphatically than ever; it was as if I could not put whatever it was behind me, even if I'd wanted to. Which I half did and half did not. This thing was not something for men to snigger at in corners; it was archetypal; you could almost say elemental.

It gave me some satisfaction, I admit, as much satisfaction as unease. Even though I was as surprised as any. In fact you could probably say she did most of it, she bewitched me, or rather her effect on me bewitched me. My love, my fear, my hate. Hers too. Also Terry's love and fear and hate, don't tell me he had nothing to do with it. An eternal triangle, you could say, except there's no such thing as an eternal triangle, there are many different triangles with many different corners. A man and two women. A woman and two men. Father, wife, son. Husband, mother and daughter. My piece was another triangle; the two figures; the maker. You could feel the maker in the figures. You could feel the maker sucked into what he'd made, what he was making, along with all his fear and lust and loathing.

Leaving aside which, it's not to say I have no practical problems. The main figure's huge, that's one problem, much bigger than any of the others. I could have done with some help, but in the circumstances couldn't expect, let alone ask for help and get it. I work alone all evening, it's ten o'clock before I've finished, the two of them will be cosily tucked up in her bed already. Oh yes, I know what's going on, how can I help it? I know why the spotty youth dares to be so cheeky sometimes, so what, he'd better watch it. Not that I think he's ecstatic about it, exactly. I'm not the only one she bugs, I see how he looks sometimes, eyeing her across the room. I don't trust him as far as I see him. But no matter what she's done to him, or what she's doing, — or what she's done to me come to that — if he dares take it out on her, the runt, in any way whatever, I'll knock his ugly little block off.

It was Grace, usually, got to the glasshouse first in the morning; checked the heat of the furnace and the amount of glass in the crucible — topped up with cullet the night before, it should have been, usually was, good and full, but just occasionally there were slip ups — then took yesterday's products out of the cooled-down lehr.

One morning in early September, however, standing in the doorway, she suspected someone had been there before her. Not that it concerned her, not at first. She had been feeling better than for some little while. A sense of oppression had as if lifted from her, along with the grey cloud and heavy air which had sat itself down on them throughout the second half of August, and now peeled off the country as suddenly, her mother would have said, as a woman lifting a veil. This morning it had been cool enough early for there to have been a dew. Coming down through the wood, her nostrils had caught a faint cold smell, an almost autumnal hint of sadness and rotting leaves, though everything else about her still spoke summer. Every green leaf, every frond of bracken glittered, shafts of fretted sunlight fell through the trees, each one swimming, dancing with delicate particles and motes in which she could see, at the same time, everything and nothing. The whole filled Grace as she turned her key in the glasshouse lock with a subliminal, thankful, terrifying sense of not only end but beginning.

'Tis thi glasshouse, dozzie. You're right, dozzie, it's mine, it's no one else's.

I do not have to look to know exactly what I'm going to see. Apart from Betsy's voice it's the only reality I'm still capable of understanding. To the left of the door, for instance, is the cupboard in which I keep my supplies of coloured rods and powders, of small tools and reference books. Jas has pinned postcards to the door — I did not ask him to, I try not to look at them if I can help it. One, recently, he insisted on showing me before he pinned it. I don't doubt he had some reason for it — Jas never did anything without some reason for it. Leda and the Swan, it was. By Michelangelo? I am not sure and do not intend to check, I've always hated that story and always will do. I see no reason why women should be remembered or praised only for being fucked by one God and giving birth to others. (Also I know the tale. It wor in one book or other, in my lady's library, where they learned us. Nor did *I* like it.) In front of the cupboard is the rack in which the blowing irons are kept. Straight out of the furnace the irons hit the water in the little trough at the bottom with a hiss of heat and the tinkling sound of overstressed glass when it's breaking.

To the right of the door is such office as we have the room for; a desk, a telephone, two large filing cabinets, all of which Jas has taken charge of. Beyond that is the display area; a table for seconds; the good stuff set out on shelves. Beyond, on the far wall opposite the door, stands the marver, behind it more shelves holding cutting and grinding tools, moulds of various shapes and kinds, junk I never get round to sorting. Alongside, two round vats full of cullet ready for melting. Next to the shelves there is a sink for washing tools and coffee mugs and the jars in which we keep the colours. Next to that, set back in an alcove, the sandblaster, a clumsy, lumpish thing to my eye, like farm machinery, except that it sits still, has not so much as one wheel to move it.

All that stuff's necessary; but no more than necessary. What's to my left as I stand in the doorway, on the long wall opposite the display area and the two small windows (we work by electric light, always) is the essential part. The lehr; the furnace; standing in front of the furnace, the chair; the heart of the business as they always have been, always will be for glass-blowers, if the old prints are anything to go by. Lehr; furnace; chair. As Jas is always pointing out, as Reg always used to, the source of the heat may be different, but it's the only difference.

What I can say, what I assert, though, is that this glasshouse here is mine and no one else's. Which means I do not understand what gives me the sense this morning that someone has been here already. Nor what I am so afraid of.

(Tek care of thissen, ond of mi, doz. Con thi not reck the danger?)

At first Grace did not know why Betsy had turned restless suddenly; why she herself had not only become uneasy but also felt, in some way, usurped. But as soon as she opened the lehr she knew. It had been emptied already. When she turned her head, she saw all yesterday's work laid out neatly on the table used for that purpose. And when she looked the other way, towards the furnace, saw yet another piece set on top. Not one she had made. Not one she had previously clapped eyes on. There was a label attached to it, stating, in large red letters: WITCH'S PIECE.

Chapter Ten

"It is friable with cold, which made our proverb 'as brittle as glass' . . ."

Do thi not see, doz, what he has done. Is't certain he has meant to harm the both on us, not only me, thi also. That way con keep us powerless, con lock us up and kep us from t'fire. Does not matter they hang us, we mun play with fire, be it metals or magic we play with; t'power us gets by it's mighty. They know it well. Why is it oll the same to them, why is work wi' fire not women's? Because woman working wi' fire is witchcraft, be more con ony man stand for. Did never reck was trouble in it? Did thi not think, like me, to tek that trouble never mind what man con say thi? Never mind what magic might to use to hold thi? Never mind noose he'll set about thi neck. Never mind he worships thi, he'll bind soon as worship, 's oll the same to him. Thus keeps fire, t'knowing to hissen. What we know, grows more important thon things he knows. Is why we work in secret ollus, to thwart him. Why he fears us work in secret, even more than fears us work by t'light of day.

Mek it now then, doz, what thi wishes. Mek it now and mek it well. If not thi's done for, and not by scragging either, the way hourlong I went, nor by yearslong way my lady tek when one she wed teks her birthright. Did her lass inherit house and oll went wi' it? Nay, was not her lad tek oll t'booty. Beware of sons still more than husbands. Cast the buggers out thi bed.

I overslept a bit that morning, didn't I, came in expecting a tonguelash from my lady, even if it were her fault and she should of woke me, after all I were sleeping in her bed.

We're supposed to work non-stop at the moment; Jas has fixed an open day in two weeks, to help us get in with all those well-heeled and nosy neighbours who are too polite just to turn up if we don't ask them. Anyways I came in whistling like I didn't know the time, and if I did know wasn't about to start feeling guilty. But soon as I gets in the fucking door I see that Grace ain't got the furnace open as she would of usually by this time. She's got her back to me, gawping at something on top of the furnace. Then I sees what she were staring at. And start staring with her. How could anyone keep their eyes off a thing like that?

The point being it were not only bleeding horrible, it were also amazing. Like something in a museum, the kind of thing sir used to tell us some gits worshipped, so hideous you can't see why, on the one hand, on the other you can see worshipping might be safer than not. At first look it weren't so different from the other females Jas were friggering lately, apart from being a whole lot bigger. The tits were bigger. The head was bigger. It had no face if you looked closer, just a load of lumps; if you stood back though, like from where I first saw it, it had a face all right, if it were as much a mask as face. The hair on its head was like a helmet. It was also like writhing snakes. One look at it was enough; any more, you think, might freeze you.

It had two stiff arms spread out. It had two great tits — their nipples plain glass not coloured like on the ones Jas used to make, they were like two blown goblets, let fall a bit out of shape; you knew this chick weren't a young one. It had a neat waist though, and great hips swelling out under and a great butt jutting out behind. It had a belly button 'n all, it had everything it should have, including a cunt. And how do I know it had a cunt without picking the lady up to look underneath her? I tell you how I know, and the way I learned's the worst thing. Because, standing there upright with her mask of a face and her helmet of snakes and her goblet breasts and her neat little belly button, she were fucking, weren't she. Not fucking with a man, though; slung on her tits, hooked into her navel, were a kind of bleeding dwarf, or baby, with a great cock on him, tucked neat inside her. While I stands there watching — I don't think she'd seen me — Grace picks up the figure, she gets her mitts on the creature and takes him out, you could see his great cock standing.

At which she turns round and sees me; herself in one hand, in a manner of speaking, me, poor bloody Terry, in the other. Don't tell me that's not how Jas meant it, never mind how any witch would have turned it. Don't tell me he was afraid of witches, if not he was afraid of this one. Don't tell me — God help me, I'm as near I ever was to being embarrassed — all those times I could've wished I hadn't met her, all those times I'd sooner have been on the dole than have to climb into bed with her, weren't nothing to what I were feeling on that instant. Why's she so shiny, I were thinking? Why can you see through her? Why does she look as if she bloody moves and dances, even though she's standing stock still, staring at me, like a bleeding statue?

I could feel myself turning red as beet. To make it worse *she* were turning red as beet. Out of nowhere, like, I felt a blast of rage — fucking huge it were. Against her? Against the piece? How do I know — weren't they the same, if you think of it, weren't yours truly the fucking dwarf, the toyboy? I don't know if I meant to hit her. Maybe all I meant was to smash the monster out of her hands. I lifted my hand, but if I'd been near enough to reach her, if I'd wanted to save the piece rather than smash it, I couldn't never of caught it when it started falling. Her startled hands slipped, she half dropped the thing, without my help. Then, somehow, she caught it; the only thing that kept on falling, though we both made a grab for it, were her stupid little dwarfish lover. Which the floor, nothing if not stony-hearted, smashes on the blooming spot.

We stared at each other after. The first time, come to think of it, she'd ever looked me in the eye, straight, except she was challenging me for something. She weren't challenging me now. She were more like asking a question. Not knowing what she were asking I didn't know how to answer, no more than she knew how to answer the questions I'd of been asking, if I'd known how to find the words. I couldn't stand it no more, soonest, I picked up one of the pieces. Not paying proper attention; serve me right it bit me, good as. Haven't I always said glass is dangerous, if it don't burn, it cuts you? It were only a little nick this time, on the end of a finger, but spouted blood like beer from a barrel. I looks at it stupid for a moment. Then I starts laughing. And Grace starts laughing. What else could we bloody do? You tell me.

(I saw thi ope thi gob, I heard thi gostering with the mardy loon — is it thi now mocks mi also? Do not reck thi may regret it? Cannot see thi may mock thissen wi' it?)

Terry sweeps up the pieces. I place the figure back on the furnace. It's no less monstrous for what it's lost, the top of the furnace is the place for it.

Jas appears five minutes later. He is playing cowboy as usual, in tight jeans and t-shirt; he looks at once cocksure and shifty, inasmuch as I can bear to look at him. He means me to look, of course; he means Terry to look also. His legs are still long, he still has neat buttocks, I grant you. Maybe he expects me to fancy them again — it's not that I can't accept that each one of us gets older. On his belt, beneath his paunch, he wears an indecent silver buckle. It was made by the Navaho, he told me. I know nothing about the Navaho. Not even where they live, exactly.

Beside him Terry appears still punier. His narrow face a mere paring, a sliver off Jas' man in the moon extravaganza. The more so these days because he has not cut his hair lately, ties it back with a bootlace to keep it out of his eyes while he is working. The sweat sits as greasy on his brow as it sits on the nostrils of a pig being slaughtered.

Neither of us has said one word so far about the Witch's Piece. Jas is annoyed, clearly, he keeps on glancing between us. He must know we've seen her, she's still sitting up on the furnace. He looks at her himself sometimes, I notice, his mouth so tight, his teeth are not for show on this occasion. But it is not clear to me, nor do I intend to ask him, if he's noticed that something is missing from her.

We work the whole day from then intently, as if our lives hang on it. All three of us are sweating still more than usual from the heat of the furnace. When we go outside for a breather the light, even in the wood, seems dazzling. Inside my glasshouse the furnace sucks in all light that is not itself; we scarcely have enough to see by. We can scarcely breathe either, the air smells like a stableful of sick horses.

As soon as I walk into the glasshouse I cannot believe what I am seeing. I had to have been possessed to have set that thing up there to mimic them on the furnace. My foolhardiness is calculated usually. I am here, after all, working my guts out, unpaid, for my ex-wife, because I can afford to and because it suits me. And because I like glass. And because I am mischievous, which may be my undoing, but give or take a few warning signs hasn't yet succeeded in ruining me.

I noticed the dwarf had gone from her belly. Did they break it, I wondered, did they hide it, what did they do with it? And do they feel the malevolence thick as ash in the air this morning? Sure they must have felt it, you only had to look at them. What was kind of strange was that though we were all in part its instigators, we also made common cause against it. You could hardly blame them for hating when we started working. But our mutual malevolence was overtaken after a bit by one much less easy to attribute. It came from Grace partly. But it was also against her, the three of us on one side, the malevolence on the other. I don't know how they found it; me, it exhausted. My skin felt both airless and sagging; on my face; on my belly. I felt the power I used making that figure leak slowly away from me. Thick as ash, it was like I said, what sat among us in the glasshouse. Also it smelt like ash, like the reek from the dump, old food and old metal, organic and mineral. The air from the dump was sweeter.

Don't know what got into us the way we was working; like our hate drove us on and pulled us together at the same time.

Jas soon lost the cocky look he came with, I'm glad to say. He took his boots off to work; his shrinking an inch or two began the business. Then he got sweaty and shirty, one of his buttons came from off of his belly. By the end of the afternoon, his hair were greasy with sweat, he kept rubbing his hand across his forehead, he had his mouth puckered up like an arse, fair enough, the shit he brings out of it.

I didn't want to stop working that day; it were like working were the only safety. Besides, once we'd closed up, I'd have to go home with Grace; remembering that *thing*, I couldn't look her in the face hardly, let alone sit at the same table with her, let alone get into her bed. Remembering how she turned so red, I supposed she couldn't face these things neither. So when we'd finished a series of pieces I said I wanted to work on my own for a while, if it was all the same to her. It weren't bullshit entirely. I'd had some new ideas lately; they were good ones, I wanted to try 'em.

Up till this time I'd made scent bottles mostly. Fiddly kinds of things, what Grace had no patience for. They were good practice, leastways. Getting the stoppers to fit was hardest, it took me a long time to learn it. But I could fit them now all right, no problem. In fact it were too easy, I wanted to move on a bit, the things Grace had been trying lately had given me a few ideas. I don't have the patience for slumping and so forth, I like to see the glass taking its shape as I work it. Just the same I thought I might make a mould or two out of the casting sand, put the hot glass straight in and shape it that way, same as when you want to put colour on the outside of a vase to make a spiral pattern. You plunge the glass into a mould then, what you lined with rods of colour. You spin the shape of the mould out in the furnace, after. But weren't no reason you had to spin it out, it seemed to me. You could let glass keep the shape of the mould, set a bubble of blown glass in the centre, the size of a scent bottle. That way you'd still have a scent bottle, but a rough, sculpted thing, not so dainty. And made in whatever shape you wanted, so long as the casting sand takes it.

When I asked if I could do some friggering, Grace just nodded. Jas went off then. She went off. Leaving me alone to do what I wanted — which is, ain't it always with glass, much harder than I'd expected; having no help I had to use the system Grace just rigged up for blowing glass on her ownsome. And then just how was I to make the lip on them for the stopper? All kinds of problems. Which I can't say I'd got sorted by the time she came back. Still I'd two pieces in the lehr, was putting in a third when she came to check it and close up. It were late enough, she said, if it was to cool down in time by morning.

I was pleased with that third piece. Though things wasn't right yet, I could see they soon might be. All the same I were surprised the way she looked when she saw it. Of course she don't say nothing. Her face and her voice's like fixed in glass, but then, the way things were, I daresay my face weren't saying no different.

Grace had driven her old car up from the road, instead of walking down through the wood. Her voice cool if not conciliatory, she offered to take Terry for a drink at the pub, or even to the chippy if he was hungry. But he wasn't hungry. He didn't feel like the pub. Drained and exhausted — between fear and enthusiasm and desire to shut out all else, he had been working at white heat — his longing for sleep became so acute suddenly, it wiped out the fear his employer would want to share his bed with him. Besides he could feel that she was as resistant to the idea as he was; a wariness between them forbade even the most innocent, accidental of touches. In the glasshouse, as they filled up the furnace with cullet, then checked its setting, saw that the lehr was properly closed and set to cool down by morning, they all but circled each other to avoid them.

Afterwards, outside, Grace locked up, then pulled at the door several times to make sure that she had done so; Terry scarcely would have noticed usually; he was maddened this evening. To make matters worse, she kept shaking the door without speaking. Not that there was anything to say, not that she ever spoke at such moments. All the same, standing there in silence, just able to distinguish her face, he did not know how he could endure it.

"Suit yourself," he answered, determined not to show her how relieved he felt when she turned round and, flinging the keys at him, asked, almost humbly, if he would mind walking home alone. Even that trek through the dark wood, even the cries of owls, he thought, would be preferable to her company. To walk with her tonight would be like his dream, like being locked once more in the solitary room of his nightmare. The fact that in her too he had observed — inasmuch as he was capable of observing — a kind of disarray, even helplessness, did not reassure him. On the contrary, he thought, he preferred her angry. Which is not to say she was not angry. She was angry. Very. Exactly why he was not sure. Unless it was his scent bottles upset her — but why should they do that? She did not have to fear competition from him. In the past she had made things not just as good; much better.

He was too tired to eat. He went to bed immediately, even forgetting to hang up the keys as he had been asked to. They stayed in his pocket all night, as he stayed in his bed all night, unmolested. He woke when she came in, his hand throbbing from the cut he'd almost forgotten. But she did not come to his room. Even the ache in his hand did not bother him for long; soon, thankfully, oblivion took him.

As for Grace, having filled herself up with beer, in neutral male company, she arrived back to find her empty kitchen as if mocking her. Thi mother wor the better woman it might have said. Belt up, she answered, mechanically; assuming it was Betsy speaking there was as little — or as much — between them that evening as there had been between her and Terry. Though ravenously hungry — she, too, had gone without supper — she scarcely had the energy to take cheese and butter from the fridge and cut herself a hunk of bread; noticed only in passing that the keys had not been hung on their usual hook on the dresser below the ram's head. The spasm of irritation she felt was succeeded almost at once by a forgotten, unfamiliar longing to lay her head for simple comfort on some soft and motherly breast. (And to this, she heard herself saying — she was definitely a little drunk — to this am us come to.)

Only very occasionally now did the unsought, unwelcome

images of what Terry had been making disturb her. It was not that there weren't things wrong with them, she had been thinking; all the same — and this was the whole problem — he had caught something that she'd felt she'd lost for the moment, worse, without even knowing she had lost it. To add insult to injury he had done so using the very casting sand, even, in some sense, the techniques, with which she herself had been trying to flee this impasse. He had caught the solidity of glass, for instance, its crystalline earthiness, its sedimentary origins; but how had he done so? In the way he had used colour? In the way the glass had as if folded itself into the mould with all the awkward elegance of pleat and corrugation? At the same time there was the airy bubble inside it. She could not endure that he had reached such a thing so easily; how, she wondered, could he have done it so easily? And how could she ask such a question? When she of all people understood that such things were reached against the odds; were never, in fact, easy. Damn him, she thought. Or Betsy thought. Or both of them thought; given the vicious weight to the words — DAMN HIM — it could have been both of them together.

Terry had gone to bed so tired he even left his clothes on. He only recollected the keys still sitting in his pocket when at some point he rolled over on them. When he woke, though, they were the first thing he thought of. He hunted in his jeans first, with momentary panic — for a brief moment, thought they had gone altogether. It was from instinct rather than memory he located them, at last, under the pillow. Presumably he had put them there? After a while, though still fuddled with sleep, he remembered rolling on them, so assumed he must have.

In which case, assuming they were under his head all night, the problem was how the lehr came, next morning, to be open. Both Grace and Terry could swear they had left it closed. They had gone down through the wood together. She asked him as they set out if he still had the keys; just nodded when he assented, instead of giving him the scolding he expected for not having hung them in the proper place. The door of the glasshouse was locked, of course, as expected. The eye of the furnace was closed up, the way they left it. Everything, in fact, was just as it should have been. Apart from the lehr.

Grace reached it first. Perhaps she was still hoping against hope that the disaster could somehow be averted, that not all the pieces had cooled down too fast for the glass to have attained its balance. She had been able to see, at least, the moment they entered the glasshouse, that the contents of the shelves had not been touched. Terry's scent bottles, for instance, thicker and heavier than the rest of the pieces, still stood towards the rear of the top shelf where he had placed them to cool more slowly. Grace put up a hand. She only touched one of them with a finger, but that was enough. She done it on purpose, thought Terry, unfairly, when it shattered; more or less blew up. As a result of that explosion, everything, virtually, went with it; the shards split open other pieces as it met them, set up echo and re-echo of shatter and splinter of harmless yet lethal tinkle, finding further echoes from the crunch and smash of glass on the floor beneath their feet. Grace had to duck to avoid a faceful.

It couldn't of been no one else but Grace did it. I saw her face. Last night and this morning. Yet how could it of been? I can't see no sense to it. I had the keys to the fucking place. She didn't.

The floor in front of the lehr's so covered in glass, it's a wonder our shoes aren't cut to ribbons. And there's this stench; like all the rotten food you'd ever eaten. I tell you what I feels when I sees all that stuff exploding, starting with those things I made last night, that I worked out my guts on. I wants to smash up the whole fucking glasshouse. There and then. For two pins, I'd of grabbed up a punty, there wouldn't have been a bleeding goblet whole by the time I'd finished. That's what happens when you see something smashed up, let alone hear it, it shows you everything can be smashed to pieces, every last bit of it. And I tell you what else it shows me; that I've had it up to here now, one way and another; that one touch more aggro I'll get Dave and the rest of the bike boys up like he wanted. Dave's not the type for art appreciation, a smash-up's more like it. A crash, bang an' wallop. Did he think there'd be a safe full of lolly to follow? If so he's in for some surprises, but then he's not the only one, so's Grace in for some surprises.

The glass was one thing; the stench another. Also *she* still stood on the furnace, of course, looking down on us, on the breakage. I could even have sworn at one point that the incubus I dropped yesterday had been remade and replaced. But when I looked closer I saw that it had not been. No doubt it was all, dozzie, a trick of the September light.

This is not a trick of the light, though. The card underneath no longer says Witch's Piece. It has written, in red, in letters that writhe like a mouth mocking (thi mouth? mi mouth? Con't tell which, these days thi will not speak separate from mi) words that till now belonged only in my head, your head; my mouth, your mouth. We are back to that beginning; do you never let up? Do you never trust me? Words that have no power now, you have destroyed them or I have. That they are still true is besides the point, I think, as I pull down the card, tear it up, hoping no one else sees it. Whether 'tis or 'tis not, this is what it said: WEDLOCK IS PADLOCK.

It's what happens to that supercooled liquid, glass, in the circumstance. (Amidst her glittering fragments Grace herself appears fragmented; another trick of the light, I daresay, which is splitting off everything, you can't tell transparent from opacity, wholeness from little pieces.) Now what? In the mining museum I copied down a rhyme about the fate of miners who stole ore from their fellows. We, I guess, have also stolen something, we seem in the same fix, pretty much.

> *But the third time that he commits such theft*
> *Shall have the knife through his hand to the heft*
> *Into the stone and there till death shall stand,*
> *Unless he loose himself by cutting off his hand.*

The only difference, apart from not knowing what we stole exactly, is that it's not necessarily our hands that have been nailed. It could be that in each of our cases, cutting off the nailed part, whatever it is, might not just be mutilating but as fatal as not cutting it off. It's a lottery; a different lottery for each of us, I suspect, lover. Like everything else in this bloody world, it's a matter of choose your poison.

Chapter Eleven

"'Tis the last effect of the fire . . ."

The young rooks were grown now in the wood above the cottage. But though when they flew they looked just like their parents, they didn't sound like the parents. All three of them noticed — not one of them said — how the harsh notes of the adults were cut by the higher notes of their young ones.

Throughout the latter part of September, it rained incessantly. The trees, the fields, the stone in the drystone walls, on the walls of houses, grew ever darker and more sodden. In the breaks between showers, dismally sharp light drew lethal gleams from the wet roads; from pools and puddles of water. The path down to the glasshouse not so much a path as a stream in places, Grace went out and bought herself the first pair of gumboots she had owned since leaving Somerset. She also bought the first pair Terry had ever owned, town boy as he was. Up to the ankles sometimes in the blackish mud, she was alarmed to find herself wishing it was red. A wish she quashed no less firmly than she quashed Terry's tendency these days to cheek her not openly but slyly, as if he hoped she wouldn't notice. But she did notice. One day, staring at some of the little iridescent bowls Jas was still making them turn out, he'd muttered, half under his breath, that he knew where he'd like to put them. She turned round and boxed his ears. In just the same way her father used to box her ears.

They were at that time working particularly hard. It was about all they did do; after what had happened about all they dared do. The ravages to the glass was the least of their problems; it took work only to replace their losses. Terry even made more of the big scent bottles that had so agitated Grace.

Though she looked at them and said nothing, she put one sample in the next batch she sent out to a gallery. They rang up and asked for more; a message which Jas relayed without comment to both of them. "Get on with it then," was all she said. The sense of triumph that he felt — it in no way ignored Grace, he acknowledged he'd never have got so far without her — mollified him for a few days. His lurking fury, the longing to smash everything in sight, retreated slightly, if not entirely.

In the same order came requests for what Jas called Grace's thunder and lightning bowls, that is the almost opaque black ones streaked with white lightning she had virtually given up making. She went back to making them. Also some that were lighter, cloudier, altogether more delicate-looking. (Was the storm breaking, Jas wondered? God only knew what would follow.) She stopped all her experiments fusing glass for the moment. The layered, sedimentary hunks — in no way had she yet caught the ordered chaos of actual geological strata — sat on the supply shelves where she left them. Every now and then she would pick one piece up, weigh it in her hand and consider for a while, before setting it back down.

"Feel like braining someone?" Terry asked her. To which she replied as he'd expected, "Yes, you." Not a flicker in her voice or face to show if she was joking.

One day she turned round to Jas, who was just shouldering his bag, ready to leave for his lodgings, and said, "Has it occurred to you we should begin from the beginning? We should make our own glass. Before we start making anything from it."

"According to that argument," he said, "you should start by making your own ash and sand."

"I'd do that," she said, "if it were possible."

"Once you accused me of wanting to play God, Gracie," he said. "But I doubt if you remember."

"Of course I don't remember." Her voice was even.

"Well what about now? Aren't *you* wanting to play God?"

"Goddess," she said, without polemic; she was simply putting him right on a matter of fact.

The business of making glass did interest Jas, however. Having read the histories he knew a bit more about it, academically speaking, than she did. On this first evening since he had moved out that they had spent together, they sat in a pub, eating crisps and Cornish pasties and discussing the properties of silica, potash, sand, manganese, flint, the necessary for glassmaking. In the end they concluded — or rather Jas concluded — that, given the technical problems, not least of getting the proportions of each substance right, and of needing another furnace for it — they could hardly put their rather crude mixture in the same crucible as the one they were using for their commercially acquired cullet — the idea was not practicable. Jas did not know, though, if Grace accepted all these arguments. Let alone if it had occurred to her that this was the first real conversation they'd had since early in their marriage.

He almost put his arm about her. He did actually touch her arm. Though she stiffened she did not draw away. For a moment she looked him in the eye in a way which might have been meant to be provocative; or equally, being Grace, might not. She did not know either. Any more than she knew what she felt about him in that moment, or any other moment come to that, what with her recent eruptions of anger, of passion, of confusion that had nothing to do with the here and now.

Jas meanwhile, felt more reckless, more exhilarated by the uncertainties than he had felt in years. The mingled sense of threat and invitation emanating both from her and her glasshouse was an attraction to him, if anything. As he also knew, or suspected, that these confusions of threat and rivalry, that ought to have been centrifugal, driving everyone apart, were in fact centripetal, pulling together; all of them, even Terry.

He took to joking, about "Our friendly local poltergeist. The one slaughtered Matrimony," he suggested, ironically; "Also the one that opened up the lehr? Now you know," he said, "why Reg always insisted on a witch's piece."

Neither of the others reminded him that the lehr door had been left open after the making of the witch's piece. Perhaps both of them dared hope, as he did, that it hadn't yet had time to do its work. That the malevolence had, perhaps, been having its final fling. Certainly he was reassured, he could not help it, by the sight of the monstrous object still sitting atop the furnace. It's wonderful, he thought, both then and still more after, when the folly of it became too apparent, how the human mind gets to contain, even organise the intolerable if it has to.

Where's Betsy these days? Do I want her? Do I need to want her? I have the feeling she is now just where I choose to keep her, aren't you Betsy, mi dozzie? In my head. On top of the furnace. I feel contained and complete. I hum as I work. If the others don't like it, that is their problem.

One day, for instance, I have to go down with Terry to the garage at Cromford to get a tyre fixed. There's a joker there always gets a bit cheeky; today he says such things as, "I know yow ladies olways liike 'em 'ard," to which I give back as good as I get; and all the time Terry, whose eye I'd blacked for much less, is gawping away behind me. I don't think he knew I'd such words in me. Nor did I come to that.

"You come up to my place," I tell the man as we are leaving. "I'll teach you how to put in another kind of air. I'll teach you to blow glass. Among other things."

"I'll tek yow up on that, me duck. Yow'll see me coom by termorrow," he promises. "'ll be worth a pint of bitter."

But of course he does not come by. And nor does anyone expect it.

The glasshouse smells of glasshouse these days. The kitchen smells of food. Sometimes I've cooked it. Occasionally Terry has. Not Jas. He's sulking. He never comes near us. Sometimes I wish he would come, if only to eat supper.

It helped, of course, that they had something specific to work for, Jas' open morning for the locals. Not the locals he and Grace got on with so well in the pub down on the main road — he invited them of course, for the sake of public relations, but he did not rate them commercially as he rated the other locals.

He spent a whole weekend and some evenings taking the invitations himself, round Timbersley and further. The alarm on people's faces when they found this tall man in boots and jeans and anorak looming on their very doorsteps, smiling his man-in-the-moon smile — he smiles a bit like Ken Dodd, one said, not very accurately — was soon dispelled by his charming patter. Everyone knew of the glasshouse. Most of them were curious about it. "Even if they don't buy anything this time," Jas said, "it's coming up to Christmas, they'll remember afterwards. And they'll have well-heeled friends. They're likely to tell some of them about us."

Grace, who had grown up among neighbours almost all farmers, knew nothing about such people; they were businessmen mostly, some active, some retired, manufacturers of shoes or underwear, coal managers, railway managers, commuting to Derby or Nottingham. All the same, she was impressed by the number Jas seemed to have persuaded that there could be no better way of spending a Saturday morning in October than drinking wine next to the local dump while watching her and Terry glassblowing.

Work only. Nothing but work. Sometimes the one thing I wish for is that the boy would go away. For his sake as well as my sake. I remember Reg sacking a bloke once because they got on each other's nerves. He said quarrels are dangerous in a glasshouse. But how am I to get rid of Terry? Even if he does so rub me up I have to clench my hands not to belt him. Sometimes I do belt him. I tell him he earned it for being cheeky, which he is, or else for being clumsy which he's not except I make him nervous. All the same he drives me crazy; for the way he gives me often a ducking sideways look, as if he both hates and fears, yet can't keep his eyes off me; for his air of pigheaded resentment. It's got so even his hair looks like it resents me. I never knew such a thing before. I don't know how to handle her. No more than I know how to handle the feelings Betsy gives me. No more the feelings Jas gives me neither. Sometimes I think Terry only maddens me so much because of Jas. Because it's getting like I can't do without Jas, and I cannot accept or endure it and no more can Betsy. Who'll have her own back if she's able, won't you, dozzie, I don't doubt it.

Maybe it's because I'm so tired these days. It's not the work, I'm used to work. It's more not sleeping. And when I do sleep, dreaming such hard dreams they wear me to a frazzle. The same dreams, usually. I'm shut in the dark inside that level up on the Brendons. Or I'm at mum's funeral again, seeing them lower her coffin into the rectangular red hole. With Betsy muttering beside me. And not knowing if it's her or me being lowered into that hole, or neither.

One morning I even woke up knowing just why mum stayed with dad and not wanting to know that I knew it. Because she really loved him, that's why, that was the fact of the matter, the ultimate treachery, the one for which we shouldn't forgive her. Terry got his black eye the morning after. I pretended I hadn't given it him on purpose, that my hand slipped; but it hadn't. As he knew. As I did. I wish he'd return the blow sooner and that's a fact. I deserved it. But all he did was show his teeth like a rat and then look at me back and forth as if he was about to burst out weeping. My head full of gleeful laughter, I was saying to myself meanwhile, "That's it, treat 'em rough, the way I did my girl; the one wor scragged wi' me, nor I for one moment rued it."

I try not to listen. I make the whole thing a joke, as much as I'm able, seeing that eye swell up, the poor lummock looks sulkier by the minute. Jas is out at the time, soon as he comes back we're both pretending an accident happened. This hateful collusion makes it worse, somehow. "You don't know your own strength, dozzie," says Jas smiling. When I look at him in horror — "Dozzie?" I ask faintly — he adds airily, "Just a Derbyshire dialect word. Don't you think it's neat?"

All the same I take Terry into my bed that night. I do it for revenge mostly. Though I'm fair enough to do it in such a way he can refuse if he wants to. I don't know why he accepts me. Unless he, too, wants to take out on us our mutual humiliation.

I teach the lad one more thing this night, it's certain. Perhaps it's the last thing I teach him in his life. At the same time I teach it to myself. I am both professor and pupil. That lovemaking turned to hatemaking is still worse than the kind of love that mixes desire with indifference.

Next morning, I wake before the lad does. I lie alongside him looking up at the sloping ceiling. It's as if I inhabit the room all over like ether, am not in bed only, own the eyes of many others. From no particular location I eye our clothes in heaps before the empty stone fireplace — I can hardly believe now the passion in which we tore them off where we were standing. I eye the damp place on the wall where the gutter keeps overflowing, the striped rug on the uneven floorboards; our two bodies prone on the bed, not touching by so much as a finger.

The boy's body, sprawled as if dead, makes me think of the baby that died inside me. The thought puts me back in my eyes and skull and anger; I push him out of my bed at once, still sleeping. Crying out at such a vicious awakening, he puts a hand over his head in self protection, lies as gawky and puny as a terrified fledgling. Though his eye is still more swollen I don't feel sorry in the slightest. That damn witch's screaming for joy, instantly her joy's my joy — is't not a good sight, to see t'ugly lout laid low? I burst out laughing.

From now my dreams are not of graves or coffins; I dream of helpless things, infant things, fledglings and leverets and unlicked kittens, naked new-born mice; that die between my hands or at my feet, no matter how hard I try to save they.

Maybe I'll buy the lad some new jeans to make up, the seat's almost out of his old ones. Maybe I'll send him and Jas away and live alone in my glasshouse in the wood like the woman in Jas' story. But if anyone comes cracking my glass, she won't get away with it, no she won't, I'll have her for dinner, probably. And maybe for breakfast even.

Tell me why, dozzie, as in the minute before dying, my whole life keeps flashing past me? Because I'm not dying, death's not my luck. Her's for past, older people like my dad and mum. Her's for the young and vulnerable like Terry. Just the same, I keep thinking, if it were me, which way would I choose, to have they dig me a deep red hole like mum's or feed me into a curtained trap like dad's? Everyone knows the fire's down there waiting to be fed, but they don't let you see her, maybe they ought to.

But then I think I'm more frightened of fire than most, in my work I must be. At the same time I am less frightened of it than I am of that earth and its creatures. Which I also work in.

I want both how can I have they? Once I choose I'm yours, dozzie, or you're mine, isn't that what we've wanted, isn't that why you plague me?

Would you have plagued another I'd like to know? What was it in me that called you? What was in you called me? It was not your death or the reason for it, you lying hinny. Did you hang for melting your coins? Or because they thought you some kind of witch, and rightly? Seems just as likely you plagued others all your life and died soberly in your bed thereafter.

You're like glass, I think, I can see right through you. Which makes you the real fraud, the mystery. Clarity in dirt, what can I be thinking?

What you are made of does not tell me who you are. I will never know, your smooth flank will always repel me, the way the flanks of my horses never did; that left the taste of their sweat on my palm when I brushed they.

It was just as well we were busy all these weeks. I did not feel like thinking any more than I do at the moment. Not that I can avoid it, now, having all the time in the world for it. Whereas then I was so busy that for almost a whole week before the open day I hardly touched a blowing iron or punty, I was reorganising the glasshouse, putting up more display shelves, for instance, seconds on one side, good stuff on the other. Also it was me got in all the food and drink for the party, Grace not having time for such domestic things. Most of the food came from the cheese shop in Wirksworth. Not just cheese either. I got hummus and taramosalata, onion bahjis, parathas and samosas, those chilly looking Greeks and Asians hanging round Derby seem to have spread their goodies to the furthest outputs. (Most of them have Derby accents, which is something else I can't get used to. When I left England, it wasn't like the USA, people who looked different sounded different also. And you couldn't get much above faggots in places like Matlock and Wirksworth.) Of course it's all just sprats to catch herring; as I used to say to Reg years ago, when I was trying to persuade him, too, to get new customers into his glasshouse.

He didn't listen to me, though Grace tends to, on such matters. Yet I am missing the old bastard badly. Or perhaps I am just missing the days when blowing glass was a simple matter. (Before women got in on the act I'd say, if I dared to. Do dare, so long as I'm not in Grace's hearing.)

But if the edibles change in these places, the original people don't seem to. Please don't get me wrong. I like them. Much more than I used to like the people who came visiting my parents. These days, maybe, I'd find even that lot more tolerable, less sure of themselves anyway, like my mother, back in the sixties, smiling benignly on our music and our gurus, whereas she thought sense was coming to the world at last.

I like the wholesomeness and niceness of the people who come to our open day. I like their noisy good humour, their tentative expressions in relation to the glasshouse, their look of having grown inside the weather. The wrinkles on the faces of old women are soft as tissue paper — there's too much sun for such softness in California. I love their dangerously ignorant, almost religious innocence; they have the pinkness, the pious merriment of nuns and deacons.

Who'd think that for centuries men hacked rock, coughed blood, here, beneath their very feet and still could not make enough to live on? It's not they don't know about such things, these people. They study them even, they're all very keen on local history. There's a group of ladies behind me talking about an evening class they're attending on the history of the

Derbyshire leadmines. Someone even just mentioned the word unemployment. But then, during a sudden silence, there comes up from the road a great roar of motor bikes, on their way up to Matlock Bath, most likely.

"Just listen to them," says someone. "I hardly dare set foot in Matlock Bath on a Saturday," says another.

A man with a red nose and beard, who's been knocking back the red wine I notice, proclaims, in a Scots accent, "Don't talk to me about unemployment. Don't expect me to feel sorry for the young yobs. Where do you think they get the money from for their Yamahas and their Suzukis, their Nortons and their Harley Davidsons?" One up to him, I think, for knowing there are Harley Davidsons.

I like nothing else about this guy. Not least the way he's eyeing Grace, who looks fantastic today to my eyes. Perhaps after all I prefer metal-boned Athenes to soft-fleshed Ledas; perhaps the odd pliant woman I've picked up in the pub lately and taken to my solitary room, perhaps even these well-clad locals responding so profitably this morning to my pullulating male hormones, have got my libido back into working order. So that when I look at Grace, like a female Vulcan today at her sweaty labours, mistress of her liquid metal, her seething furnace, she appears so superbly dangerous, to hell, I think, with not only Leda but Athene. Forgetting to be a good salesman, briefly, I glower at the Scotsman; he looks like he just came for the booze, anyway, he's not going to be buying anything. And I feel, I swear it, such a stirring in my loins suddenly, it could be embarrassing in this public situation, if I did not stand with my crotch concealed by one of Grace's thunder and lightning vases.

Yet more women are advancing with things they want to buy; cheap things of course, but who's complaining. I smile and congratulate them on their choice, keep a weather eye on their kids — kids and glasshouses are not, to my mind, a healthy combination — with the other half of my mind hear that the Scotsman is still banging on about the awfulness of the bikers. Only his wife dares suddenly to contradict him.

"I asked one of the shopkeepers in Matlock Bath if they

caused any trouble," she says hesitatingly. "She said not in the least. They may look dreadful, she said, but she's had far more trouble with some of the old age pensioners on day trips from Derby."

I smile at her, encouragingly. Not least because her Scots husband having nudged his wife to make her shut up, turns his back on her smartly. No one else appears to be listening either; maybe no one dares to listen. You can identify dirty devils in black leather. The others are harder to check on. They may hide in your backyard. They may even be called husband.

But then isn't everything deceptive? Looking at me now, at magnificent Grace, at Terry spruced up in the new jeans she bought him, who'd dare not think we were some great big happy family?

"Is that your son?" asks the Scotsman's wife, who has latched on to me, gratefully. "Is that your son working with your wife? He does look a bit like her."

She has to be bloody well joking. But then I suppose it's always been true of everywhere that one half of any given country doesn't know who the other half are and vice versa. And no matter how many Johnny Ruskins bewail the fact, they never will know, either,

Jas works hard at it, I grant him. From eleven o'clock on the dot when they started coming, he ain't stopped passing round wine and tit bits, wrapping up dishes and goblets in return for the notes he clamps in our cash box. Explaining all the while what Grace and I are up to. "You mean glass *melts*?" I heard someone saying. I shouldn't laugh, less than two years ago I didn't know nothing, neither. Next moment he's listening politely to some people who've seen glassblowing in Venice, so wanted to tell *him* how we did it.

They lap up his attentions mostly. Even the men seem to, like Jas is a good bloke really, and if he's a bit arty, most like you have to be arty for the job he's into. As for the women, they want to eat him, the way they hang on to every fucking word he gives them, I bet all their knickers are dripping. I bet they envy Grace like crazy. I bet they never guess it's me the assistant what gets to put it in; or any road, used to.

Some of these people of course, I recognise. There's the bloke from over the road, his fat wife bought three of the iridescent dishes and can't stop unwrapping the paper to peek at them. (Judging by the way she looks at him, I ain't sure but what like all the rest, it's Jas she'd sooner be unwrapping.)

Then there's the red-nosed Scots git and his wife who isn't wearing a kilt this morning. It's quite cold outside, she's got a thick tweed coat she don't take off, even when everyone else is complaining of the heat and begging for somewhere to hang their macs and jackets; another way in which Jas manages to be obliging. She keeps picking up things and saying "Look at this, Dick, isn't it lovely?" When Dick keeps knocking back the booze, taking not a blind bit of notice, she puts it down and moves on to the next piece. "Isn't this one a beauty, Dick?" She might as well save her breath. He holds the purse strings clearly. He ain't in a mood for buying, just for drinking.

There's a lot of kids here. Jas don't trust 'em, no more I do with their clean socks an' shiny hair. Even the ones in jeans look so shiny they might be polished. They look like the kids in the Ladybird books we had in the juniors, that my mum bought me sometimes when she got worried about my education. I used to look at them in amazement, there'd Jane be helping mum do the washing up and Peter helping dad clean the car, those buggers might of lived in Timbuctoo as far as I was concerned.

I tell you what the Peter and Jane books'd of said, if it had been me writing. Things like "Peter's nicked some fags for mummy just like she asked him." Or "Jane's getting daddy in her knickers tonight" (which had happened to some poor little bint in my class, it turned out when the welfare took her). Or "Peter is putting Mummy to bed, she's plastered." (At least Grace is sober usually.) Or "Peter is a very good boy today, he puts it into mummy just the way she told him." (In this case I leave you to fucking imagine who's playing mum and who's playing junior.)

Today of course Junior, in his new jeans, is so well-behaved he ain't hardly said a word, all morning. Not even when the people started talking about the bikers, like they weren't proper humans. Jas meanwhile makes out he runs the bleeding outfit; Grace is the ever-so-talented artist. Yours truly's the fucking assistant. OK, I am the assistant. But who wants to keep having their nose rubbed in it, by Lord High and Mighty in his little silk neckscarf and cowboy boots? (Don't he know he's out of date? These days Rambo'd be more like it.)

Still some people seem to notice my existence. There's two old birds I rate. They love the glassblowing as much as I do. They keep pushing their way to the front and standing just behind me, asking me questions which I do my best to answer. I didn't never know there were old birds like these ones, kind of beat-up versions of Miss Marple on telly, only more so. One's thin, got eyes sunk in her head, behind huge, jutting, wrinkled, blue-veined eyelids. The other's fat, her hair's so fine and white and thin you can see the pink scalp through it. Though they're doddery enough, though they can't hardly stand up by the look of it, they won't take the chairs no one offers, they keep on pushing nearer and nearer to see what Grace and me are up to. Times I think I'm going to give 'em a crack with the punty if I'm not very careful. And all the time they're asking questions in high, fluting, wavering voices, a bit like the Queen's, only older.

"Look, Effie," they says, or, "Look May," then repeat what Grace or Jas or yours truly just told them, as if to make sure their friend's not missed a single word of wisdom. And all the time they're knocking back the booze and nibbling stuff off the plates of goodies. It's the thin one, I notice, eats by far the most; maybe the fat one keeps her short at home, she looks like the one that owns the green stuff, I mean the boodle.

But actually I likes 'em. I keep thinking I hope I enjoys myself that much when I get old, if I get to be that old, ever. The whole sodding day they're the only thing I like. For all it's such a success, for all Jas has flogged plenty, bum stuff and good stuff. He sold one of Grace's thunder bowls for 175 nicker; it should of been £75 only the man misheard him. Seeing he wrote one seven five in his chequebook without blinking so much as an eyelash, Jas wasn't going to stop him. The bloke went away a bit startled, the way he gets thanked ten times over.

Jas seems to be taking a lot of money. That's the only thing to be said for it. In all other respects it's intolerable. You can scarcely breathe now, let alone hear yourself think, let alone blow glass. He seems to think it's his duty to entertain the whole of Derbyshire. It'll be a miracle if we get through without some damn kid starting a holocaust. Not that, here, we aren't familiar with holocausts. Nor that they don't have their merits, holocausts.

I say to Terry at one point that I can't stand it. He looks astonished. My usual way of making complaints these days is to swipe at him, no questions. I say nothing to Jas, however. Even when we take a break from working I can't get near him for customers; female customers, mostly. I don't catch him looking at me much, except to make technical explanations. Even Betsy'll be hanging on him the way he is going; maybe she is already, maybe he knows it, he thinks he's the cat's whiskers, doesn't he, the bastard. I drink wine, and watch him. Betsy is watching him. We see his mouth moving. We cannot hear a word he's saying. There are red spots on his cheek, this time our furnace made them, perhaps he imagines getting under our armour, thinks virginity's once more for the losing. (Is't that your thinking, is't mine, what's the difference, cooms to the same thing, don't it?)

I take gulp upon gulp of red wine. To hell with everything and everyone; we make delicate adjustments meanwhile to the stem of a Reg-type goblet. It's all right when our armour's on, God help you if we take it off, we are thinking. How we'll start is by snatching back everything we've always wanted from you.

I see Grace getting a bit boozed. I see her looking at Jas, when he don't notice. I see him looking at her when she don't. It'd be obvious to a baby the way things are going. At the end of the day when we've finished clearing up, we put the remains of the nosh and the wine in the back of the old banger and head for Grace's place for a booze-up.

It's the first time since Jas walked out he's been here of an evening. I don't like the ways he looks at Grace, nor how she looks at him, neither. She's pleased with all that boodle, she makes no bones to hide it. There's plenty of booze left over. More booze than food to be honest. Grace was pissed to start with, soon I'm pissed as she is. Nothing's left but getting pissed, the way things seem to be going. Not that I couldn't celebrate on my own account; those Derbyshire biddies bought up my scent bottles, all of 'em. What they puts in is up to them, and might smell worse than sheep shit.

The smell of Grace tonight is another I don't fancy. I never saw her like this before; never. There's something wicked about it. She's the most pissed of the three of us, she's good as dancing round the table. Rubbing herself all over Jas one minute, shameless, the next minute rubbing herself all over me. Looking at her smarmy and sexy, he thinks he's playing her nicely. What he don't see is what I see; that actually it's her playing him. That she always has played him the way she wanted, the way she plays me also. Like she did the very first night when he were standing in the fucking doorway.

If I'd wanted to come off worst in the game of mummies and daddies, I couldn't of gone about it better. I see it in the way they're looking at each other — oh yes I bloody see it. If I could of stood steady on my pins for two whole seconds I'd of upped and clocked them. Or maybe it were just nerve not legs what I was lacking. I had good enough reason to clock them. It's not before the fucking infant time, I realise, sure enough, Jas begins to talk to me the next minute just like I were his bleeding infant.

"Isn't it after your bedtime, pal?" he says. I can't hardly believe what I am hearing. I looks round the kitchen for help, but that ram's head is glaring at me as usual, tonight he gets to turn my bowels to water. And Grace, God help us, is giggling. Like I never imagined Grace giggling. She's looking me straight in the eye, giggling like some loony; she ain't who she is usually, she's turned into another.

"Do what you're told, dozzie;" she can't hardly speak for giggles. "Didn't you hear what daddy told you?"

Jas looks stunned on hearing this, I give him. Not that it stops him leching her for long, the next moment he looks like a man Joan Collins made a pass at. As for me I'm lost, the bloody witch/bitch nicked the sense clean out of me. Mummies and daddies, I mumble. Daddies and mummies. Peter and Jane. I'm so bloody pissed I can't do no more about it; I stagger to my feet, swipe at them vaguely, then pass out under the table.

They put me to bed between them. Leastways I think they must of. Seeing as it's on my bed I find myself later, not that they'd bothered to undress me. Judging by the stink I'd done some puking; it don't seem to have put them off, all the signs are next morning they'd not even bothered to get themselves upstairs, that daddy got his oats off mummy right under the kitchen table. As if he hadn't meant to from the first moment. What chance have the likes of me, against the likes of them?

There are three kinds of people. Grace is one kind, the kind doesn't even bleed when they lose their virginity. Which is not to say they don't have to work hard for it, nor that they can't use a stroke or two of luck. People like me, on the other hand, don't even need luck. We can land in the cooler, you still couldn't call us losers except in the sense of the things we never discover; the passion and the fear we have to imagine — or steal — from other people. Not like the third kind, the Terrys. The Terrys of this world are never anything but losers.

Apart from talent, I give him talent, what hope did he have, poor little sod? OK, we seem kinder now than a century or so back, once we took the whole lives of his lot the day they came into it, which was the end of them before they'd even started. (What was the life expectancy of a miner, for instance? Let alone a crossing-sweeper?) We're more subtle these days. We just steal all their hope. And when they think they've won it back for a moment, we let them celebrate for a day, wait till their backs are turned and give them a crack on the head to remind them.

Which is in bad taste, you might think, in the circumstance. But then I've got plenty of time right now to reflect on the nature of bad taste. By this I don't mean the kind of taste I had in my mouth the morning that Terry erupted. That taste was the result of our long night's excesses; who can blame the kid for freaking out? Though there was something about Terry made you want to kick him in the balls in the first place, it's not to say he should have been given what we gave him. Not for one single second. You could say it was a measure of his rotten luck, that having gotten to be Oedipus, in a manner of speaking, at least having gotten to fuck mummy, he never got to thump daddy on the head before or after; on the contrary it was daddy who did the thumping.

(What Grace thought about it wasn't clear then or later. Why should I have cared what she thought, all the time I was buried in her? All the time I was making free of those delights I had so wilfully abandoned? Most women, even the softest, have wire wool for pubic hair — how come that Grace, my lady Vulcan, retains a silky, exuberant bush almost reddish in colour, more than long enough to wind around my fingers? She even bled for me again, much more generously than last time — if it was for a different reason, I accepted it gladly, gratefully, as a token of her — and my — surrender.

Whether she'd agree she'd surrendered is something else I can't be certain. I only know that she's tougher than I am and always has been. In relation to Terry, for instance, I can imagine her saying, 'every man his own master; if you can't stand the heat, get out of the kitchen.' Yet she loved the runt in her way, to judge by her face after. Which I knew. I'd always known. In the final analysis that's why he got it, and why I find myself pleading guilty, rather than innocent.)

Coming into Grace's bed that night, later, after tending Terry (almost tenderly, she noticed), after their furious writhing all over the kitchen floor, Jas said it felt like homecoming.

"It weren't I ever told you to leave home though, was it?" Grace responded.

"But you never asked me to come back, did you?"

"I never asked anything of anyone," she told him, her voice very Somerset and deeper than usual.

"That, lover," he said, "was always the problem."

Grace knew what he meant, in one way; in another she didn't. Never having cared for homecomings. Besides she was too drunk, so drunk that lying in her bed, in his arms, she floated. He felt that she floated. Her flesh, at first touch, felt at once hard as iron and insubstantial. To her he felt if not hard exactly, as insubstantial. Even she accepted him between need and drink and demon. Was it surrender after all these years? Or just more taking? Either way she might or might not blame herself for what this consequence of need and drink and demon did to Terry, both on Saturday night and Sunday morning.

That's fond talk, dozzie, what's thi clacking — did thi not bleed for a warning? Wor not mi had thi follow the dance in thi glasshouse, noon after. Wor not mi, also, shut door on thi sense, set thi burrowin' inside thi liike a mowdiwarp knows his own country. Wor not mi little lady another, that had all t' men betray her, yet would not hearken and died of it sooner? I tell thi, Grace *is* mi, thi sense and body. *Be* this same sense and this body, sets thi bleeding first, then puts thi to glass dance on t'morrow, never reck whur it do lead thi. Nor were glass dance part of bed dance, neither, not the way t' nesh wherret thought it.

Did I make the Witch's Piece then? No I did not. And for good reason. Wasn't it always heads we intended breaking, from the moment I hefted open thi door, caught t' whiff of thi leek and coney puddin'? From the moment I heard thi voice in my head and hearkened to it? From the moment I gave thi questions and answer? Till it's got so's I can't tell t' Good Lord from Old Nick, question from answer. Leave alone his flesh from mi flesh, surrender from taking. Mi bleeding from thi bleeding. Blood flow from ebbing.

★

It were lucky nobody expects any work of me on Sunday. I felt like death went and gobbled me up, for tea, breakfast and dinner. I don't suppose those others felt any better, not that I saw them, I daresay they were snuggled up together in her bed, fuck them. Of course I didn't let the thought stop me. T'other way about, it drove me. I walked all the way down the hill without seeing a living soul, and got the train to Matlock Bath twenty minutes later.

I didn't hold much hope of it. If the bikers were along here yesterday, stood to reason they wouldn't be back today. But maybe it were another lot of fucking bikers. It took me three boozers to find Dave's bike but that were all it took me. Inside, the way he were leaning on the bar, the way the mate of his was leaning even harder, it looked like I weren't the only one had a rough Saturday night, and still rougher Sunday morning. I went over to him, never mind it. "How's things, cock?" I says all cheerful. He don't look like he recognises me at first, another day I'd of scarpered the way he glares me. But today I weren't going to scarper; I went on the way I intended.

"It's your mate, Terry," I remind him. "The one what works in the glasshouse. The place you says you'd like to take a look at."

He don't seem to want to now. He's going to tell me to piss off, any minute, but seeing how he looked like Jas I wasn't having any. My head jangling and thudding, I were a bloody madman, I buys a pint of bitter and bangs it down in front of him. "Now you listen to me, mate," I says to him. "Don't tell me you're going to miss the best fucking smash-up of a lifetime."

That had him interested; especially when he got to hear about the new loot in Grace's cashbox, what the three of us might share out between us, before I set my road for London. As for Grace and Jas, my gaffers, I couldn't see them turning up on a Sunday, not with their likely hangovers; it wouldn't be heads, only glass we'd be smashing. That were all right, then, he'd never gone for GBH, Dave tells me, "That's grievous bodily to yow, lad," he added. "You a bleeding pacifist?" I asks him. I don't know why the hell the bugger thought I needed telling. Mind you, I don't think he believes me when I calls it the best outing ever. But there ain't nothing much else he could do here on a Sunday, once he's done the rounds of the boozers and wiped out the space invaders. (He weren't the type for the museum and the Lover's Walk, were he?)

I rode the back of his bike to the bottom of the hill after. He had to drop me there, so I could fetch the key from the cottage.

Dave and his mate were to give me half an hour or so. I'd hoped for greater numbers; but I reckoned the three of us was enough for a good bit of aggro. We could smash the glass to smithereens, for instance, wreck the sandblaster and the lehr, for instance, fill the woods full of cullet, for instance. If Jas turned up, the two of them could keep him off me. (Dave and his mate would put in some GBH all right, I thought, if they had to.) I'd told them how to get across the river, what track to go up; and so on.

But the key weren't hanging in the kitchen. And when I'd skidded down through the wood, my jeans mud to here, my trainers so heavy I couldn't hardly lift them, when my head not that much lighter, I chucked open the door of the glasshouse, there they both were standing in front of the furnace. Not Dave and his mate, the fucking bikers. Grace and Jas. The fucking bosses.

"Talk of the devil. Just the guy we wanted," Jas says cheerfully. And would you believe it, before I knew what was happening, never mind that Dave and his mate would be appearing any minute, they'd fixed me, had me in, alongside Grace, on the business end of a punty.

If it wasn't hard to see that the kid was up to no good, what with satisfied desire and headache it didn't seem hard to start deflecting his devils, either. This of course, was my mistake; and his misfortune.

Grace had gathered her glass, was waiting. Terry looked dazed for a minute, the next moment it was like a dance he'd been swept into by some ungainsayable partner. Since she didn't get much further than smoothing up the gather, I didn't know, I still don't know, what it was she intended making. Though I know it was me this time, not Terry, she'd chosen for her assistant. That was, of course, what we were there for; it wasn't, simply, that she couldn't keep away from glassmaking; or that in the middle of our lousy hangovers we weren't both still a little tipsy — on each other, as much as anything. It had to be me she was angry with, not Terry, when I pushed him at her.

Like I said, Terry did what he had to at first. Though I could see that his mind wasn't in it. If he got things right, if he was there when Grace wanted, it was purely out of instinct. He looked like someone travelling through motions he'd learned before the right sense left him. Like a blind man seeing; or like a deaf man hearing. Alternatively he looked like a puppet; Grace pulling his little strings and levers.

I don't know what I'm doing, do I? I'm listening for them coming, I need them, they're my sort, not like all these others, didn't mum warn me, didn't she always know it? My head is aching and aching. I hand Grace tools, I spray glass for her, I put the punty to heat in the furnace ready. And all the time I'm listening for Dave's coming. Like I listened for my mum coming, locked up in that empty room, not suspecting she wouldn't come alone, that there'd be a fancy man laughing along of her.

Jas is fiddling around behind us all this time, I can't see what he's up to. Nor don't I hear what he's up to, I'm too busy straining my ears for the bikes. Grace is on the bench now, twiddling the iron with one hand, working on the glass with her other, her head bent like it were the only thought she had in it. Perhaps, so to speak, she hasn't never had no other thought in it. I envy her in a way. I want to be like that now but can't be. But then I think, maybe she can't be it neither. Maybe she needs the glass for other reasons. Maybe that's why she's come down to work on a Sunday, not because she loves it, because she needs to.

For a moment, seeing into her head, or thinking I might do,

I pity her almost. Which don't make me hate her any less. If anything I hate her more, how dare she be like me, like anyone else, I think; like a human being. (Any more of that, I'll have to see my mum as fucking human.)

I look at the door then, hearing a sound from that way, something like a door opening; maybe Dave and his mate are coming, I am praying it's Dave and his mate are coming. But it's not them, fuck it, it's Jas opening the cupboard, the one whose door he went and covered with pictures, of some nude bint, for instance, getting fucked by a swan — who says education's not sexy? He's taking something out of the cupboard, I know what before I see it, I'd seen him put it there yesterday before we opened; you can't open things like that to the public, they've got to be protected from it.

When he turns with her in his hand, she's still uglier than I remembered. If all he's doing is taking her back to the furnace, it's not back there yet, is it, we aren't safe are we, seeing what I swear is a smirk across his great fat chops, as though he's remembering that cunt he spent last night inside of; I know he's doing it to bug me. I can't stand nothing no longer. I grabs the punty I've been heating from the furnace, I swipe against the witch's piece. Which is the end or the beginning, whichever way you like to put it. I knock it out of his hand, of course. That stone smash, glass tinkle is the best sound I heard my whole life ever. Too bad Dave and his mate'll miss some of the action, I ain't going to wait for them now, maybe they ratted on me, maybe they aren't even coming. A thought which drives me still more crazy, I let rip, don't I, I run berserk with the iron, laying it about me, the way I always wanted.

(Let him rip, dozzie, keep grinnin' before you know he'll smash himself, or other will, it's them 'll be greetin, you and I happy on our own, for ever. Oh yes I'm smiling. I don't know what I'm smiling at or who for. Not for you, dozzie; not for them either. My head is aching. And I am smiling. I con do no other.)

They can't stop me, though they try to. Not least it's them I'm really after. Why's Grace smiling? I'm breaking up her life aren't I? Like she broke mine up. Like mum did. I'll kill them both for it, and with the same weapon. There ain't no difference no more, between her and the thing Jas is holding, no good breaking it, there she still is, it always was her, her belly is enormous, her hair snakes, her tips tipped with roses, if I look at her a moment longer I'm done for. I *am* done for. I takes a swipe at her first, but I'm a good way off still, I miss her. I takes a swipe at Jas, at her he's not holding in his hand only, but in his head, I miss her. And all the time my ears are roaring all the time the heat beats at them all the time I'm screaming and cursing at the buggers like they was everyone done me wrong my mum and dad for starters more like she's the bloody witch she's everyone done me wrong smiling at me she knows it she loves it she wants and this is the end of her ain't it I take aim I have her she's screaming what's she screaming screaming scream . . .in

Not for one moment do we regret it, dozzie, thi recks little, don' thi, of t' terrible little demon advancing on us — he's our demon and not our demon, his face is his own entirely, twisted way we never saw, but always wanted; who can love an incubus like that, we wither him with our look, we hate him; our hate makes his strength, in't it ollus t'way of it? Such strength it'll have us, it almost had us then, but we're past caring. If he missed un' this fust time, 'twill not do the next time. Thi voice is in mi head, is my voice, I wait for its orders. KILL HIM. But no, I will not kill him, that's not the way of it, sooner he kills us first, which in't t' proper way of it neither. KILL THE MARDY BASTARD. We are screaming. We have our weapon. But 'tis not our weapon's needed.

We wait. Smiling our stony smile. Screaming our stony, our silent screams. The man in the moon has found his way to us, has burnt his mouth, to judge by the look of her, has snatched the hot iron, that till this very moment we've been holding in the furnace, twisting and turning, to stop the glass from falling. Bye Baby Bunting on the Tree Tops, momma's gonna buy thi a looking, a cooking glass, next time she goes to the shops.

Does he need to hit so hard, then? Does he need such a cruel weapon to do it? Could have taken another, couldn't he? Would have felled him just as well, was no need was there to make of him another glass baby?

The hole in the side of the boy's head is hair and glass and blood. The glass hardening as it meets its target, they can see the changes of colour as it cools and settles across his features. They can hear its little cracking about his eyes and nose and mouth. He is a glass creature. With a mask of glass where before he had a face. The glass itself heats the livid colour that burns into his cheeks, bringing them to life again, even while his blood is cooling. The glasshouse smells of burnt hair; cooked flesh; roast pork almost. As for us, we are no longer a burning demon. We are icy. We survey this thing at our feet, Betsy, the memory of the crucible with its molten white metal is diminishing inside us, the burning eye which surrounded us is a dwindling golden speck, going going gone, for ever. Dies. (*Dies.*) Like the small word in italics in our red-covered school Shakespeares. Was it really so simple with people, I used to wonder? It wasn't that simple even with pigs. (*Dies.*) We are left surrounded by pale water, the colour of the sea on the maps at the end of my mother's little Bible. And by the smell of cooking.

And yet it is simple, after all. Mostly because we cannot grasp it. One moment he is alive; the next (dies) isn't. Poor mardy bastard. With his glass hair and eyes, his glass face burning. Coom Betsy, cradle our baby, rock a bye baby, momma's mocking bird. The noise we hear's not from our throats is it, this deep unassuageable mourning; art thi mourning also? has the furnace inside us been drowned by the bottomless ocean?

I'll never forget the faces as long as I live. Didn't know whether it was Grace standing there or my hand-blown figure. Couldn't believe I'd really made anything so monstrous. If I had done, that was my crime, I knew it, not what I did, so much, not even what I'd wanted to do to that wretched little bastard. Whom, maybe, I hadn't intended to kill, really. Or at least wouldn't have without he'd given me such a good excuse. For you can't keep anything straight, let alone stick to the right rituals (young king should kill old king, not vice versa) with your head full of flying glass and hangover. (I got a splinter on my face, for instance, and didn't notice it till after, assuming, reasonably enough, that the blood I had on me must, every bit of it, be Terry's.)

Nor was it fore-ordained, not even by Terry, it was just his usual bad luck, that those leather guys he'd conjured turned up too late to help him. "That you, Terry?" one of them said as they threw the door open. To find it was Terry all right, but lying on the floor, with me standing over, still holding the incriminating weapon, its bloody tail of glass leading, inexorably, to the wound it had inflicted. It did not take them long to take in this Shakespearian drama; there was no way they'd stick around, not bloody likely. They didn't even take off their helmets, what with them and the amulets and the black leather, they looked like aliens from outer space, or frogmen. "*Fuc*-king Jesus," said one of them. Then they scarpered. The use they were to Terry, they might as well have been from Mars or Venus. Or from the bottom of a distant ocean.

Glass congeals maybe ten times quicker than blood. Terry lay twitching a bit after I'd hit him, his head cracked twice over, from the iron I wielded, from the stone he fell on. The blood streamed over the glass in his matted wound. Over his eyes and down his nose on which the hot glass settled, cracked and tinkled. It was hissing a bit, I could swear it; it was actually steaming. His left arm, the punty alongside it, lay flung on one of those pink polishing pads we make from the Financial Times. His amazingly thin little white ankles stuck out of his too short jeans, all of them mud-coated. Why were his new jeans so short, I wondered vaguely. His black trainers were like the plimsolls I used to wear at school; his feet looked enormous, much too big for the rest; as if he hadn't yet stopped growing; or at least hadn't till I topped him. I never felt before just how young the poor bastard was. Young enough to be my son. Or Grace's. Or ours come to that, the way she was cradling his head. Like a parody of the first time I'd seen them, except that this time she was weeping. At times throwing back her head and howling; like a dog; or like someone laughing. Now and then, to my horror, singing; crooning; in a high, high voice.

There was a murder indictment; Jas agreed to plead guilty of manslaughter, could even have got off that, his lawyer said, the judge would have accepted a plea of self-defence, better still of defending a woman from the murderous assault of a hooligan. Jas would have none of it, however. It was a brawl, he said, that they had both been mixed up in. He'd hit Terry far harder than necessary — neither he nor Grace could swear the boy was actually going to hit her. The judge looked him up and down — Jas had not cut his hair, wore his boots and silk-neckerchief, for all his mother's long-distance attempts to dissuade him; then gave him three years in prison. (It meant two years allowing for good behaviour.)

Even to me such a reaction seemed quixotic. My taking the rap for the thing entirely had more to do with Grace, perhaps, than with either me or Terry. Forget the basic English decency — my guilty conscience is a luxury, it costs XXX pounds a week to keep me at Her Majesty's Pleasure. The price of my opting, you might say, for one glasshouse rather than another. But tell me how else I could escape her? Inasmuch as I have escaped her. Waking or sleeping I feel her flesh under my hands. Dream her eyes and skin and hair turning me to stone and glass and paper. Her whole place, the whole country these days is one monstrous regiment of woman. With nowhere to run to. Except here, where I've run to. You're still right, Johnny Ruskin, but it's a hundred and twenty years too late, the only possible courses of action sound too much like hard work for me and you to get involved in — I mean it needs serious subversion.

What happened is not, of course, the end of mothers. Terry's mother, for instance, screamed vengeance during my trial, for one she chose to call her baby; despite respect for her grief — it was legitimate, if alcoholic — she had to be removed from the public gallery. Grace could not come at all, except as a witness. Nor would my mother. This does not stop her visiting me in prison, bearing flowers, she prefers to imagine me sick, by the look of it, the guest of the Health Service not the Home Office.

I will not give in, ever. I do not give in. Though for the first time in my life, I acknowledge mourning. If not yet exactly for what I am mourning. The snow is deep up here already. It covers all faults, everything, even the wrongs done to me by others, that Betsy won't let me forget, though there are times I'd like to.

There are some matters I know now, for instance, are too dangerous to play with. It's for that, begging Betsy's pardon, I make another witch's piece. And set it on the furnace for her and my protection. As I always should have done, not left her to Jas to make. Afterwards I choose a hunk of laminated glass. It was Jas started it, while he was still out on bail, he carved out the first pebble; then sandblasted its surface. But it was me after the trial, after he'd gone to prison, who ground one facet of that opaque surface to make a window to the transparency within, to the layers and sediments it's holding; the layers are still too even, but now I have the notion I make more and more of these pebbles, working alone, slowly, the long weekend evenings, in front of my closed-up furnace.

It is not my intention to take another helper, even for the glassblowing. "What is thi about now, mi dozzie?" I hear the old voice pleading. "Can't you tell, can't you tell?" I answer — it is even harder for me now not to keep up these conversations. Yet there is no reason not to. Sometimes we both laugh madly, because neither of us can do much more damage, we are both as bad as the other. Sometimes I think it's good they don't burn women like us any more, no matter how much we may deserve it. Sometimes I change my mind, I think it a bad thing.

One night, for instance, I dream Jas has hung himself in his cell in the prison I never visited; I see him choking and twitching and pissing hissen, his tongue out his gob, his cheeks turning to blue, liike he wor celebrating his dead wedding, death hersen the bride, not the bridegroom on this occasion. When I wake in the morning, I'm so convinced I did more than dream it, I do not go to my glasshouse. I sit waiting in my empty-smelling kitchen for news that has not come. I sit waiting for the note they will bring me also. That in my dream I saw him leave on his mattress. I do not want to read it. There will be too many words as always, clever words, naive words, words of cynicism, despair, of reproach and of mockery inextricable from words of undying love, irrepressible passion. (These last are the ultimate mockery, not to say the final reproach. It is these words I clung to so long, thinking of our dead son, and now wish to turn my back on.)

While I am waiting, I lift down from the top of the dresser in the kitchen the jar Jas dug up that day, that he never, after all, took to London. I carry it down to the glasshouse. Under the gaze of my witch's piece I open my furnace, with all my strength, I swing the pot towards it. A stream of dull silver parings pours into the crucible; as many scatter hither and thither, I am crunching them under foot, dancing on them. One only I take in my hand, I set it round my wedding finger. It is not a ring, but a crescent; unlike Jas' golden band — the other ring I have taken to wearing again lately — it does not meet, it cannot bind me, cannot get children on me; that is the one I keep, thereafter. The wedding band I heft from my finger, throw into my glass fire, to be melted along with the silver.

"Connot thi tell, mi dozzie," I cry, laughing madly as the sweat pours off me — I have been thinking of such things day and night, before such a relentless and burning eye the thoughts are endurable no longer. "Connot thi tell what 'tis I am about? Connot tell whose grave I am dancing on? Connot see, that t'glass — and what it coom from — is oll that's left us, that today at long last, I'm dancing on us deep red grave and no other?"

RIDING THE DESERT TRAIL
BETTINA SELBY

Armed with a sun-hat, insect repellent, a Swiss army knife and an 'all terrain' bicycle, Bettina Selby set off. 4,500 miles later she reached her destination – the source of the Nile. Her journey took her from the sites of one of the most ancient civilizations to some of the last discovered places on the planet. From the Mediterranean to the mysterious Mountains of the Moon; from the Pyramids, the great temples of Luxor, the Valley of the Kings and all the magnificence of Egypt to the empty burning sands of the Nubian Desert, war-torn southern Sudan and Uganda. She endured endless miles of yielding sand, swamps, deserts and jungles, was arrested and nearly killed – and emerged at her journey's end to tell the fascinating tale of the encounters that befall a solitary traveller in remote and often dangerous lands.

THE BRIDE WHO RAN AWAY
DIANA O'HEHIR

The town of French Ford was founded by Grace Dowell's great-great-great grandfather as a Utopian community. But by 1950 the roads are still unpaved, the telephone exchange is a hut on the hill, and the population consists, largely, of Dowells. Utopia it is not; and Grace, aged nineteen and newly engaged, has had enough.

Even for a self-confessed 'odd lot' the Dowells' behaviour is bizarre. Aunt Sybil, eccentric and over eighty, lives in the back of a Buick. Grace's father lives mainly in the clouds, and her beautiful cousin Indiana has recently taken her own life, leaving a disturbing diary – and a broken triangle of love.

Grace, improbably and unwillingly at the heart of every odd relationship, abandons them all. The consequences are more than startling . . .

Also by Diana O'Hehir in Abacus:
I WISH THIS WAR WERE OVER

The Rattlesnake Stradivarius
TERESA KENNEDY

Louisiana 1830 or thereabouts: Mary Faith Beaudine, rich slave-owning mute, is jilted by her gypsy music teacher and switches his Stradivarius violin for her own inferior instrument.

Later that century: Icy Fee Moulder, sorceress, adds a rattle to it.

Atlantis County, Texas, the present: Boo Strait, enchanted fool, grabs the fiddle and runs like hell.

It is when the Strait family comes together for the reading of a will that the Stradivarius and its passionate power ties the past with the present—the lives and loves of those who have gone before with those who come after. The object of love, lust and intrigue, the violin makes its way through a wonderful tale of thieves and preachers, cowboys and conjure-women, and cranky old ladies with more secrets than they can shake their Bibles at.

0 349 101027   FICTION   £4.99

THE WAR AGAINST CHAOS

Anita Mason

THE SOCIETY OPERATED WITH A NIGHTMARE LOGIC. CURIOSITY HAD NO PLACE. NOR DID READING, STROLLING, JUNK-COLLECTING – ALL THE THINGS JOHN HARE RELISHED

He had been upwardly mobile on the ladder of Universal Goods when his wife left him and his career in jeopardy. He seemed the ideal, expendable scapegoat in a powerful company official's much-needed cover-up. And with a trumped-up charge worthy of Kafka, Hare found himself cast into the netherworld of a dreaded population known as the 'marginals'.

What the authorities never reckoned on was the reawakened cunning and imagination of these outcasts. Or the greater threat to them that Hare was to discover – based on self-respect and humour – steeling itself in the bowels of the city.

ZERO db

MADISON SMARTT BELL

Consider the pitfalls of a would-be streetwise vigilante, a lovesick shrimp fisherman, an officer of conscience at the battle of Little Big Horn. Tune into Manhattan through a hidden mike in a sleazy downtown bar or observe an old widower negotiate the hostile zones of his living room and prepare to do battle.

From the dining halls of Princeton to the hog farms of Tennessee, Bell's vision sets humour against raw and dramatic realities, private ambitions against uncertain futures. The result is one of compelling artistry.

'Considered separately, the stories in this collection are astonishing; considered together, they are even more astonishing, for they indicate a dazzling range of voice'
New York Times Book Review

The Truth About Lorin Jones

ALISON LURIE

Lorin Jones, an undervalued artist, died of pneumonia contracted from snorkelling in a cold sea. Polly Alter, art historian, feminist and fugitive from emotional chaos, has a mission—to wrest her from her ill-deserved obscurity and reveal for the world's judgement the truth about Lorin Jones . . .

'Alison Lurie's tone is unerring, no word wasted. As slyly cool as Jane Austen, she subjects to pleasantly relentless examination the woman's movement, art and the deep flaws in us all'
Daily Mail

'Miss Lurie's skill and lightness of touch conceal a highly elaborate technique. Her book is funny and shrewd . . . a polished example of the American comedy of manners'
Daily Telegraph

Also by Alison Lurie in Abacus:
REAL PEOPLE
FOREIGN AFFAIRS
IMAGINARY FRIENDS
LOVE AND FRIENDSHIP
THE NOWHERE CITY
THE WAR BETWEEN THE TATES

M. CHARLESWORTH

LIFE CLASS

Marriage to a beautiful woman barely half his age hadn't seemed fraught with hazard until Jack Ruffey took Annette on a belated honeymoon in Java. There, on the slopes of Mount Bromo, they encountered the enigmatic John Ridinghouse – a figure from Annette's past, an obsession for Jack's future. A tantalizing intrigue developed; a voyage – like Jack's paintings – of discovery, but with the twisted threads of jealousy, a hilariously egotistical misogynist philosopher and eerie Javanese spirits teasingly playing their parts.

'The reader is completely entranced . . . a masterpiece of perplexities'
Literary Review

Also by Monique Charlesworth in Abacus:
THE GLASS HOUSE

A
CAPOTE
READER

A Capote Reader contains virtually all of the author's published work – including several short pieces that have never before been published in book form. It is divided into six parts: *Short Stories* (twelve of them, all that Capote ever wrote); two *Novellas*, *The Glass Harp* and *Breakfast at Tiffany's*; *Travel Sketches* (thirteen of them, mostly around the Mediterranean); *Reportage*, including the famous Porgy and Bess trip to Russia *The Muses Are Heard*, and the bizarre murders in *Handcarved Coffins*; *Portraits* of the famous, among them Picasso, Mae West, Isak Dinesen, Chaplin, André Gide, Elizabeth Taylor – who radiated 'a hectic allure' – and 'the beautiful child' Marilyn Monroe; and *Essays* (seventeen of them, including *A Day's Work*). Each section is in chronological order of publication, demonstrating the evolution of the author's style and interests.

Also by Truman Capote in Abacus:
**ANSWERED PRAYERS
MUSIC FOR CHAMELEONS
IN COLD BLOOD
BREAKFAST AT TIFFANY'S**

0 3491 0095 0   FICTION   £6.99

Nancy Thayer
MORNING

'THERE HE WAS, THE PERFECT HUSBAND, AND HERE SHE SAT, NOT PREGNANT, THE IMPERFECT WIFE. THE FLAWED WIFE. THE INFERIOR WIFE. THE RAPIDLY-MENTALLY-DETERIORATING WIFE.

SHE WANTED TO BREAK ALL THE DISHES OVER HIS PERFECT, UNDERSTANDING, LOVING HEAD.'

But it wasn't Steve's fault. It was nobody's fault that she couldn't have the child she so desperately wanted. So Sara channelled her energies into her work as an editor. And then she read a manuscript that led her to a creative life of a different kind; the autobiographical novel of a beautiful, terrifying recluse with a mysterious past . . . and a painful obsession.

Also by Nancy Thayer in Sphere Books:
NELL
STEPPING
THREE WOMEN
BODIES AND SOULS